CARDBOY

Mervin Etienne (signature)

A Novel by
Mervin Etienne

SPECIAL DEDICATION & RESPECT TO THE FOLLOWING:

The working girls of London: .

The CardBoys: .

The Maids: .

The Met Police: For the inspiration of conflict and tension to the story.

The Cleaners: For making it possible for the CardBoys to succeed.

British Telecom: For providing the telephone boxes that made this tale possible to tell.

The Punters: For keeping the business alive, long enough for me to research properly and Write this book.

LONDON 1996

Fuck, it's hard holding down a job you don't like these days. I'm all over the place: working in factories, then off to work in warehouses. I don't enjoy any of 'em. Same as a lot of us really. Just doing it for the money with zero love for the job. I've gotta at least like the job I'm doing. Fuck it! I should love the job I'm doing. It's easy to get a job, but getting one you love is a concept a lot of people just can't seem to grasp. Including me. Anytime I'd had enough of a job, I'd just walk out. I remember my first day at one factory, a fizzy drinks place, where my job was to help prepare the packing. There wasn't much that the foreman had to teach me about this work.

'Grab that flat cardboard pack would ya?'

I gave him the cardboard, to which he pushed the sides in, bent the flaps closed, slammed it in a staple machine, stamped on the foot pedal a couple of times. And boom! One cardboard box was made.

'Just keep doing that, and there's a pile of boxes over there.'

I looked up to see seven piles of flat stacked boxes from the floor to the ceiling, and d'ya know what I said to him?

Where's the toilet?

'Right there near the back door.'

And with that, he pissed off. And so did I. Right out the back door. A job that I didn't give one second of a chance to. When I look back at the jobs I let go so easily, I could whip myself with a stick for being such an idiot.

My name is Tony. I'm twenty-six years old. I'm a white lad with a black soul. All my life I've had family and women comment on how good looking I am, making comments like,

'Ah, he's gonna be a heartbreaker this one, I can tell.'

But I don't give a shit about that, all I've done is won the gene pool lottery. Down to my mum and dad. Nothing to do with me. I'm in East London, in a small town called Buston Manor. This is where I was born. Let's just say, it's not glamorous around here. Any decent car is owned by one of the local gangsters, and even the mail-order delivery companies have crossed out delivering to anyone who orders their goods from the area for fear of getting their vans robbed. It was, however, a normal upbringing for me as a young boy. That's if street fighting two or three times a year is considered normal, but I did have fun too. For the most part, everyone gets along here, and a lot of the residents know me. I'm normally quite upbeat, but it's been a month since my last job.

MAY

No fucking money. Jobs have gone dry, and I regret walking out on so many. Thoughts of crime are creeping in. It can be hard to keep away from crime when you have no money, and you come from where I come from because everyone is at it. Well, most of the people that I know are. Deep down though, I know I won't go down the route of crime, but having no money for the last three months is no fun. I feel a bit old to be living with my mum, but my dad is not around anymore. Divorced. I never saw much of him as a boy, and then he was out of my life for keepsies by the time I was twelve. So I feel a great need to be there to support my mum. She's great. I know everybody has got to love their mothers, but not everybody loves theirs. I love mine. She's always looked out for everyone in the family, and always did her best. Even when she had fuck all. We live in a big four-bedroom semi-detached house, which can be described as being in need of a 'major overhaul.' The carpet is so old that it's beyond ever looking clean. I can barely determine what colour it is. The small, square opening in the back door where there once was glass is now just a boarded-up hole. You can't even lock it properly. I can't even remember what happened to it because it has been like that for so long. There's never really been any sort of decent garden. Big piles of dirt with plenty of house bricks from the broken-down wall are half-buried in the packed, tight, mini dirt mountain. But as a kid, that made for a wicked bike track of instant speed.

Geronimo!

From the top of the mountain to skidding up at the back, broken door. It's cold in our house in the winter. No central heating. There's never been any central heating fitted in this house. That costs a small fortune now to install, about fourteen hundred quid. And we need everything: radiators, boiler, all the copper pipework, and of course, the plumber to put it all in. The heaters that are in the house are two gas heaters fitted where the coal fires used to be back in the Victorian days. One in my mum's bedroom, and one in the living room below it. Electric, move-around heaters are kept in the other bedrooms to keep warm, but the kitchen, bathroom, toilet, and hallways have never been warm in the winter.

Going to the toilet in the night from my bedroom is a long, cold walk. Or in my case, a quick march. The light switch to the upstairs hallway is downstairs, and in my early to mid-teens, I was still a bit scared of the dark. So on a few occasions, if I woke up after a bad dream and wanted to go to the toilet, I would piss behind the wardrobe in my bedroom. My older brother Jacob, whom I shared a room with, was just about to move out.

'You're free to do whatever you want here now.'

I soon stopped pissing up the wall though, when it began to stink a rotten, ammonia-like stench in my bedroom. Jacob is six years older than me and very clever. But his punches really hurt. We get on well, and growing up, he always had a knack for learning stuff really fast and building stuff really well.

'Go on then. Try and work that one out.'

Wooden cases with hidden compartments were his specialty. I could never find how the compartment opened unless he showed me. It was genius stuff.

'You give up?'

Yeah, I give up. When have I ever sussed out how to open 'em?

'Alright, I'll show ya. See this left-hand corner? Well, you grab it with the tips of your three fingers and turn it ninety degrees to your left like this, then open the corner. Now, you see that tiny bump underneath? Push that.'

I pushed the nodule, and a whole section, the entire width of the box, came sliding out from the lid.

Fucking hell Jacob! That's amazing!

'I knew you'd like this one Tony. You can't fit anything bulky in it, but you can get about a hundred quid in twenty-pound notes in there if they're flat.'

Fuck knows whatever happened to those boxes. My sisters, Maggie, Charlene, and Cynthia, shared the other two bedrooms. Charlene was hardly ever indoors growing up. Always with a different guy too in her late teenage years. She's twenty-nine now, and hardly anybody sees her. She shows up at Christmas time but didn't last year. Maggie is the youngest in the family and spent most of her infant life following Cynthia, who is the oldest, around the house. She's twenty-four and lives in the north of England with another girl. I think she's gay. Maggie is so shy and quiet, and I do feel quite protective towards her. She still looks up to Cynthia and does almost anything she wants her to do. I think Cynthia takes advantage of her. I think Cynthia takes advantage of everyone. She takes advantage of Mum, and I don't like that. I don't like Cynthia; she's not very nice to people or animals. She once put caustic soda in our cat's drinking water bowl and gloated about it.

'Stupid old cat, I put this stuff in its drinking water, and now it's coughing.'

MUM! MUM! Cynthia hurt the cat!

The cat died with a swollen belly and froth coming out of its mouth. I loved that cat. Freddy was his name. I didn't speak a single word to Cynthia for a whole year after she did that. She lives alone without a boyfriend. I've never known her to have a boyfriend. but I don't think she's gay. I think she's just horrible.

As the bathroom and toilet are the coldest rooms in the house, the time I spend there is minimal. I've learned to shit really quickly because of that. My dad used to spend ages in the toilet having a shit. He'd take a newspaper in there with him and a cigarette. The toilet seat was always warm when I went in after him, and I hated that. The thought of my dad's butt warming my butt put me off a warm toilet seat for life. In fact, any seat warmed by another person puts me off because of my dad. Warm bus seat, no thanks. If I had a ride on someone's bike and the seat was warm, I'd stand up until it cooled down. I'd much rather have a warm house and a cold seat.

My dad never taught me anything about life. He took me out to play when I was a kid once, to fly a kite in the park. And even then, it was only for fifteen minutes. I'll never forget it because the string snapped, and the kite soared into the air and lodged itself into the canopy of the biggest sycamore tree there.

'We cannot get that, it's gone. Come on, let's go home.'

I cried all the way as we left the park, crossed the main road, and went home. Having dinner that evening, I looked out the window to the back garden, and stuck on the fence was my eagle kite!

I can't believe it, it's there. It's come home all by itself!

I ran out to the back garden to retrieve my perfectly intact kite. That is a good memory. There were bad memories though. I can't remember what I did, but I do remember the punishment. And I remember thinking that if I went to bed before Dad got home, I'd be safe. I tucked myself into bed while it was still light outside and slept. I woke up because the blanket was off me, and I was cold. I was crying a little and stinging a bit. I rose up to drag the blanket back onto me and noticed a two-inch wide belt mark on my thigh where Dad had beaten me while I was sleeping. I was crying, yet didn't feel a thing. Apart from the little stinging once I woke up. I was about eight years old, and he never hit me again after that. I had four years left before I would never see him again.

The jobs I've had have not even paid one hundred and fifty pounds a week. I can get food, but that's about it.

Mum, we've gotta get some warmth in here.

'Don't worry Tony, it's summer soon. I'll just put layers on when it gets colder.'

Nah Mum, that's not happening.

I must get a decent job to get this central heating for Mum to be warm this coming winter. I can't stand to see her shivering every year. I've had enough of it. I'm glad it's coming into summer now, but I'm still determined. One day this year, there will be central heating here. There's a local minicab office in the area called Derricks. And sometimes you'd have to wait half an hour outside until a cab comes back from a job to become available again. Pain in the fucking arse. It's Friday night, and I want some money. I'm driving down the road in my immaculate white Honda. Old, but immaculate. I bought it for three hundred pounds from the father of one of the most decent families in the area, the "Moyas." They were one of the only families I knew that didn't house one of the local thugs amongst them. I'm driving up towards Derricks, and because it's party night, there's eight to ten people waiting outside for a cab. Fuck it! I'm pulling in.

Allo mate, you looking for a cab? I'll take ya for a bit cheaper. Where ya going?

'Green Gate Street.'

Jump in, I'll take ya.

Boom. Four quid. Now, I know four quid is not a lot of money, but it was only five minutes away, and after a few fares like this, I soon had twenty-five quid. The last fare I nicked tonight was a girl that I'd always seen around but never spoke to. Lovely looker. Shane Zipp is her name. Long, straight dark hair with a cracking smile. Anyway, she got in my car, and by the time I got to her destination, Ilford city, six quid, I knew she had the hots for me. Needless to say, she gave me her number. I'll be following this one up later.

There's a well-known character that lives near me, Big D. We just like to say D. A staunch Manchester United fan. White. And when I say white I mean a really light kind of mozzarella white. I've never seen someone so white, with a good head of blonde hair. Travels for miles each week to watch the team play. Funny as fuck, with a sharp wit and has always driven a nice car. I found a wallet once with seventy-five pounds in it and a driving licence with D's picture on it. My first thought was to keep the money, but because I knew D, I felt that I should return it. I knocked on the door, and D could not believe that I had brought it back.

'The seventy-five quid is still in it!'

Yeah. And your licence.

'I can't believe you brought it back to me. Who does that in this area? You're a top man. It's nice to know there are people around here you can trust. There you go. Take a twenty. Thanks a lot.'

You don't have to give me this D. But I will take it, 'coz I'm a bit brassic.

'A bit brassic? What, you've got no work?'

Nah, it's shit at the moment.

'I might have a bit of work for ya.'

Yeah? What do you do?

'These cards. It's a pucker earner. West End girls.'

So what can I do then?

'I can't explain it now 'coz I've gotta go out, but come round at the end of the week and we'll have a chat then.'

'OK, I will. Is Friday OK?'

'Yep. Friday night is sweet. I'll be home by eight-thirty.'

FRIDAY

I got to D's house, a fair-sized Victorian terraced house. I'm feeling curious and excited to know what this is all about. I'm standing in D's living room, and there's a massage table opened up in the middle. D has just had one of the weekly full-body massages, and the masseuse is still there.

'Once a week I have this; I couldn't live without it. Misha, meet Tony.'

Misha is a short, slightly fat but perfectly formed girl.

Hello Misha, I could do with a full-body massage myself.

'Take my card. Doesn't your girlfriend give you massages?'

I ain't got one. The last girlfriend I had, as much as I asked her, never gave me a massage. That's a prime example of low interest right there. I don't know how she lasted eighteen months before I fucked her off.

'She was a selfish cow. Good riddance to her.'

I'm looking around the room, and there's a stack of money on D's ironing board. It's at least five grand.

'I need someone I can trust to do the top-up for me.'

What the fuck is that D?

'I'll show ya.'

D went to the closet and pulled out a large box of prostitutes' advert cards.

'I've been out in the city this morning putting these cards out in the telephone boxes for the girls. I need someone to go out there in the afternoons and just replace any that have been taken down.'

I think I can do that D. Doesn't sound too difficult.

'It can have its good and bad points. You'll bump into a few other CardBoys out there, but don't worry. I'm the top dog down Tottenham Court Road and the sur-rounding areas, so you'll have no trouble. I had to pay a few boys to get down there to protect that position from some other boys trying to take over. It was carnage. Someone's always trying it on. We had 'em running around scared everywhere.'

OK D, you're the boss. I'll do it.

'Good, I'll give you a hundred and fifty pounds for a couple of hours of work.'

What's the risk out there D?

'I can assure you that it's all gonna be alright, and don't worry about the police. They can be funny with us sometimes, mainly when they get a complaint. Then they have to be seen doing something about it, but it's not often. Come round on Monday afternoon at about two-thirty.'

OK then D. I'll see ya later. Cheers.

MONDAY, JUNE, 2:26PM

I arrive at the house to pick up the cards.

'Right, I'll lend you this waistcoat for now, but if you carry on working after today, you've got to get your own one.'

These waistcoats are made of canvas. They're fishing waistcoats with big pockets everywhere. They are ideal and the uniform of the Cardboy. The cards were premixed, which means two girls' cards were mixed one on top of the other. This means that for twelve pockets, you could have twenty-four different girls' cards on your person. I had a bit less than that amount on my run. I was given two packets of blue tack, or sticky putty as it's called in America, which is the only tool needed for the job. I stuffed the pockets with the cards and headed for the station to catch a train to the city of London.

Getting off at Tottenham Court Road station, the first task was to do the whole of Tottenham Court Road. Then walk to Euston Station and do all the phone boxes round there. Then onto Kings Cross, then back to Oxford Street and the backstreets there. I was even told how many boxes I'd see in each area, which all sounded easy enough to remember.

I've started to feel a little bit nervous as I leave Tottenham Court Road station and head for the first eight red telephone boxes directly outside the Dominion Theatre, an architecturally beautiful building that opened in nineteen twenty-nine as a musical theatre before becoming a cinema a year later. Charlie Chaplin was there for the London premiere of his film "City Lights." Now it's back as a theatre. Someone gave me tickets to see a show there just because they couldn't go: "We Will Rock You," the Queen musical. It was fucking brilliant. I also have a pal of mine who even performed there in the musical called "Buddy," all about Buddy Holly. I never saw that show. We became friends after the show had finished its run, but it's a great venue, hosting all sorts of shows. Even the Queen of England hosted the Royal Variety Performance there a few times. I look in the phone boxes, and to my delight, the cards I was looking for are all still up. I don't have to do anything here. And I still get paid. Is it really as easy as this? OK, it's not over yet. I walk to the next set of four boxes on Tottenham Court Road. This side they're up. That side they're up. This is very good. Onto the next two. This is a breeze. It's so busy down here with people and traffic. Messy too, with empty burger boxes and other rubbish scattered around on the ground. There's a funny smell too. I don't know what it is, but it comes and goes with the wind. Don't they clean these streets during the day? There's electronic shops everywhere down here. I've counted twelve shops in just the first little stretch of the road. If you wanna buy a television, You come here. If you need a decent camera, this is the place to come. You can buy electronic parts as well to fix it all. Some cards are up in this phone box. There's fuck all in the other one though. Here we go. This is it. My first attempt at putting the cards up. Why am I feeling nervous? I was told there was nothing to worry about, I can't start panicking now.

Right. So these cards get the priority position, just above the phone. Most of the boxes here are jam-packed with 100-plus cards in each one, all offering the services of the oldest profession in the world. They measure six inches by four inches, and in the box, they are on the backboard, both sides of the windows, and even on the ceiling. I can't imagine a client wanting to stand there dialling a number from the ceiling. It would look way too obvious to everyone looking in. Hence, the girls on the ceiling would get fewer calls, I should imagine. Above the phone is always best. It's a good eyeshot with minimal headturn.

I'm standing in the box, looking out for the police, but there's none about. I feel like Clint Eastwood, just about to draw his guns. I'm a little nervous, but I think of the money and soon calm down. I have twelve girls' cards on me, and two of each card must go up: one above the phone and one on the side window. My blue tack is in a big ball in my hand, and I pick big, booger-sized pieces from it to stick each card up as quickly and as neatly as I can. One, two, three, four, five, six, seven, eight, nine, ten all on the backboard. Another quick look around, and I'm off again, whacking the same amount of cards on the window at supersonic speed, and I'm out! Twenty cards up in less than a minute.

I'm way less nervous already, and I wanna speed up. As I leave the phone box, I take a look back to admire how neatly I placed the cards up. That's the first box out of the way. That wasn't too bad. I'm walking down Tottenham Court Road, and every box I'm approaching where cards were put up this morning has remained in place. Most of the other CardBoys' cards are still up too. This is easy money. I walk the remaining length of the road up to Warren Street train station, and all the cards are still up. I turn left into Warren Street, where the residential houses and a few backstreet phone boxes are. These are all up too. I get to Grafton Mews, where there's a few basement flats, and the two phone boxes there are bare. Not a card in sight, but there is a man in there on the phone, so I wait outside for him to finish his call. It's a nice day, and there's no stress at all as I wait patiently. My mobile phone rings, and I see that it's D calling.

'How's it going Tony?'

Really well, only one box was down on Tottenham Court Road, and I'm waiting outside this box in the backstreets for the bloke to finish his call.

'You're in the backstreets, off of Tottenham Court Road? Great, can you do me a favour and pick up some cards from one of the flats there?'

Yeah, course D, where do you want me to go?

'Sixty one, the basement, Grafton Mews. Her name is Mandy. I'll call her now and tell her you'll be coming.'

OK, D.

I grab the appropriate cards from my waistcoat that need to go into this phone box when the guy has finished and hold them ready. The man in there glances out at me now and again. I smile at him, and at this point, he knows what I am waiting for and motions with his head that I can enter the phone box and put the cards up while he is still on his phone call.

This man may well be expecting only one card to go up, but he doesn't know that I'm about to resemble 'Animal,' the drummer from the Muppet Show, with my arms flying all over the place. And now I'm in full flow. Bunch of cards on the backboard, quick quick. A bunch of cards on the side window, bosh bosh. I'm stretching over his shoulder and whipping my hand just past his nose real quick to slap the cards up, and he just seems fascinated by it all. I feel like I'm taking the piss a little bit, but it's got to be done, so I carry on. He tries to continue his phone call normally, but the fascination of it all slows his conversation down.

'There's a man in here putting up prostitute cards.'

I need to get out of here quickly; I don't want to listen to him explaining what I'm doing to whoever on the phone. Last card, and I'm out! All nice and neat.

Thanks, mate.

I'm loving that most of these boxes are up. Only the one on Tottenham Court Road and that last one had to be done. Took me about ten minutes in total so far, and I'm gonna pick up one hundred and fifty pounds. That'll do. I put a couple of cards in two of the side street boxes before emerging onto Oxford Street. It's a bit different around here. It's a lot busier for a start, with lots of black taxis and double-decker buses. There's plenty of people walking up and down and crossing the road everywhere. It's noisy and smokey from vehicle exhausts. There are huge department stores with busy phone boxes outside of them that I definitely don't want to do, so I'm glad the cards are still up. I'm feeling a bit nervous now as I've got to check the four boxes right on the junction of Oxford Street and Regent Street. Two of the busiest streets in London. And it's as busy as fuck at four in the afternoon.

Bollocks. There's a box down, and there's someone in it. I've gotta do this. I look around for the police while I'm waiting, but not one in sight. They'll probably be in plain clothes anyway down here. It's the only way they're gonna catch the rogue and petty street criminals. I have to keep telling myself I'm not committing any crime. I'm putting cards in a phone box. That's no fucking crime. When that man comes out, I'm just gonna march in there and get it done.

He's out. And I'm in. And feeling calm again. Right then, let's get my flow going, ten on the back and ten on the side at lightning speed, bosh bosh bosh. Slapping all the cards up. I'm getting the hang of this. And I'm out. There's no looking back at this one. I'm off to Mandy's, job done. Here it is. Grafton Mews. Fuck knows why I'm feeling nervous again. I'm just knocking on a house door. I've gotta liven myself up. The door opens, and a dark-haired woman is standing there. Out pops this quarter of a smile. I can see she has a liking for me.

Hello there, D sent me over.

She sounded like she was from the north of England, with a kind of accent similar to how the Beatles would talk.

'Yeah, come in love.'

She's checking me out and smiling as I walk in past her. I know that look, but she ain't gonna be doing anything with me. You dirty cow.

'Do you want a drink?'

Nah thanks, I've gotta shoot off.

'OK love. The cards are there. I'll get you a bag. Are you gonna be coming over in the future for D then?'

I don't know. It's just for today at the moment.

She wraps the cards in a white plastic carrier bag and hands them over.

'There's six hundred there love. Give my love to D'

OK, I'll mention it. I'll see ya later.

'Bye love.'

And with that, I'm out the door. I walk back to Goodge Street train station, which is situated halfway up Tottenham Court Road. I walk down the very long and very old spiral staircase that takes me down to the underground platform. I jump on the train and roll on out of there.

One hundred and fifty quid for doing this bit of work is not bad money, and of course, I would like to explore the possibilities of continuing this line of business as I think this is the answer for the central heating. So, I will be speaking to D to extend my services in this game. When I got to D's house, I stopped and stood to listen at the front door because I could hear swearing being shouted out from behind it.

'YOU FUCKING IDIOT!'

I ring the bell. D's full name is Devon, Irish name I think, the voice doesn't sound Irish though. Devon is as Cockney as you like.

'Alright Tony, come in." Man United are on, this fucking player, he's.. never mind, did you get the cards?'

Yeah, they're here.

D grabs the cards from me and moves around the room, picking things up and moving them around while shouting at Manchester United on the television.

'YOU FUCKING IDIOT! MY FUCKING GRANDMOTHER, WHO'S BLIND AND FUCKING EIGHTY, COULD KICK A BALL HARDER THAN THAT!' And then turned to speak to me. 'How'd it go?'

Easy really, there were only a couple of boxes down.

'Wicked, here's your money, do you wanna do it again?'

Yeah I'll give it another go.

'OK then, Can you do the round tomorrow?'

Yeah D, I can do that.

I took some more cards and went home to smoke a nice joint and grab my guitar. I'll go to the supermarket later for food but for now I will indulge in my two passions. Rock'n'Roll and weed. Nice. I sit back and take a good few puffs on it. It makes me think of the time my friend Pauly handed me some strawberry flavoured weed, such good stuff.

'There you go Tony smoke that, tell me what you think'

I got home and wrapped one up. A nice taste of strawberry. It makes me wanna play the guitar too. I ain't ever felt such a leap in my guitar playing. There's this amazing shit pouring out of me that I've never played before. The next day I phoned Pauly just to tell him how amazing it was.

Pauly, that smoke was so good last night. I grabbed the guitar and I was playing all sorts of complex shit. It's that fucking spliff, I'm sure of it, it was so smooth, and no coughing up.

Pauly plays the drums, he's in a three piece band called Sky Above. Not the greatest of names but an amazing band who have definitely got what it takes to captivate an audience. The bass player Nile is as cool as fuck and gives the band that jumping force. The guitarist who is also the vocalist, well, how shall I put it. I have a favourite list of two guitarists and it goes like this. Jimi Hendrix and then the guitarist Benji from this band. He's that good. Pauly, who sweats a lot when he plays, said the same thing.

'That's fucking mad hearing you say that. I got home and after I had one I got on the drums and I'll tell you what Tony, I was hitting all sorts of shots on the kit, I was playing like I've never played. I felt like a completely different drummer. The old strawberry surprise. Yeah, it was definitely that. I'll never forget it.'

That smoke gave me the strain hunter mentality, to seek out that perfect strain for the perfect frame. I'm so stoned, I can't even play the guitar now.

JULY

After falling asleep fully clothed I wake up at twelve thirty and I make a decent lunch that gets me ready for the top up. The day seems to be going along at some pace and by the time I make my way to D's house, it's already three in the afternoon.

'Alright, Tony? Come in. Yeah, it was extra cards yesterday that I gave you. Today there's not so many. I know I gave you one hundred and fifty quid but the job pays one hundred a day normally, yeah that's what it is. Are you happy with that?'

I'm thinking. Five hundred quid a week for doing that.

Yeah D, I can live with that.

'Cool, there's ten girls here. I've mixed the cards already for ya and you can use my old waistcoat, Have you got blue tack?'

Nah, I haven't. Thanks for the jacket.

'You've gotta pay for it though'

How much do I owe ya?

'Just get me ten packets of blue tack and we're even'

I grabbed a packet of blue tack from him and proceeded to load my waistcoat with the cards. London in the summer can get a bit too much for a lot of people, I can feel the tension. Men and women with short fuses, rush rush rush everywhere, but I still like to watch them. Observing human behaviour, it's fascinating. I'm walking through the backstreets of Oxford Street before making my way to the set of four phone boxes on that busy junction, and as I walk up a bit, there's a policeman standing right there on the corner. Just casually looking in my direction as I walk towards him, just my luck, why don't you just fuck off. Right, what am I gonna do here, he's maybe fifty yards or so in front of me and in between him and me are the two phone boxes that look empty so I've got to do them. Well he can't see me if I do the phone box on this side so I casually stroll to the first box and open the door, as soon as I'm in there I'm off, I feel like I'm in a race, there's commentating in my head, it's jeering me on and makes me go faster, it's like a horse race commentator " IT'S 'RED RUM' COMING UP IN THE LEAD BATTLING ALONG THE RAILS, CLOSELY FOLLOWED BY 'HOOF HEARTED' IN SECOND PLACE, IN THIRD IS THE FAVOURITE 'DUNARF CHUCKUP' AND IN FOURTH PLACE IS 'HOODUN IT.'

Quick as I can, get 'em up, first the left pocket. Then the right pocket, aah yeah baby, this is flowing, one on the back one on the side, next girl's cards, one on the side one on the back, pinch blue tack quick time, bosh it on the middle of the card, sticks up nicely, quick as I can, all up now count the cards. One, two, three, four, five. Another one to five on the window and done! Grab some fucking change outta my pocket, must go quicker than this, go, go, bosh! Bit of change in my hand, elbow on the door to open it and out! At exactly the same time as Mr Constable walks close by. I'm coming out, fumbling with the change in my hand. He looks straight at me. Time for the performance of the day.

'Fucking phone boxes, they never work. Excuse my language officer, it just stole my money.'

He smiled a little and slowly carried on walking, and I walked straight into the phone box on the other side and quickly smashed the cards up. Bang bang bang bang. Is he coming back? Adrenaline is flowing, and I'm not stopping till I'm done. Bosh bosh, one two three. Aah, last one, and out of the box! Take a deep breath, Tony. Take a deep breath.

Huhhh, aaaah.

A quick check behind. Ah shit, he's looking. I don't want you to catch me looking, Mister Constable. You fucker. I walk to the end of the road and turn right into the crazy hustle and bustle of Oxford Circus. Which basically is just the end of Oxford Street, and there are people everywhere. Let's get this done. No cards in these phone boxes, but this is bollocks. Every single box has someone in it. Fucking jabbering on the phone. Ah, quick, someone's coming out. Get in there, one to five, ah this is fast, another five on the glass side, two of each in the box, go go go, blue tack, quick quick, cards on the backboard, one two three go go, quick as I can, last one and out!

Gotta breathe, inhale, exhale. Relax, I'm alright. I'll stand closer to the next phone box. I'm next in there when he comes out. The man looks at me and smiles. It looks like one of those guilty smiles. You're smiling at me, mate, because you're feeling guilty about looking at that fucking filofax and not even on the fucking phone. I'm gonna say something to him in a minute. He knows I wanna use it. He comes out the box and says to me,

'Sorry, you can use it before me if you like. I've got to go through this paperwork.'

Thanks, mate.

And I'm in! Pinch a bit of blue tack, and the first cards up on the backboard. one to ten in no time, next five for the window, and up they go. One two three. Faster Tony. Get 'em up. Any police? None about. Last two cards. Quick check around. Ooh, she's getting ready to come out of the next box. Quick Tony, get in there before someone else does. I'm out, and so is she. Perfect. It's like a circus trapeze act, grabbing the door handles before they even close and swinging into the box. Aah, that smell. That perfume makes me think of sex. Get on with the job Tony. Purpose first. Cards out on the quick. Bosh, bosh, three four five. That perfume. Last sniff of it, and out. Next box, already empty. What a result. Here we go again, and I'm in. Hurry up and get out. Bish, bash, bosh. Cards are flying up. I should time myself, cause I'm getting so quick at this. I'm done and out the box. As soon as I'm out, I bump into the same policeman from the side street who looks at me, so I just smile and walk off. I'll come back for that last box. Time to hit Soho. Now, this is notoriously the red light district where sex workers' front doors are very much on display with handwritten signs on cards that just read 'Model.' Well, I know what goes on there. The neon lights suggest the advertising of all sorts of kinky stuff. It is one of the scruffiest sets of phone boxes in the city. Cards are always skew whiff and bent up, around this area. I like these traditional red telephone boxes, but they ain't got that much space for everyone to put their cards up like the new metal phone boxes have, and D is still the first to get the cards up. Just above the phone, they're all up there in that first box, so I ain't gotta do that, but gotta do this next empty box, so off I go whilst having a quick look around for the police. My face scrunches as I smell the stink that hits me as I pull that door open. Someone has done a humongous shit in there and wiped their arse on some of the cards.

I feel sick. I wouldn't wanna be the person who has to clean that up. It was just a tidy-up of D's cards in the next box after that. Right then, Charing Cross Road. This road houses the biggest collection of musical instrument shops in the whole of the city. There's at least fifteen scattered about here. But it's not on D's route, so I can walk past them. Who's that playing rock'n'roll I can hear woofing out of the doorway of that guitar shop? I think I'll stop off here at this cafe for a quick bite and listen to some more of that sweet rock'n'roll. After my sandwich, I carry on walking up to the Dominion Theatre, the starting point of the day, and the ending point. I grab a newspaper from the seller on the corner there. He has his pitch on the junction of Tottenham Court Road, Oxford Street, and Charing Cross Road. I jumped on the train and was on my way back home by five thirty. Not bad, an hour and a half's work for one hundred quid. Can't complain. I went to D's to collect my money.

'How was it today?'

Alright, coppers were on me a bit though.

'Ah yeah, it's like a cat and mouse game with them. We piss 'em off sometimes, they see us out there, we don't take the piss, and nine times out of ten they leave us alone. But they have purges sometimes, or you might get a copper who just doesn't take a liking to ya. Nothing you can do about that. And if you do get one of those, he'll just have it in for ya. He can make it his mission to fuck you up. Did he see ya putting them up?'

No, I slipped him.

'Do me a favour tomorrow, would ya Tony? Can you pick up some cards from a girl in Gloucester Place for me? She's a bit of a pain in the arse to be honest. I might get rid of her. She never has the cards ready, and I don't like driving all the way up the West End twice because of one girl.'

I can do that D, no worries. What's the address?

'I'll text it to ya. It's not a bad job eh?'

Nah, I like it D. Kind of funny, putting up cards in phone boxes and going to the flats to pick up cash from working girls. It's not normal, but I think I could get used to it.

'Good, I'm glad.'

TUESDAY MORNING

What time is it? Eight. I'm not fucking getting out of bed. I'm having a fucking lay in. I ain't gotta go to work till three o'clock, so fuck it. I'm going to have a motherfucking lay in. Perfect. I am not getting out of this bed. Let's see if I can drift off back to sleep.

12PM

Fucking hell, that was a proper sleep. My fucking eyes are stuck together, and that fucking crazy helicopter dream with my mate in it. So fucking real. I feel refreshed, though. I've always wanted to go in a helicopter. This dream felt so real. I have a friend called Tony. Let's just call him Tony two. We may have bonded because of our names, but what I do know is that I love him dearly. When we spend time together, it's always a good laugh. His dad's name is Tony as well. Let's just call him Tony three. So it was always surreal and a bit of a laugh when I rang Tony two up and his dad answered. The conversation would go something like this:

ME: *Hello, Tony, it's Tony.*

DAD: *'Hello Tony, you alright?'*

ME: *Yeah, I'm alright thanks Tony. Is Tony there please?*

DAD: *'Yes Tony, I'll just call him. TONY! Tony is on the phone for you. He's coming Tony.'*

ME: *OK Tony, thanks.*

Anyway, about this dream. The helicopter picked up my friend Tony and was hovering about twenty feet above my head. Wind from the helicopter blades was blowing stuff everywhere, and slowly up they went. They went so high as I whispered to myself, wow, right up into the clouds. The helicopter then slowly came back down and hovered about twenty feet above me again, but Tony wasn't in it this time. I shouted to the pilot,

TAKE ME WITH YOU, TAKE ME UP?

but the pilot said,

'No. You can't come.'

What! Take me with you?

'No, you can't come.'

After saying that, he drifted back up into the sky. I couldn't fulfil my dream of going into a helicopter even in my dreams!

I fancy scrambled eggs and smoked salmon for breakfast, lunch, or brunch. On a bit of toast I think. Where's my guitar? I'm gonna play a bit of Hendrix. Rock'n'roll style, ladies and gentlemen, If six was nine. Before long, it was already three o'clock. I've gotta leave for the top-up. Here we go, another train to Tottenham Court Road Station. I get to the first eight phone boxes outside the Dominion Theatre. Right, there's only two boxes down. That one first. Any police? No police, right. Fucking smash it and as quick as you can Tony, quick as you can. One two three four five. Doubling up on the window, two of each card in a box. Another quick look around for police. Mustn't get too brave. Mustn't get complacent. I don't want to get caught. Right, get the other box done. Bollocks. I'm too slow. How long is he gonna take in there? I've gotta fucking stand here and wait for you now. I don't like waiting for people in the boxes around here. It's too open. Ah, great, looks like he's coming out. He's taking his time. He wants to say something to me.

'I'm going to be here for a while, I'm afraid.'

OK mate.

Think Tony. What ya gonna do? I've got two options. Shall I come back later and do this or go for it now? Fuck it, I'll go for it now. With a smile I said,

Excuse me mate. Can I just put a couple of these cards up, please?

'Yeah, go on then, quickly.'

Cheers mate.

I didn't expect that. Go quick, go quick. One two three, cards on the back, quick time. One two three, on the side window. Poor bloke, he's moving left to right, trying to dodge my elbows and arms. I've gotta get out. Bosh, bosh, and done!

Thank you.

Right then, quick march to the next set of four. Fucking bare. not a single card in these boxes that back is usually completely full of cards, and the windows. Even the ceiling gets covered in these boxes. It could be a set up. Someone might be watching these boxes to see who puts them up. I don't like it.

I'll just go and pick up the phone for a little bit, pretend I'm using it. Fuck this fucking paranoid shit, it's slowing me down. shake it off. Right, there's no suspicious people around. I'm fucking going in. One on the back, one on the side, quick quick, got eight to go, pinch a little bit of blue tack, one two three four on the back and four on the side, next one. C'mon Tony faster one two three four five on the window, the backboard and out! Next one, I've got my work cut out for me today but still it must have taken me no more than ninety seconds to have all four boxes done. Nice and neat, right then, hotfoot it up the road to the next four. They're down, what's going on today? Yesterday everything was up, it was piss easy but today, it's full on. A quick look around, no police, c'mon, c'mon lets get this shit done quick. Nice and neat, in and out, no time to fuck about. Next set of four, who's that fucker in there taking 'em down? He's been taking 'em down all along the road. I've gotta stop this fucker, he's giving me loads of fucking work to do. How is he going to respond to me when I confront him? How shall I approach this? The man walks out of the box with a bunch of cards in his hand and walks into the next box to do the same. I've got to stop him now, I'm just gonna pull that fucking door wide open and give it to him.

WHAT ARE YOU DOING!?

The man shook with fright as he spun round quicker than an ice skater with his hands full of cards,

'I was just taking them down'

Yeah I know what you was fucking doing, now leave them alone, and don't touch any more cards down this fucking road.

'OK, sorry, I didn't know'

Well you know now, go on, fuck off!

Why would someone go out of their way to pull all these cards down? As if they've got nothing else better to do.

I feel a bit bad having a pop at him the way I did but I had to do something to stop him. He would have had the whole of Tottenham court road down if I hadn't. Right, let's get D's cards up. Five on the back board as quickly as I can. Five on the side window. D's cards are the only cards up now so there goes the competition. I'm glad I'm on the case for the top up. It's important. OK then, on to the next set of two. Thank fuck that bloke listened, these cards are up, and those are still up. Now this is how I prefer my top ups to go. Hassle free and cards still up.

I wonder if that homeless man who dwells down Warren Street is there today, in his doorway camp site, with his wooden pallet and plastic sheeting over it to shield him from the weather.

There he is. What's he up to? Is he pissing between those parked cars? As I'm getting closer I know he's not pissing but what's he got that wooden crate for? What's he up to… is he gonna shit in that? Here comes another car driving up the wrong way, they always do it on this road. Shit, I can't believe he just threw that crate at that car for no reason. What, now he's fucking rolling on the ground screaming. I know what he's up to, he's after a claim up. The car screeches to a halt and the lady jumps out and runs towards the man panicking as she shouts

'I'M SORRY, ARE YOU ALRIGHT?'

But the bloke is now just laying there. Don't look at me like that lady, I didn't see anything, don't even bother asking me. You're fucked. A one way street and you've just come across a chancer who's gonna make a nice few quid out of you, and there's no way I'm fucking up his chances of getting it. And as for you old man. You clever fucker, you planned this all along. Your secret's safe with me. The man is now looking at me as I walk past as if to say, 'Did you see anything?'

I just wink at him and walk past. Then I got to the phone boxes round Grafton street that were down and then off to the dreaded Oxford Street via the other backstreet boxes. All seems good as most of the cards are up, It's so fucking busy here so they'll be more police here too so there'll be a higher chance of getting caught. All this waiting around for people to come out of these boxes is a drag and there's even a fucking queue before me. The perils of a Cardboy. I'll come back to these main boxes, I'll get the others first

I jumped in to do this bare box on Cavendish street. A quick look around, nothing suspicious, so away I go, boom boom, two cards up on the backboard, Shit! The door opens just as hard and as fast as I opened the door on that bloke earlier in Tottenham court road. Now I'm the one nearly jumping out of my skin. What's this fucking badge in my face? Oh bollocks.

'Police. Come out of the phone box please,'

He's in a pair of trainers, jeans, t-shirt and a dark blue, thin, Harrington jacket.

'Stand over here for a minute, have you got anything else on you apart from the cards?'

No, just the cards

He's joined by his colleague, again in plain clothes as he gets out his notebook and asks,

'What's your name?'

I gave him my name and address, and after writing it all down, checking my ID and all that bollocks he says to me,

'You'll be hearing from the courts in due time. In the meantime, I suggest you go home.'

And off they went. Fuck knows what's going to happen now. Why didn't they take my cards? I'm not going home before I do what I've got to do. Fuck it, I'm gonna carry on. It's best I come back here once it's cooled down a bit and do the Soho boxes first. All lovely and still up in Soho, so fucking nothing at all to do here. Sweet, onto Cambridge Circus. There's the odd couple of cards to put up in the boxes here outside the Palace Theatre. "Les Miserables," that show's been up here for ages. Right, back to Oxford Street for the main four boxes.

But I'm dreading going back there after seeing those two plainclothes. At least I now know what they look like. This feels like what D was explaining about a cat and mouse game. Great, someone's coming out of that box so I'd better get in there quick. Come on, walk faster, get there before someone else does. A quick look around and bang! I'm off, two three four five on the backboard and five on the window. I don't give a shit about those police at this moment, just gotta get it done and get the fuck out of here. Last one and out! No police, and I disappear into the backstreets. I've still got a few cards on me, but if they're mostly up, then they're up. I don't need these ones anymore and I've still got to go to Gloucester Place to pick up some more cards from the pain-in-the-arse girl for D. I'll throw these few cards I have left in the bin and head for the nearest tube station. Thirty-three Gloucester Place, D said to go. I jump on the train to Marylebone Station and walk the rest of the journey to Gloucester Place. Nice looking flat from the outside, so here goes. With the sound of a classic doorbell, there's a lady who looks about sixty standing there.

Hello, are you Trilly? D sent me to pick up some cards.

'Oh, come in love, you must be Tony?'

Yeah, that's me.

'I'm not Trilly. I'm the maid.'

The last place I picked some cards up from on Grafton Street was a bit shabby, but this place looks quite plush. She leads me into the kitchen. And there I'm greeted by the girl.

'Hi, I'm Trilly. What's your name?'

I'm standing silent there for a brief second because she took my breath away. I'm just looking into her eyes while she stands there with her outstretched hand. I'm eventually shaking her hand and I've got an instant hard-on. Fucking hell, the blood gushing through me with attraction for this woman is so powerful. The last time I felt this way instantly when I met a woman was when I was twenty years old. That was six years ago. I've had a few women in my past, but this kind of crazy attraction is definitely rare.

I never did a thing about the strong attraction I had for that last woman for some reason. I was young and probably wasn't confident enough. What a pussy. I fucking regret not acting on that. All the girlfriends I've had since have never had the same effect on me when I first met them. And here I am again, six years later, with that same feeling for someone else. And it's bollocks 'cause I need to let this one slide. She's a working girl. And I ain't fucking a working girl. What the fuck is going on? I feel like I'm magnetised to her and it's obvious she is attracted to me.

Hi Trilly, I'm Tony.

'So, D sent you to pick up the cards then, everything OK?'

D's OK.

'How long have you been a CardBoy then?'

Well, I'm just doing the top-up for D, just helping out a bit.

'Well, you can top up anytime for me.'

Oh shit, she doesn't mess about coming on like this. I've got to go, but I'm fucking rock hard for her and I don't care that she noticed it. I'm not breaking eye contact with you if that's what you're looking for. The maid comes into the kitchen with a stack of cards.

'Tell D this is all we've got for now. I know it's better to take the full week, but we've got new cards being printed, so lazy nuts will have to come back tomorrow. I know D doesn't like coming up here for small amounts of cards." Trilly then comes back into the conversation.

'Or you can come back tomorrow to get them.'

I'm looking at her and thinking, fuck yeah I'll come back. I want to know if this feeling I have for her today will be there tomorrow. Maybe I'm just feeling extra horny today and she just happens to be the first woman I've seen in my radar while I'm feeling this way. Who the fuck am I kidding? Six years I haven't felt this way for someone. So I say to her,

If I'm around tomorrow, I'll stop by and pick 'em up.

It's so noisy on this train ride back. The rhythm of the wheels rolling on the track sounds like music. The drums. What could I play to this? Rhythm guitar I'm hearing, and oh boy do I have a good tune going round my head right now. It's quite packed on this train. That smells like expensive perfume. I wonder who it is that smells so good? Could be that Middle Eastern woman over there. I suspect it's her; they always smell good. I'm also looking at four beautiful women on my carriage, all of them look gorgeous. Any man would want to have sex with any one of these sexy, classy women, and I would not say no either, but strangely enough, none of these beauties have the same effect on me or anywhere near the same effect that Trilly had on me. I'm not attracted to any of these like Trilly. I can't choose whom I'm attracted to, and as much as I would not turn any of these women down if they threw themselves at me, that hot attraction is just not there. But I won't make a move on Trilly. That would be silly, mainly because she's a working girl. In fact, it's only because she's a working girl. If I'm fucking her, the thought of someone else fucking her or, even worse, many men fucking her is a horrible thought.

It reminds me of a girlfriend I had a little while ago whom I loved very much. As with ninety nine point nine percent of men out there, what I value most in a girlfriend is loyalty. This girlfriend, as cold as ice, went ahead and fucked this guy I knew. She even tried to get me to give him messages that would facilitate her affair. She had no integrity, and I didn't vet her first. Although I probably acted weak somewhere along the line, like a bitch beta male, a cheating woman is the worst thing that a man can be exposed to in his relationship.

Whenever someone buys a secondhand car, they run checks. They check the engine for leaks, the tires for baldness, they may look underneath for rust, check the paintwork, and test drive the car properly before they make a decision to buy it. That's how I should have been with her. Another girlfriend I had, whom I hadn't seen for a short while, involuntarily burped in my face while we were in a clinch, and all I could smell was baby gravy, cum, fucking spunk. I hadn't seen her for two weeks, so it wasn't mine, and that was it for me. She knew I could smell it; she obviously smelled it too, which is why she broke out of our clinch. I couldn't leave the house or the relationship quickly enough. I vet everyone now, including friends, and Trilly is definitely off the cards for any fun. I arrive at D's house to deliver the cards.

'Alright Tony, how did it go today?'

I got nicked.

'You got nicked? Where? What happened?'

Side turning in Oxford Street, two plainclothes old bill got me.

'Really? Did they take your cards?'

No, they didn't. They took my name and address and told me to go home.

'OK. You'll probably get a summons to go to court, but don't worry, it's only littering. It's not a criminal offence. You'll get a little fine, and that's it. You've had your first pull now; that's your cherry broke.'

It's not funny D.

'The only thing is they know what you look like now, so they might be keeping an eye out for you. Are you okay?'

Well, I don't really wanna go to court for this D.

'You don't even have to go to court Tony. You can if you want, or you can just pay the fine. I just pay the fine. They know me; half the time, they just leave me alone. They know I'm just putting out cards and drive straight past me most of the time. It will take a few weeks for that summons to come through. Did you get the cards from Gloucester Place?'

Yeah D, there you go, six hundred. She said she's getting more cards printed up and you'll have to pick up the rest tomorrow.

'See what I mean? A pain in the fucking arse, that one'

That bird in there D. She's fucking red hot.

'Ah, you fancy Trilly, eh?'

She's got something.

The speed that D is mixing those two piles of cards is incredible.

'I've got so many girls, I've not got enough pockets. I've got to mix them all now so I can get two girls in each pocket. I might employ someone just to mix the cards for me. I can't stand doing this every night. Will you go back there tomorrow to pick 'em up? I really can't be bothered with that girl, but it's money. There's twelve hundred cards left to pick up. You okay with that? Shouldn't be that bulky or heavy.'

Yeah, I'll go there tomorrow D. Fuck me, it's nine o'clock already? I'm going home to roll myself a nice joint. I'll see ya tomorrow.

'Cool Tony. Thanks for today.'

Fucking phone! Shit, it scared the life out of me. Who's that ringing at ten this morning? This fucking hammock is comfortable to sleep in. Fuck me, I must have been tired to sleep that long. Oh, it's Tony number two ringing.

Hello geezer. What's happening?

'Hello, Tony?'

Yeah?

'It's, it's Tony's dad.' Tony three. But why does he sound so sad?

Hello Tony, how are you?

'Not good. Tony died last night. He had a car accident and hit a tree. I've lost my son.'

I... I can't believe it. I was just... I'm so... I don't know what to say. I can't believe it. My mind is going crazy. It's all over the place. What? My friend is dead? I can't believe it. And that dream with the helicopter! I probably dreamt that the minute his soul left his body and floated up into the universe. That's it. That's proof of extraordinary human connection right there. This is some freaky shit and at the same time, it's so clear. I know that dream was Tony reaching out to me at his final moment. I'm convinced of that. I can't believe my mate is gone. I just feel like staying indoors after this news, but I've gotta do the top-up.

Tony, I'm so sorry. I know this is something you'll never get over. I loved him so much. He was my good friend. I'll talk to you soon, yeah?

'OK Tony, thanks for being such a good friend to him. I'll let you know about all the funeral arrangements and all of that stuff.'

Yeah, OK, thanks. I'll see ya later.

I jumped on a train and headed for Tottenham Court Road station. I've been standing outside this box at the Dominion for over five minutes now, waiting for this bloke to get out of the only box that needs doing. Right, here we go. He's coming out, and I'm going in. Quick Tony, get stuck in today. I've got to go to Gloucester Place to pick up cards. Bollocks to keeping a diary. I'll just keep on repeating it to myself in my head. Keeps the brain working. I write fuck all down. Risky sometimes, but that's how it works for me. I never use an alarm clock either. Once I had to catch a plane at three-forty one morning. I went to bed at twelve-twenty, didn't set an alarm, and still got the plane in time. I fucking hate alarm clocks, and thank fuck I don't need one. Just the thought of being abruptly woken up by a ringing bell puts a frown on my face. I mean, who would want to wake up to that? He's out of the phone box, and I'm in. Right, Tony. Get to work and get this shit done. Two on the back, one two, and two on the side window. Bish, bosh. A quick look around for police and another two on the back and two on the window. One two three four. Four more girls to do… and done, out!

I'm off walking up Tottenham Court Road to the first set of four boxes. What a result. I can see this first one is untouched from this morning. All the cards are neatly up. There must be about a hundred cards in that box. The backboard, both sides of the windows, and a section of the ceiling are just covered in cards. I think they all look really good in there. They're all placed so neatly and straight. Nothing like the scruffy boxes of Soho. I wonder who cleaned that stinky shit up down there.

I don't think these pictures are the actual girls on these cards. I'm almost sure they just use random photos they found in a magazine or somewhere. It's like a piece of art in this box, and there's not a single missing card that needs to go up. I'm loving how easy this job is. I'm off to the next set of four. What a fucking breeze, they're all up! This is good. Right, cross the road and check the two boxes over here. There's a couple of cards missing from this box. Bosh these up. Right, let's go and have a look at these two boxes opposite Goodge Street station. They're up! Fucking brilliant, no one's touching D's cards today. I'll stock up on blue tack. Our man's shop is not too far from here. Such a small shop. I like going there. Always a good bit of banter going on, and I love his Pakistani accent. Standing next in the queue, I can hear someone behind me drumming on the magazine he's going to buy. Sounds like he really knows how to play the drums. That shopkeeper is so fucking loud.

'NEXT PLEASE. Oh no, not you again. What can I get you? Blue tack? One packet, two packets?' There's a magazine on the counter with someone I recognize on the front cover.

Ah, look at that! I met her last week.

'Who? This famous person? She's on front cover of magazine, you say you meet her? My customer is funny'.

I did meet her. I kissed her on the cheek. Both cheeks.

'Oh, bloody blimey. You are funny. This lady is in soap opera, British television. She doesn't spend time with people who put cards in telephone boxes.'

No, you don't understand. She's a friend of my brother. He took me to a party about three weeks ago and introduced me to her.

'OHHH, you tell me last week you meet her. My customer doesn't know the truth. Nobody is believing you.'

Look, you may not believe me, but I assure you it's all fucking true. I kissed her.

'OK, see you tomorrow, after you've had tea with the queen. NEXT PLEASE.'

I'm watching the man behind me throw his windsurfing magazine on the counter. I look at the man, then the shopkeeper.

'Is there anything else you want to buy?'

No. I know the inventor of the windsurf.

'OOHH bloody blimey, here we go again. Did you meet him for dinner last week?'

Actually, it was about two months ago.

'AAHH you say you meet him for dinner, I cannot believe it.'

No, I didn't say I met him for dinner, I went on his boat, his name is Peter.

'Stop telling bullshit.'

I went to visit him on his boat in the Docklands in East London through another friend of mine. He loves to play live music which is what brought us together.

'Nobody is believing you.'

You might not believe me but I assure you it's all true.

'Yes OK, everything you say is telling the truth.'

Alright, you's fucking laugh, I aint fucking lying though.

I'm out of there, and I walk a little bit further down past Goodge Street station to the two phone boxes outside the American International Church. Funny how I always think of the story around that rough bit of ground outside there. Under that big tree. How can it be forgotten that there is a cemetery just there, and to think there was a murder investigation after revealing human bones, the whole road must have come to a halt while that investigation went ahead. I can't imagine how they felt once they realised there was a cemetery there. Nice that they put that tombstone there after to honour all the buried there. They don't give a fuck about it now though 'coz it's all broken. I wonder if it will stay there right in the middle of Tottenham Court Road forever. There's work to do in these two boxes so I'm in. I'm a bit careless in these because I don't look around much for the police so five on the back and three four five on the side window, and I'm out of there.

I cross the road to the next two phone boxes, brilliant, all cards are still up, back across the road to the next two, both up. This is how I love my days to go. Onto the next four, oh fuck. Why's that dirty-looking man pissing in the phone box? Fucking disgusting. I wonder if he's the shitter from Soho. I'm not going in that box, there's only a couple of cards down anyway, I walk into the next phone box, the backboard is up so I just need to put the window side up, one, two, three, POLICE! They screech to a stop right outside the phone box and I grab the phone receiver to pretend I'm using the phone. Did they see me? I guess I'll soon find out. I'm standing there looking out the window towards them while I hold the phone to my ear pretending I'm laughing at what the phantom person on the other end of the phone might be saying.

They get out of the car and walk towards me, here we go again, another nicking. I slowly put the phone down but they walk straight past me and up to the nasty man pissing in the phone box on the other side. While they get him out and start giving him the bollocking he deserves, I slowly slip into the next box and proceed to smash up the odd few cards that are missing. It's a bit cocky but I've got to get these boxes done. I'm smashing this phone box as quickly as I can, one, two, three, four; I won't do the side window on this one whilst they're there, I don't want to push my luck. Onto the last two of Tottenham Court Road outside the McDonalds. I'm not feeling like doing the rest of this route now, what with my mate being dead. He'd be pushing me forward to crack on with it anyway. I gotta make sure I finish D's work for that money, so I push on through the backstreet phone boxes around Grafton Street, hitting the few boxes that are down and then onto Oxford Street. Thank fuck these boxes are up, I really want to finish this round quickly today so onto the Soho area. I hope that shit has been cleaned up properly, I'm not doing it if it still stinks.

I get to the four red boxes in Soho, the cards are a right fucking mess. Makes it harder to see if D's cards are up but they are, I just need to tidy them up a bit in a nice neat square. I open the shit phone box and it's clean. A few sniffs but I can't smell anything so I go in and arrange the cards neatly, replacing a couple that have been scrunched up. Right, just Cambridge Circus to do before I head up Charing Cross road and back to the starting point.

It's four thirty and fucking hot. I'm glad I've finished, I'll jump on a train to Gloucester Place to get those cards from Trilly's flat.

I wonder if she'll still have that effect on me, we'll see. I ring the bell and the maid opens the door with a big smile on her face.

'Hello love, come to pick up the cards? Come through, she's in the kitchen.'

I walk along the passageway into the kitchen and there she is. Just standing there, looking stunning, it's not just her looks that sends a shiver down my spine, there's an electricity forming between us, I stand next to the kitchen island in the middle of the room just staring at her. Sparks are flying all over my body, my cheeks, my ears, right down to my feet. I'm controlling my lust for her while we stand there just looking at each other, and without me even realising it I'm rubbing my full hard on against the corner of the kitchen island, what the fuck! She can feel me big time, what the fuck! These thoughts running through my head, Tony, no, she's a working girl, I've got to keep away from her, don't stare, do not stare; how often do we ever feel this much attraction for someone. Last time, I let it go. I knew what a fucking regret that was, but I've gotta let this one go. She fucking likes me too. I can feel that. And then she speaks to me.

'Would you like a cup of tea?'

Holy fucking shit! I want her even more now. I'm not fucking leaving, and this tea will keep me here for at least ten minutes. That's ten minutes of this wonderful feeling running through me, but it's better she feels like this and not me. I wouldn't wanna rob her of this feeling. It's better that way too. Always better to be the adored, not the adorer. She won't run off so easily. Why am I teasing myself like this? Nope, I refuse to take this any further. She's a working girl, so it's best I just enjoy the feeling right now and forget about her. The maid is removing cards from a big cardboard box and putting them in a big white carrier bag for me while I stand there, still rubbing my hard-on slowly against the island. I don't even want to try to hide or stop it. I don't fucking care. I should take her right now. It's my duty to be direct and go for anything I want, right? But I just can't bring myself to do it. The maid hands me the cards, so I no longer need to be here. I leave the rest of the tea, and hand her the cup.

'Aww, you didn't finish your tea. Thanks for coming.'

The maid slowly looked at Trilly with a look that said "What the fuck was going on between you two?" before turning to me and saying,

'I'm sure we'll see you again.'

OK, see ya later.

I started to walk out of the kitchen to the passageway. Trilly came behind to see me out. As I'm walking towards the door, I felt the gentle finger of Trilly's left hand just touch my shoulder. Well, like I said before, attraction is not a choice. It's either there, or it's not, and this kind of attraction only comes by once every six years in my case. My body and soul just did their own thing without me even realising it. As bolts of passion for her rang through my body, I spun around and spun her around in the passage with her hands up against the wall, my hands grabbing at her tits from behind her as we both groaned in unison. My cock rubbed along the crack of her beautifully formed arse while my breath on the back of her neck made the hairs on it stand up. It was paradise! We would have done it right there and then had I not snapped back into my mind the fact that the maid was in the kitchen and that I was here to grab some cards. I growled myself back into reality, and with a deep breath, I left. I got the train back to my home station, jumped in my car, and headed to D's house.

'Hello Tony. Manchester United are top of the league by seven clear points. They're my boys, they're just my boys. Are those the cards?'

Yeah D.

'OK. Pain in the arse that girl.'

Yeah, you said, D.

'How did it go out there? Were there many cards down?'

A few D. I sorted 'em though.

'Good boy. Listen, Tony, I can't do the round tomorrow. Do you wanna do the route in the morning?'

Er, yeah, OK.

'It's easy, you'll be OK. You'll have to mix the cards tonight though. I really can't do any of it. Just go round the flats after and take the money. I'll text you the addresses later. When you get to Euston Station and King's Cross Station, you'll see the British Transport Police there. Don't do the boxes directly in the station. There are a couple right close to the wall outside, but it's still the Station's land, and the old bill there love a Cardboy. They'll fucking stick it on ya big time. I've been dragged into the room they've got there for interrogation before, but they've got no jurisdiction anywhere outside of the stations. So the ones across the road from King's Cross are not in their jurisdiction. You can do those, and they can't stop ya.'

D gives me a big box of cards and three packets of blue tack, which I put in the boot of my car and drive home. There are twelve girls in total, six hundred cards from each girl. That's over seven thousand cards I've got to mix. There's enough cards for the morning and the afternoon top-up, and they all need to be mixed so they all will fit in just six pockets. I'd better start mixing. I make a cup of coffee, roll a big fat joint, and put on some good old Rock'n'Roll ready for the task ahead. I lay the cards out on the table and start to mix with six piles of cards on my right and six on my left and with a bowl of water for my fingers to grip. Both hands are at work, flicking out cards from each pile and slamming them together in the middle. I immediately stop to answer the front door. It's my next-door neighbour.

'Got any cigarette papers, Tony?'

Yeah Steve, come in.

'What's all those cards about then?'

Ah, just fucking work. I'm putting them out in the West End for a little while, get some money to get this house fucking sorted. It's freezing here in the winter.

'What! How much do you get paid for that?'

Well, Cardboys get paid ten pounds for every hundred cards they put out. I normally just do a top-up in the afternoons, but tomorrow's different. I've got six hundred cards of each girl to put out, and I've got twelve girls, so that's sixty pounds a girl times twelve, leaving me to earn seven hundred and twenty pounds for one day's work. Let's get one thing straight though Steve, I ain't no pimp. That's not my bag. The Cardboys work for the girls, not the other way round. They don't control them or tell 'em what to do or who to see. I'm about to make some good money tomorrow Steve, but I'll have to be up early to get the space just above the phone.

'Is it dodgy?'

I'm a bit nervous. You do get fined if you get caught, but it's not a lot, and the thought of all that money gives me all the courage I need. Can you help me mix 'em?

'Yeah, go on then. I've got fuck all else to do, let me roll a joint first.'

I'm glad he helped me tonight. I would have been here for ages otherwise. I'm quite stoned now and it's fucking nine o'clock. I load the cards into each pocket of my waistcoat. It's very heavy now, and I hang it up, ready for the morning.

3:15AM

I'm fucking nervous this morning. Come on Tony, you can do it, you can do it. Eat a good breakfast and get the fuck up there. It's still dark outside when I leave my house at four and head for Tottenham Court Road. It's nice at this time of the morning: nobody walking about, no traffic around to contend with, just me in my car, music on. It takes me just under fifteen minutes to reach Tottenham Court Road. I pull into Great Russell Street, the first turning off that road, park up, and get myself ready. I put my waistcoat on and a light jacket over the top to hide it. I open up a packet of blue tack and make it into one big round ball. Nerves are kicking in, so I take a deep breath. In the name of the Father, and of the Son, and of the Holy Spirit, Amen. Right then, get the fuck out of the car, here we go.

As I approach the first set of eight phone boxes at the Dominion, I can see there are no cards in any of the boxes. Is someone watching these boxes, waiting for a Cardboy to walk in so they can catch me red-handed? I can't get my cards taken off me this early, but I haven't got all the cards on me, so I'm safe in that respect. Just think of the money Tony, think of what you'll earn today. Grr, right, here we go, first box. Fucking stinks of detergent, where's that fucking cleaner gone? A quick look around for police—none about—so time to crack on at full speed, bang bang. I whip out the cards from my pocket at lightning speed and slam the first two on the back. C'mon, next two. Fuck. Stay up, you bastard. It's too fucking wet! That fucking cleaner, what do I do here? I ain't got a fucking cloth. They just won't fucking stick. I try again, but blue tack will just not stick on a wet surface, and they've got to go up, so I keep fucking trying, but it's no fucking good.

I grab one of the cards and desperately try to dry the back with it, but it's pretty much useless. I scramble around in my pockets looking for a tissue or a receipt or anything that I may have on me to get this box dry. I'm taking way too long here now. Don't panic Tony, just look for something. Fuck yes, a rotten bit of tissue in the corner of D's waistcoat pocket. What's on this, I wonder? Fuck the boogers, I've gotta get this dry. I dunno how this tissue can clean the next few boxes here; it's falling apart already. I get the cards to eventually stay up, but it's taken me four times as long to get this box done and out of there. The other boxes are also wet but not as wet as the first one, and I do all of the boxes eventually.

I continue walking up Tottenham Court Road to the first set of four boxes, but the cleaner is there. It's a company called NTN who are contracted to clean the telephone boxes in the west end of London. They do a good job, but this for me is a pain now. I just want to charge my way up Tottenham Court Road and get these boxes done, but it looks like he'll be going along the whole road at his own pace.

Who's that bloke standing by the box? Got a waistcoat like mine. A bit obvious that he's a Cardboy. I'll watch to see what he does first when the cleaner leaves. And when the cleaner eventually jumps in his little van and drives off to the next set of phone boxes, the other guy steps into the phone box. He's putting at least eight cards on the backboard, and then he puts the duplicate card of each girl on the left-hand side window. He's not put any of his cards in D's space. He's not smiling at all when he comes out. And he just stands there watching to see what I'm about to do. I look at him as I enter the box, and he's still standing there, just staring. I ain't got time for this bollocks, so I start smashing the cards up on the backboard in D's space. He quickly pulls the door open.

'Ere mate, you can't put your cards up there. Oh, you're doing D's cards? Where is D?'

Not about today, so I've been given the cards to do.

'Ah, that's alright then, 'cause that's D's space above the phone. No one's allowed to go there."

These fucking cards keep falling off. The fucking cleaner has soaked this.

'Here you go, use this.'

He hands me a cloth, and I rapidly wipe the backboard and hand it back to him.

Cheers mate.

'Nah, keep it. I've got another one. You're gonna need it 'cause we've gotta go behind the cleaner, and he's fucking slow today. He's late. He's a fucking pain in the arse. I've gotta go somewhere at ten this morning. I had plenty of time to do my round and get out of here, but this cunt is fucking holding me back. I hate going behind these cleaners. He's gotta take all the cards down from yesterday, about hundred of 'em. Then he cleans it, and it's always soaking. That's why I carry a cloth, even a spare! You've got that. You'll be here ages waiting for him today, you watch.'

Think Tony, think. How can I get this job done quicker? Shall I go off and do other boxes first and then come back to this road? Fuck knows if he's going to be the same cleaner on the route that I'm on. I might get to the backstreets, and all the cards are still up from yesterday. Then what? I can't put my cards up. He'll just take them all down. The Cardboy turns to speak to me.

'What's your name mate?'

Tony.

'Alright Tony, my name's Terry.'

You're a bit of a lump ain't ya Terry.

He's holding back his smile, so I don't know how friendly he is unless he doesn't smile much at all because of that missing front tooth I can see he's trying to hide. People get so insecure about these things. Everyone I talk to who has rank teeth tries to hide them from me when they're talking, and because I'm making the fuckers laugh, they really try to close those lips while they're laughing. Looks so obvious. The eyes are another one. Talking to someone who has a crossed eye, they always seem to look away, trying to hide it. I see your eye, motherfucker. Don't try and hide that shit. Own it. I won't judge you, motherfucker. In fact, when I meet someone with tombstone teeth or missing teeth altogether, I look them straight in the eye when we're talking. I do not look at the fucked-up teeth at all, although I can see them in my peripheral view. They don't know that, and it's remarkable how quickly you see them stop trying to hide them. The confidence in them is instant. As soon as you stop looking at them, they open up and relax. So it's you motherfuckers that look at them that gives them the complex. Same as the eyes. I always look at the eye that's looking at me. Sometimes those motherfuckers catch me out and change the one that looks at me. That's when it gets awkward because as soon as I slip up and look at the wrong eye, they fucking look away. Own that shit, motherfucker. There's a very pretty woman who lives near me, but her teeth are hooked and twisted up to a degree you really don't see often. But she owns it. She smiles confidently, so it doesn't make her look unattractive.

Fuck standing here, I need to sort out what I'm going to do about these cards and that fucking cleaner. I can't stay out all day because of him. I'm gonna have a word with him. The fucking cards this cleaner collects each day are something to see. Those black sacks are full. The fucking van is full. Right then, time to work this fucker. Look how slowly he's washing that box. Put on the friendly smile Tony. I open the door of the phone box to have a chat with him.

Hello mate, how are ya?

'What, oh, morning, alright?'

I bet we're a pain in the neck to you cleaners, us Cardboys, eh?

'Nah mate, we don't mind. I don't mind, we're used to them. I think some of those cards are funny. You've gotta do your job, and we've gotta do ours.'

Where are you from?

'I am from Lithuania.'

I'll tell you what mate, we can help each other out here. I'll go down the rest of Tottenham Court Road before you, and all the backstreets—Cleveland Street, Maple Street, Fitzroy Street, and all around there—and I'll take down all of yesterday's cards. Then I'll put my cards up all neatly just above the phone box. There are six girls I've got here. I'll put six cards just above the phone. You leave them up there, and I'll give you fifty quid now.

I pull out two twenty-pound notes and a tenner and rub them all between my thumb and finger at him.

'Fifty quid?'

He takes a very quick look around before snatching the money from me.

'OK mate, I'll leave them up. Six cards yeah? All nice and neat above the phone box, yeah?'

That's it mate, see ya later.

I left him to it. What a result. I can now crack on and get this round done and out of here before it gets busy. I quickly march to the next set of two boxes. Cards everywhere. Both sides of the glass windows are eight stacks high and five stacks deep. All the back is covered with cards. Some Cardboys have slotted their cards in between little panels and gaps that make up the booth. I look up to see about ten cards on the ceiling. That's funny. If I was a punter, I'm not going to feel comfortable looking up to the moon for the numbers and back down again to the phone keypad. Those girls must struggle to get the punters in when their Cardboy gets them that position. Above the phone is perfect.

I like that there's a code, and it's frowned upon to move another Cardboy's work. Throughout the day, everyone is jostling to get the cards up fairly and keep them up, including me again this afternoon when I come back out to do the top-up, but that's cool. I'm making over seven hundred pounds today for two to three hours of work this morning and a possible hour and a half later, and that fifty quid spent on the cleaner was well worth it. With a big smile, I start to rip down all the cards in the box. I put them down in one big pile on the little metal shelf that's in all of the phone boxes and put my cards up nice and neat above the phone. Darting into the next box quickly, I carry on ripping the cards down. Just as I'm starting to do this, a police car slowly draws up alongside the phone box and stops. I stop with a smile and shout out to them.

IT'S DISGUSTING!

Thank fuck they drove off, but I've got a feeling they'll be back for me. At double the speed, I finished taking down yesterday's cards and got these boxes done. The rest of the road was just the same. Some of the boxes that were still up from yesterday were all nice and neat, so I just took the rest down and left D's cards up. With Tottenham Court Road done, I walked back up the road to get my car.

By the time I get Euston, a cleaner has already been, and the boxes are dry. Before I arrive at the box, I'm looking around for police, just moving my eyes around everywhere with my neck still. Any up the stairs of Euston Station? No. I'll never know who are plainclothes police around the area watching out for the likes of me. I better grow some balls. I ain't gonna be a Cardboy who's not doing every box. I can see why some of 'em skip a few here and there. I don't like it myself when someone is taking ages using the phone. I wonder how long all the other boys are prepared to wait for that when there are one hundred-odd boxes to do. But if I'm gonna do this job, I'm gonna do it properly. That's the whole purpose of getting up this fucking early in the first place. And what girl wants a Cardboy who doesn't make 'em good money? No police about, so quick, get in there. One two three four five six on the back. Same on the side window, quick look about, and out. Into the next box. One two three four five six. Quick quick, hit the window. One to six. Done. Out! There are about sixteen of these to do around Euston and the station, so I walk to do those, leaving my car at Euston Square. There are no traffic wardens at this time of the morning, so parking ain't a problem. Finishing the boxes there, I head back to the car.

Next stop is Kings Cross. I park my car round the backstreets there and reload my waistcoat with more cards. A deep breath is needed, and I jump out of the car, up to the first set of two empty boxes on the route, and off I go. The sound of that door opening has embedded itself into my mind as I systematically move in exactly the same way to enter each box, neatly and quickly putting my cards up. Onto the next two. Bollocks! All the cards are still up from yesterday. Is the cleaner gonna come today, I wonder. Bollocks, I'll take the fucking risk. Yesterday's cards have got to come down, so I put them in a neat pile on the shelf while I continue to put my cards up. I then chuck yesterday's cards in the bin and carry on to the main set of boxes directly opposite Kings Cross Station. These ones are all still up from yesterday, and they're a right mess too, but this shit needs to be done, and I've gotta fucking do it. Why do I feel so fucking nervous? I better liven myself up; it's only a silly fucking fine. So I hit that first box and stripped it in under fifteen seconds, leaving the old cards on the shelf. I quickly put my cards up. One, three, six, and six on the window, and out! Next one, there's a copper across the road right outside Kings Cross Station peeking over at me. Maybe he thinks I can't see him looking at me because it's dark, but I can see ya, and I do these four boxes without him coming over. Even though D told me about these British Transport Police, it still feels weird doing it right in front of him like this. I cross the road and go to the box on the side of Kings Cross Station, strip yesterday's cards down, and put mine up. I look up to see the policeman slowly walk behind a pillar and peek round it at me. Yeah, I can see you looking at me, and you can do fuck all while I'm not over there. With all boxes up, I put yesterday's cards in the bin and walked back to my car. Come to think of it, I'd better go and check Tottenham Court Road to see how the fifty quid I spent on the cleaner has worked out. Right then, first stop, Dominion Theatre. Drive nice and slowly down, that one's up, next two, up, up, up, Goodge Street station boxes, both up, next two, up, wicked, they're all up. I get to the bottom of Tottenham Court Road and turn left for the backstreet boxes, up, up. Here's the cleaner at Cleveland Street. I love watching him use that squeegee on the outside of the box on all that soap, and I know he's already done the inside 'cause he does that first and my cards are still up. They're not going anywhere. I've got to toot him. He waves and smiles at me as I drive past. Time to go home, job done until this afternoon for the top-up.

The return from the West End at this time of the morning to my house is about a twenty-minute drive, and I get home at eight. I feel good about how this morning went and have some breakfast before getting my head down for a rest.

MIDDAY

And what a rest that was. Three and a half hours of sleep, and I feel great. I've done a day's work already, for good money, and it's only twelve o'clock. The sun is out, and I'm going for a walk. I could get used to this lifestyle. I've still got the top-up to do, but I know that's way easier than it was this morning, so right now, I'm gonna enjoy a bit of lunch out somewhere. That time out soon passes by. I've never had hot steamed pear and Roquefort cheese for dessert before, but I can tell ya that combination works a treat. I'm not gonna use the car for the top-up; the train is much better, no worries about parking tickets. I could put money in the metres here, but it works out to four quid an hour in some places, and I can't be guaranteed I'll have the space to park where the phone boxes are, so it can stay at home.

On the train for the top-up, I'm feeling good. I have a hundred cards of each girl in my pockets, and the sound of those wheels on the train track is bringing up the beat of the old Rock'n'Roll song by Chuck Berry, and I can imagine myself playing the guitar to '**Let It Rock**'. I love Chuck Berry. My brother calls him 'Throw Pineapple' but that groove—when it rocks, oh man, I just love Rock'n'Roll. All this puts a smile on my face, but I can't see anyone else on this train smiling or talking. I close my eyes and imagine that everyone on this train is talking, laughing, and meeting each other, just like at a bar on a Friday night.

As I am meditating further into this thought, the familiar smell of shit begins to make its way across my nostrils, which first puts a damper on the smile I had on my face, but it got a little stronger, a little worse, which in turn made my eyebrows drop. At this point, I still had my eyes closed, hoping it would go away, but then disaster struck. It became one of the worst-smelling farts I have ever encountered. I could not keep my eyes closed any longer. This had to be addressed. I stood up and said,

WHOEVER DID THAT, IT'S ROTTEN!

I have a quick look around for the culprit. Anyone looking suspicious? There's a woman sitting opposite the chair that I had just vacated, trying her best to stifle her laugh. It must have been her. If it wasn't, she would have laughed out loud or not laughed at all. Thankfully, this next stop is mine. Tottenham Court Road Station.

When the top-ups are like this, it puts a big smile on my face. All the cards at the Dominion Theatre are up. I walk up to the next set of four, and they are the same as they have been all day. Next two, up. Only one box down at the next set of four and nobody using the phone, beautiful. I go in there and neatly put my cards up. I take my time in this box, like I haven't got a care in the world. It's more like, one......two......three......four. Strolling out of the box and casually walking along the road towards Goodge Street station before crossing the road to the next set of two. No one has a clue what I'm up to; I'm just looking at cards. All up. It's a lovely day today, and doing this is so sweet. I'm getting paid for just going for a stroll and slipping up the odd card. Only one box to do on the whole of Tottenham Court Road. That saves so much time, I'll pop into McDonald's for a drink.

Standing there in the queue, there's a cool-looking Rastaman in front of me waiting for his order. The worker puts it on the counter in front of him. He opens the bag, looks inside, and shouts at her, questioning what she gave him.

'A-WHA-DAT?'

You ordered two cheeseburgers and two hot chocolates.

'NAH, MAN. ME-SAY ME WAN TWO MCDONALDS AND TWO CHOCOLATE MILKSHAKE!'

I have to bite my lip to stop this laughter from bursting out. What the fuck is a McDonald? The girl behind the counter is just the same; she wants to laugh too. I grab my coffee and head on out to the backstreets. Nice and relaxed today.

I'm thinking of the homeless guy with the crate. I wonder if he managed to push his compensation claim through from the woman driving the wrong way up the road. His camp is not here anymore. I straighten up a few cards in the backstreet boxes. The odd card is down. Some blokes like to take the cards and ring later. I'm sure some just want them as souvenirs of London, and if someone needs to write something down while they're on the phone, they're perfect. I'm noticing that these pictures can sometimes be a bit graphic, and there are some with just writing on to entice the punter, but I guess the pictures are better because men are visual and most will fall in love at the drop of a hat, so it must be better to slap a little photo on the card. Surely they won't use their own picture. There's transexual, and transexual pre-op. A drastic difference there. Submissive cards, dominatrix, oriental cards, Indian. I was given a transexual card to put up this morning, and I do need to go to her house later to pick up money when I've finished. That should be interesting. I can't believe I'm going to meet a bloke who has had the full operation and is now a woman. Her name is Pearl. These backstreets are quiet, with very few people walking about as I speed up my pace a bit and swing the phone box doors open. I'm getting to appreciate the sound of the doors squeaking as I pull them, and now I've developed a Jeffrey Daniels-style robotic side foot slide into the phone box. I love his style. He was the first person to do the moonwalk, whom I learned it from before Michael Jackson learned it from him. I loved the days when I used to body pop like a motherfucker in my early teens—caterpillar crawl, cracking and popping from my knuckles through to my elbows, and straight to the body. Yeah, that was me… and of course, the moonwalk.

Time to fuck off to the phone boxes down Oxford Street. It's crazy here, so fucking busy. There are two boxes with no cards in 'em down here and people in both of them using the phone. I'll come back to these ones. I'll go to the other end first, the end where I start the route, where Tottenham Court Road meets Oxford Street, and walk up from that way. Thank fuck these first two boxes are up, especially as there are people using those phones too. I know there are plainclothes police about, so I try to blend in and not look suspicious. I've gotta be in and out of these boxes like lightning. Right then, some cards down in that one and the lady's just coming out. Quick, gotta get in there before someone else does. I swing open the door and do my now well-practised moon glide into the box as the soft closing mechanism of the door eases itself shut behind me. Shit! She fucking farted before she left the box. It doesn't smell as bad as the one on the train, but I'm holding my breath and doing this box extra fast before I suffocate or take a massive intake of breath and inhale her shitty arse smell. That's twice today that I've eaten shit.

They're not too bad, the boxes down Oxford Street today, but I've got to go to the main four boxes now at the junction of Regent Street. When I get there, all the boxes are occupied by people using the phones. There are only two boxes that need a couple of cards put back up, but there's one bloke just standing in there not even using the phone. I think I'll make my intentions clear, so hopefully, he'll let me in. I hold up my card and gesture my intentions. The man pushes the door open slightly to speak to me.

'Sorry mate, I'm waiting for a call. Can you use the other phone box?'

I only want to put a card up, is it okay to do it before your call?

'Yeah, sure, put it up.'

I step in there and proceed to put up three cards as the man stands there and reads out what I put up. *"Busty blonde, dominatrix. Transexual eh, any good?"*

I just put out the cards, mate, but check 'em out for yourself. They're not that far. Thanks for that, mate. I leave the box and make my way to King's Cross train station. I'll soon find out if the cleaner did turn up after me. I bloody hope not, especially after I did his job and ripped down all of yesterday's cards. When I get there, I'm delighted to see all of my twelve girls' cards neat and still up. Looks like the cleaner doesn't come every day like they do down Tottenham Court Road. Just as I walk off, a woman approaches me.

'Excuse me. Do you wanna have sex for ten pounds?'

Did she just ask for a tenner? A fucking tenner, what are you desperate for?

'Excuse me, did you hear me?'

Sorry love, I don't need the money.

What fucking drugs is she on? She ain't doing that for a loaf of bread and a pint of milk. Clearly, there are different levels to this game. On one hand, you've got the girls that I work for, who have plush flats in places like Mayfair and the rest of the city, and then there are the skanky ones on drugs who approach you from the streets and will ply their trade for a tenner.

It's just Euston I need to check and top up before I can go to the girls' flats and get my money. This is the best day I have ever had for taking money; it's worked out seven hundred and twenty pounds for four to five hours' work. The two boxes outside the front of Euston station are both down, and I'm not too sure if they fall under the British Transport Police jurisdiction, who are always about. But I did them this morning, and they're down, so I'll do them again. Just gotta watch for those bloody transport old bill; especially as they really go to town on Cardboys when they catch them, and that transport bobby at King's Cross was bang on my case, just waiting to get me in his little notebook. I do the last of the boxes around Euston and make my way to the first flat to get my money, which is the flat in Grafton Way. There are two close to each other there, one of them I have not been to before. I knock on Mandy's door, who takes ages to answer.

'Hello love, have you come to pick up your money?'

Yeah, I have.

'Come in, do you want a cup of tea?'

I'm standing in the living room and she's chatting away about all sorts of shit and I'm quickly losing patience because I've got another eleven flats to go round to yet and they're situated all over the place so I'll need to cut her short.

I've got to go Mandy, I've got another appointment.

'Oh alright love, am I talking too much?'

She hands over sixty pounds and I'm on my way. The next flat is literally thirty steps away. She's a Dominatrix. I ring the bell and a woman opens the door.

Hi I've come to pick up payment for doing the cards today.

She's slim, about twenty six years old, quite attractive with a sexy fitting t-shirt on. I can see her nipples poking through which of course being the visual man that I am, I'm instantly turned on by, she even shakes her tits a little at me.

'Ooh you must be Tony?'

Yeah, D sent me.

'Hold on a minute. I would let you in but I've got a punter just turned up, how much is it?'

Sixty pounds it is.

She came back and gave me the money at the door. I don't like taking money at the door like that, I'd much prefer to go in. She then shook her tits at me again when she came back so with a cheeky smile I said to her.

Show us your tits?

Quick as a flash she pulled up her t-shirt to reveal a perfectly shaped pair of tits with a bra that was just a leather strap that went under and around her tits. She smiled and then closed the door. I slowly walked away with that image firmly stuck in my head. Ten more flats to go. The next flat is in Percy Street just off Tottenham Court Road. It's Pearl's flat, the transexual. I had to ring three times before the maid answered the door, she was so ugly and about fifty years old, for a minute I thought she was the fucking tranny.

'Can I help you?'

Hello, I'm Tony the Cardboy, D sent me. I put your cards out for you today and I've just come to pick up some money.

'Ooh we've had a good day today, come in.'

Here we go, I'm about to meet a transexual for the first time, I don't know what to expect, maybe a five o'clock shadow beard? Rough voice? Who knows.

'Go through my lovely, she's in there.'

I walked into the living room and saw a very attractive woman sitting on the sofa, she has a nice oriental looking face but she's not fully oriental, smooth skin with no five o'clock shadow, she's wearing a black see through nighty with lacy underwear, lovely pair of tits too. She spoke with a slightly husky but feminine voice. I'm standing there thinking to myself, there's no way she used to be a man. I don't believe it, there's not a scrap of evidence that this person standing in front of me is, or used to be a man. She then says to me,

'You've got a lovely face. look at his face Mary, isn't it lovely?'

I feel like a fucking prized cow being forced to parade my shiny coat for the judges. I still can't see any signs of a man there, even when she speaks some more.

'How much do we owe you, sixty pounds right? You put out six hundred cards yeah?'

Yeah I did.

'Here's your money, We've had a good day today, lots of calls, you've done a good job'

I do my best.

'It's good to have a reliable Cardboy. I've had a few crappy ones over the years, D is good, are you gonna take over D's round then?'

Nah I'm just doing it for today.

'Oh, OK then.'

5:15PM

I realise that collecting this money is gonna take a bit of time, I've got to go to another nine flats yet so I'd better get going. I say goodbye and leave. I go to flats in Mayfair, Euston, Kings Cross, Soho, Piccadilly Circus, all spread out over the city.

I leave Trilly's flat till last, that fucking sexy thing gets me so hard but I've just got to resist her, there's no way I could let myself get involved with a working girl knowing all those blokes have been there, so it's business only, but she's hot as fucking hell. It must have been just how I was feeling that day.

I get to Trilly's flat at six thirty and ring the bell. The maid answers with a big smile on her face,

'Hello love, come in.'

As I walk along the corridor. I'm wondering if I will be as attracted to her as I was last time. I walk in the kitchen and Trilly is standing there, looking so fucking gorgeous in long matt black boots and sexy black lace lingerie with little red bows in the middle of the bra and knickers. What a fucking stunner, I wonder what it would be like to fuck you? No, I just can't allow myself to. I can't mix it up with the other blokes that come to see you all day, it's just not right, she can't be clean enough. Has she got any diseases? She's just standing there staring at me, not looking away once. She's looking at me as if to say "You're gonna fuck my brains out," and I know I'm looking at her as if to say, I can't fucking do this. I feel like a bit of a mug denying myself the opportunity to fuck this woman until I collapse in a heap of sweaty fucking meat but I keep telling myself it's business. Get the fucking money and get the fuck out. She hands me over the sixty pounds without losing eye contact once, fuck me she's hot. With a deep breath I grab the money and make for the front door; Trilly calls out to me.

'Give me your number in case I can't get hold of D or anything'

Oh shit, she's on me, here we go, can't let her know what I'm thinking. Take my fucking number you fucking red hot piece of ooh. She takes my number and walks slowly backwards towards the kitchen, you're so fucking hot, I've got to go. I go to the rest of the flats and collect all the money, seven hundred and twenty pounds, that'll do nicely. I go to buy myself something nice to eat and a spot of shopping is calling because I've just seen a nice jacket in that shop window over there. One hundred and sixty pounds. I can afford that today so I'm gonna buy it. That's two hundred quid on a jacket and a nice meal, five hundred quid left for a day's work is still lovely. I jump on the train and got home about seven thirty to roll a big fat fucking joint, crack open a beer and grab my guitar.

I wake up the following day at about eleven, it's just the top up to do at three so I slowly get up. My phone is ringing and it's D.

'Yeah Tony you didn't bring round the money yesterday'

What, the money I picked up from the flats?

'Yeah that money.'

Well that's my money ain't it D?

'No, I was gonna give you two hundred and fifty quid for doing the morning round and the top-up' you never said that D, you said do you fancy the work, then you said just go round and take the money.

'I didn't say take the money, you take two hundred and fifty quid and that's it!'

I'm thinking to myself as I stand there on the phone, this is bollocks. I've just spent two hundred quid of that already on a jacket and a fucking meal, I don't want to hand over all that cash, especially as I was the one who went out there and took all the risks, it was only for one day and you couldn't do it, so I stepped in. How can you expect to take all that money after I did all the work surely not. It's only right that I keep that money. So I said,

I think I earned that money, D.

'IT'S NOT YOUR FUCKING MONEY!' D shouts and puts the phone down.

Oh fuck, this is a bit uncomfortable, I guess we can sort it out when I go round there today, maybe if D's that pissed off I will not get to do the top up anymore. I don't want to lose this little number, we'll talk, we'll be alright. I go to D's house at two in the afternoon and ring the bell. I'm left standing outside for ages before the door gets answered. I can tell D's pissed off big time but appears to be holding it back well. I've known D for a while, we've been cool friends but I feel this money thing has put a wedge between us.

D, I just want to say.. before I could say anything, D interrupted me.

'Save it I don't wanna know, I think you took a liberty but that's alright. I've learnt my lesson, so what I'll do is give you your own girls. You can have that pain in the arse girl and there's a few others that I wanna get rid of anyway. I'll tell 'em you're doing the cards now and that'll be it, you just take over. I'll do the top-up myself from now on.'

D didn't have to do that. I could have just been told to fuck off. The mind was made up before I even got to the house, the cards were already in a carrier bag for me. D gave me six girls to work for, these girls put out four hundred cards each, that's forty quid from six girls coming to two hundred and forty pounds per day, over five days totalling one thousand, two hundred pounds per week. Not too bad at all I'd say. I have to put out three hundred cards in the morning and save the last hundred for the top up in the afternoon. I guess I can live with that but I should have taken better care of our friendship which is damaged now.

Can we chat D to sort things out properly?

'Nah there's no need, here's the cards, I've got things to do, you can start these tomorrow.'

I drive home to sort out the cards to make them easier to put up, I put a stack of three hundred of one girl on the table to my right and another stack of cards on the table to my left and using both hands at the same time I pick a card from the top of each side and put one on top of the other until all of the two cards are mixed together alternately. So instead of using six pockets of my waistcoat, I now only need to use three. I have my blue tack ready and the rest of the day off as D is doing the top-up. One of the cards I'm putting up is Trilly's number. She won't mind me doing her cards, that's for sure. As for the rest? We'll have to wait and see. I need to take my mind off the cards for now, so I grab my guitar and play the song that's going round in my head, **It's Alright Mamma** by Elvis Presley, written by the great Arthur Crudup in nineteen-forty-six. It was Elvis's debut single, and I would have loved to have been in the recording studio when he went in there to record that one track for Mother's Day—the very start of his career, a solid case of fate and destiny. I'm so tired; I need sleep.

4AM

I'm awake and up early. I make coffee and have a slice of toast before heading down to the car. Normally, I would listen to Rock'n'Roll in my car, so I don't hear much of the new stuff that comes out. But on this particular morning, I decided to put the radio on instead. A new song came on that grabbed my attention straight away; it was rough, heavy, a sort of dance electronic song that got me revved up. I turned up the volume to this aggressive track and couldn't stop myself from rocking my head to the fast beat. This translated to my feet pushing down harder on the pedal, which made my wheels spin a little faster, and my car left the road, mounted the pavement, and hit a lamppost. How can a song make me crash my car?

The song was called **'Firestarter'** by a band called The Prodigy. The car was not too badly damaged; I stopped just a little too late to prevent a collision, and only the bumper was bruised up a bit. So, I didn't spend much time assessing the damage; I had to get to the West End and do my round. It was five in the morning by the time I got to Tottenham Court Road; I parked my car down the first side turning, which is Great Russell Street, put my waistcoat on, and walked back to the first set of eight boxes outside the Dominion Theatre. Looks like D has already been and gone. The cards are all neatly placed on the backboard above the phone and the side window, along with Terry's cards that are placed around the outside of D's cards, meaning my cards will be placed four cards up and over to the side a little bit.

It's not the ideal spot to put them in, but I am the third Cardboy to come along this morning, so I still have a good chance of getting the girls the calls they need to be happy. There's no sign of D or Terry at the next set of four boxes, even though their cards are up. I put my cards up and carry on walking up the road. There's an Odeon cinema just up on the left, and as I am walking near it, I hear some groaning coming from the doorway of the entrance. I look over, and there in front of me, I can see two men.

One had his trousers round his ankles and bent over, while the second man is standing behind him fucking him up the arse, right there in the street. No one else is around, and I just stand there for a few seconds, not quite believing what I am looking at.

I walk off to do the next set of four boxes, where I bump into Terry, the toothless Arsenal supporter, putting up his cards in one of the boxes, while D is round the other side putting cards up in the next box. I stand there waiting for my turn. Terry comes out of the box, and as I am going inside, I tell Terry about the two men I just saw down the road.

'What! Where?'

He walked back up the road to the cinema where the two men were and proceeded to shout abuse at them. I could hear him from down the road.

'OI, THAT'S DISGUSTING, FUCKING FILTH!'

As he stood there shouting abuse at them D calls out to him to come back, and as Terry walks back, he is still ranting on.

'Nah, that's disgusting mate. He's bumming him in the street, absolute filth mate.'

Just as he says that, a police car is slowly driving up the road. Terry flags them down and proceeds to tell them what he just saw, which makes them reverse up the road to investigate. D begins to tease Terry about it as they continue to put the cards up.

'What did you do all that for Terry? Are you jealous? Do you want some yourself? Yeah, we know you like it really.'

"Nah I don't think so D. I just wanted to stop it from happening in the street."

D and Terry walk off to the next set of two boxes across the road from Goodge Street station, leaving me to put my cards up in these four boxes. I'm not being very vigilant as I do this; I'm still thinking of the two blokes I just saw having some bum fun, so I didn't notice a policeman walking straight up to me in the box until he opened the door and said to me.

'Step outside the box please. Hand me over the cards.'

I emptied one of my pockets of cards and gave them to him.

'And the rest in the other pockets.'

I gave him all the cards I had on me, and he said.

'Okay, you can go now.'

Fuck that fucking shit. What a fucking dilemma. I'm fucked! Okay Tony, don't panic, take it easy. Think. Even though they're pain-in-the-arse girls, I'll still have to smooth it over with them all to keep the work, somehow. They'll understand this shit happens, surely? I catch up to where D and Terry are putting up cards. I don't know what I'm gonna do now. I could lose everything if I don't shine today. I have to keep on top of earning this kind of money. Maybe D has more of these girls' cards in the car. I'll ask.

D, I've just had all the cards taken off of me.

'Did you hear that Terry? Tony had all his cards taken from him. That's karma for ya. You fucked me over and this is what you get.'

My mind is all over the place; I'm thinking more and more that I was out of order to take the money from the girls and keep it. I'm starting to think how greedy I came across. It was the wrong thing to do, but I've done it now. I made the choice, and now I have to live with it. It's clear that my friendship with D is not as it should be and certainly not as it was. But right now I've gotta think about these cards. I can't earn any fucking money; no fucker can. The fucking maid will turn up wanting her wages, rent on the flat has still gotta be paid, and fuck all coming in coz their Cardboy gave his cards to a policeman. Would they understand and just say it's okay and carry on as normal, giving me more cards to put up? Or would they be really pissed off? There is something I can try.

I growled to myself as I marched back up Tottenham Court Road until I saw the policeman. I walked straight up to him and said,

Let me have those cards back?

He looked at me, pausing for a few seconds, and just shoved them into my chest and said,

'Go on, get out of here, I don't want to see you again.'

What a result! I think I'll fuck off.

Cheers mate.

And off I walk back down Tottenham Court Road to finish off the rest of the boxes. D and Terry's cards were all up, and they were already off the road. I caught up with them on Cleveland Street, where Terry said to me.

'Where did ya get those cards from?'

I got 'em off the old bill.

'What, you nicked 'em back off 'im?'

No…! Nicked 'em off 'im. He gave 'em to me.

'What! What d'ya mean fucking gave 'em to ya? What, he said, 'Where's that Cardboy, I wanna give him his cards back'? Fuck off will ya, he never did that.'

He fucking did I tell ya.

'Old bill don't do things like that, sorry.'

I ain't bullshitting.

'Well, when do old bill do things like that to help people out?'

Just now.

'Yeah, right now. A one-off.'

Actually, it's not a one-off.

'D, can you hear this? He reckons the old bill keeps giving him his cards back when he gets nicked. So it's happened before, has it?'

Not with the cards no, but they've helped me out before when they didn't have to.

'With what?'

I know how we feel about the old bill, but this one was when my car broke down in Brighton last year on Madeira Drive, on the seafront, and I was right in the middle of the road. I was sitting in the car when the police slowly drove past, giving me the eye. I watched them in my rearview mirror disappear and just sat there waiting for the recovery van. About ten minutes later I could see them coming back in the mirror but this time they stopped behind me. I thought, here we go, more hassle. I got out of the car and as I was walking towards him, he said to me,

'I know what it's like to break down and thought you might be hungry or thirsty so I bought you this.' And he handed me a Snickers chocolate bar and a bottle of water!

'Yeah, but you weren't doing anything wrong there were ya? It's unheard of to get your cards back like that.'

I arrived home at eight a.m to find a brown envelope at the front door with a red stamp on it that read, 'Clerkenwell Magistrates Court'. Here we go, this will be the first fine. I rip it open and scour the page for the amount. It's a 'go to court or pay now' kind of thing. I can't help but chuckle, sweet. Thirty quid! That's it. No criminal record, just a thirty quid fine for littering. It says here I can do two things: one) I can go to the court and appeal it or just pay the fine and hear no more about it. I'm a busy man, I've got no time to go to court to contest that. It would be madness to complain about that with the money that's in this game.

No cards go out on the weekends. Well, I don't put my cards out anyway, but I know there are Cardboys out there who do the weekend shift for the girls. I like to shut off from all cards. I'm chilling at home, sipping on a shandy and smoking a lovely joint. I'm about to cook a roast dinner. My phone rings, and it's Trilly. What does she want on the weekend? I've already picked up her cards for next week, and I've been paid.

'Hello Tony.'

Hello Trilly, you alright?

'Yeah, I'm alright. You alright?'

Yeah, I'm good. What's happening?

'What are you doing?'

I'm just at home chilling.

'Come over?'

No Trilly, I'm busy doing stuff indoors.

'Leave it and come to me.'

Don't be naughty, Trilly. I can't. I've got things to do.

'Like what?'

I'm cooking a roast dinner for a start.

'I'll come to you then. What's your address?'

No Trilly, I live miles away anyway.

'I don't care, I'm coming.'

I gave her my address and put the phone down. Fuck. I can't be messing with Trilly; she's a working girl. What if she's got a disease? She's so fucking hot, and I'm getting a hard-on now just thinking of her getting into her car. I'm making chicken for my roast and preparing the bird. I've got some condoms ready. I kinda liked 'Dunkies' as everyone used to call them before AIDS was about. I sink into my spliff and guitar and strum out the opening riff of Chuck Berry's **Roll Over Beethoven.** I love getting lost in Rock'n'Roll.

The chicken has been in the oven for an hour now. A roast always takes longer than expected to cook, fan-assisted oven or not. I turn the chicken over in the dish for the juices to run through to the other side when the phone rings. I look out the window, and it's Trilly ringing me. She's parked outside in a little green Mazda MX Five. A great little car. She gets out, she's mesmerising. She can't see me looking at her as she adjusts her tits. I have a full-on boner for her at this stage, and she knocks on my door.

Looking down on the way to answer, my trousers are looking like a four-man tent, but I don't give a fuck about hiding it. And then she walks in without saying a word. So I'll say nothing too, but my mind is open as I follow her through to the kitchen and just look at her beautifully formed arse. It's so alluring. Stroking it as she walks is making me want to fuck her right now, but that can wait.

Red or white?

'Ooh, red please.'

Grab a seat. I'm gonna turn the bird over.

'You what?'

The chicken. When it's all wet down below, I like to turn it over so all the juices run to the bottom. "That sounds, erm, really nice.'

Well, you'd better try it then.

'What?'

Are you hungry?

'Yeeaah, I mean yeah.'

I'm carefully basting the chicken and turn around to see Trilly sitting upright on the end of the chair, teeth showing while biting her bottom lip as she wiggles around slowly. She is sooo ready to receive me that I cannot deny her a second longer. Taking my time to walk over to her, I plunge my lips onto her neck while I grab her sexy arse with both hands and pull her tightly into me. The sound of her groaning is such a turn-on. She's tearing at my top, and she ain't gonna stop until it's off. She's fixated on my lips while she continues to bite hers, which was so inviting to me that I went against my principles. Despite her being a working girl, despite how many cocks she's sucked on, there is just something else about this woman. I just have to kiss her, so I move in. Now I'm locked in this sensual experience that can only have one outcome. The passion burning in me now is so immense as I remove her bra, sucking and playing with her erect nipples.

I stand up in front of her, and she undoes my trousers and grabs my cock in both hands, proceeding to give me the blow job that I don't think I will ever forget. Standing up in front of me, my cock sliding down between her tits as she goes, she has a Dunky in her hand. She rips it open and hands it to me, so I slowly slide it onto my fully erect cock. She grabs it and slowly turns around with it still in her hand. She kneels on the chair with her hands on the backrest. Her gorgeous body bent over in front of me, I slowly slide my cock all the way deep down into her as far as I could push it. She groaned so beautifully as I thrusted and pulled her towards me with a firm, consistent motion. We fucked on that chair for a good fifteen minutes before I had to stop to check the other bird I was looking after. I was basting the chicken, then going back to baste that sexy arse. This is amazing. She follows me into the living room but doesn't get far.

I stopped her in the doorway, spun her round, and fucked her there from behind with my back pushed up against the inside of the door frame with her hands on the inside on the other side of the door frame. Doorway sex. This feels intense; none of us can move away as I fuck her standing up. By the time the dinner was ready, we had fucked so much I was pleased for the break. It was delicious: crispy potatoes, crispy chicken skin, carrots, broccoli, and Yorkshire puds. She's eating it faster than me! It's impressive to see such a big appetite. She also had a big appetite for my cock, and we fucked some more after we ate and again after pudding. A truly pleasurable afternoon. With Mother Nature making fucking the most pleasurable feeling a human can experience, she's not stupid.

'You were amazing. That was so good.'

We chatted after over coffee, and she left. Time for the washing up.

AUGUST, 4AM

It's the start of the week, I can't eat that much when I get up at this time, so it's a cup of coffee and maybe a biscuit or two. My cards are already mixed and are in the pockets of my hanging waistcoat. I jump in the car and head off for Tottenham Court Road. The blue tack is a bit cold and hard, so I put it on the heater outlets to make it nice and soft by the time I get there.

After parking down the side turning in Great Russell Street, I walk the few hundred yards to the first set of eight boxes outside the Dominion Theatre. The ground around the boxes is wet, so I know the cleaner has been, and D and Terry have been too, as both their cards are up, nice and neat.

There's not much room for the cards in these traditional red phone boxes. As long as I can get mine up, I don't mind, but anyone coming after me will have to put their cards up really high. The ones that follow later on after that will have nowhere to put their cards but on the ceiling. That's got to be sixty to seventy percent fewer calls for the girls if I had to put my cards up there. A quick look around for police, and I'm in the first box. One two three four five six, on the back as quick as I can go. One to six, bosh, another six on the window, and out! Next box. I'm continually scoping the area for police as I step up the speed a little. The quicker I can get out, the less chance I've got of getting caught.

I complete all eight phone boxes in under two minutes and head on to the next set of four. The cleaner is at that set of boxes, and D and Terry are standing there bantering with each other while they wait for the cleaner to finish. As I approach, the bantering stops. No good mornings, hellos, or anything, just silence as they stand there looking at the cleaner working. Not a-fuckin-gain. The last thing I wanna do is stand here with these two soppy bollocks not saying a word. D's still got it in for me for taking that money, I guess, but this is awkward. I've gotta break the ice.

Morning D.

'Morning. Have you already done the Dominion?'

Yeah, of course. They're the first ones.

'We'll be waiting forever for this cleaner. A right old ball ache. Hope you've got more time on your hands today.'

I'll tell you what D. Last week, I gave him some money and he left the cards up.

'What, all the old cards? That's bollocks. He'd get sacked.'

No D, hear me out. Not the day before cards. I went before him and stripped the whole box of the old cards and put mine up. I gave him fifty quid to wash around my cards and leave them up.

'Yeah, but that was last week.'

Well, what I'm thinking is if we give him money each week, we'd not have this problem anymore. If you gave him fifty quid a week, and so does Terry, that's a hundred and fifty quid extra for him in his pocket.

'Go on then, ask him.'

Terry agrees to the proposal too, so I go to ask him.

Mate, we'll give you one hundred and fifty quid a week for you to come after us in the morning and leave our cards up, and we'll take down all the cards from the day before so you know ours are fresh today.

'Oh, I don't know, it's a bit risky.'

It will be four o'clock in the morning; no one's gonna spot you doing anything.

'OK, fuck it, why not.'

I collect the money from the boys and hand it to the cleaner. That's it. We're clear to crack on. Terry, D, and I set a new pace up Tottenham Court Road, ripping down all of yesterday's cards and putting up all of ours. By five, we had done the whole of Tottenham Court Road. D lightened up with me a little because I had made the day a little easier, apart from all the stripping work, but I did mess with his money, so we'll see how long this lasts. By five-forty a.m. we had done all the backstreets near Tottenham Court Road and were already onto Oxford Circus's main four boxes. The cleaner there had already been; it's a different cleaner on these boxes. He comes out very early. It's nice and quiet here at this time of the morning, a completely different atmosphere compared to the afternoon. The police just drove past me. Shit, I wasn't looking. And I was putting up a card when he was looking straight at me, so I know he saw what I was doing. They just continued driving down Oxford Street. Their shift probably starts at six a.m. or finishes at six, and there are fifteen minutes to go, so I doubt if they want to deal with a petty Cardboy when they're just about to knock off or not even started work yet, but I can't get complacent. There are cameras about, so I know they can see what I'm doing. The way I look at it is as long as I've not got a big crowbar trying to break the box open to get the money out or taking a shit in the box like that filthy cunt in Soho, they must just think, 'let them get on with it.' But still, and like D said, they do have purges now and again. Fucking purge. It's only paper cards in a box, no crime there.

I finish off Oxford Street, head back to my car parked off a side turning, and drive to Euston at six fifteen a.m. I park in Euston Square and do the four boxes there before walking up Euston Road towards the station and vigilantly doing the six boxes there. It's getting light now and soon it will be busy with people and traffic wardens, so I head back to the car and drive the short distance to Gower Place. I leave the car there and walk to Kings Cross, carding the eight phone boxes further along Euston Road as I go. I'm getting that 'be extra vigilant' vibe as I approach the four main boxes in the middle of Kings Cross, and it's better doing these early than doing them on the top-up. I can see everywhere, and I'm scanning the area as I quickly approach the door and enter. One two five six quick on the back, a little scan around for police as I reach in my pockets for the next set of two girls, blue tack on the back sharpish. One two, into the two inside pockets like Clint Eastwood in a gun draw or Bruce Lee pulling out his nunchucks,   PER CHANG! I remember when I first discovered Bruce Lee. At that time, everyone was going crazy about him in the schools.

I also remember my brother making a neat pair of nunchucks out of our dad's old walking stick. He made a really good job of it. My dad came home, and my brother proudly showed him his craftsmanship, but all my dad did was beat him with them. I'm both those Bruce Lee and Clint Eastwood characters at the moment as I quickly reach for the top two pockets for the next set of two. Blue tack quickly on, bang bang! One two, on the window, next two, bosh! Done and out. Onto the next box.

After the many times that I've done this, my skill level of being able to glide into a phone box having already scanned the place for police, then having this quick, precise flowing movement is pure professionalism. I stroll away having done all four boxes and jump back into my car just as the rain starts. Driving along the backstreet of Kings Cross, there's a car parked so only room for one car to pass through at a time. I was twenty feet away from it, but there's another car coming towards me which is sixty feet away, so it's obvious that I'm gonna reach and pass through this small gap first, but no. This guy is accelerating from thirty miles per hour to fifty miles per hour in a defiant bid to make it through the gap before me, but all he's done is blocked us both in. Now what? C'mon mate, you're gonna have to reverse. But no, you've got alternative ideas.

What are you fucking smirking at? Ah, that's right, go on then, pull up your handbrake, you fucking, what, you wanna cross your arms now! Are you trying to tell me you've got all day? You ain't moving me off my centre, mate, and I ain't reversing. Let's see how you respond to this. I turn my engine off, grab an umbrella from the back seat, get out, lock the door, pop my collar, put my umbrella up, stroll away, and disappear around the corner. I've got time on my hands; I'll just stand here in the rain for as long as I want. I'll zone out here and think for a bit. I wonder what's happening to that smirk on his face while he sits there with his arms crossed, staring at an empty car. I've got to see this. I don't want him to see me, so I peek around the corner. He's gone. Reversed up the road, you fucker. There's a man sitting close by on a wall who watched the whole thing play out. He is laughing out loud and says,

'You should have seen his face. That was brilliant.'

In my mind, I did see his face. I drove back and was home around eight thirty, perfect. I had breakfast and slept from nine till midday. I could definitely get used to this, having the rest of the day to do whatever I want.

WEDNESDAY

There's a clever Cardboy challenging the court system. The littering charge that he received for putting the cards up was being fought against on the grounds that it was not littering at all, and he was in court last week to prove his point. Apparently, a littering charge cannot be enforced because the four walls of the phone box are considered 'inside,' and therefore a littering charge is only enforceable if it is out in the open. He got a fifty-pound fine, which I personally would have just paid, but if he's got the time to run up to the court and fight such a small amount, then good luck to him. Perhaps we'll all start getting away without a penalty when we get caught. Maybe the police will not stop us at all anymore. After all, what's the point of them pulling us in if nothing is going to come of it? No littering charge, no fine. We'll see.

It's four thirty in the morning and I'm walking up Tottenham Court Road to the first set of four boxes. D and Terry have already been and gone. Looks like they're getting there even earlier now that we have the cleaner in our pockets. It's good to see him there cleaning around their cards. While he's on one side, I'm in the opposite box putting up my cards. I walk to the next set of four at the junction of Percy Street, and with a quick look around for police, I slip in there. The blue tack I have in my hand is running low, so I reach for a fresh packet in my pocket only to find it empty. Shit! I didn't check. The shop where I could buy some more from is not open yet. The cleaner pulls up in his van and has headphones on. He is singing away as he jumps out to run through his cleaning routine. He's in such a good mood as he dances and smiles at me. I'm not surprised he's like that with the extra one hundred and fifty quid a week he's getting from us.

'Morning Tony, you alright?'

Nah, not really.

'Why, what's up?'

Fucking blue tack, I'm out of it and the shop's not open yet.

'Don't you worry my son, I'll sell you some.'

What, you're selling blue tack now?"

'Yep, I'll get it.'

He goes to his van and pulls out a massive ball of Blu Tack in various shades that resemble planet Earth.

'I have been collecting the little pieces of Blu Tack from the cards when I take them down. Do you like?'

Fuck me, there's enough there to last three weeks!

'I've got this smaller one for you if you want it?'

How much do you want for that?

'A tenner.'

Go on then, I'll jump on that. You could have a good little side hustle selling that. Cheaper than what I spend on blue tack each week.

I carry on doing the rest of Tottenham Court Road knowing that the cleaner will be leaving them up when he eventually gets around to it. I turn left onto Euston Road to do the four boxes there before ducking back in to do the backstreet boxes around Grafton Way. D and Terry are there putting up their cards. D does not acknowledge me; obviously there's still a bit of resentment towards me, but at least Terry says something when he sees me.

'Have you been down Tottenham Court Road yet?'

Yeah, of course.

'Has the cleaner left the cards up?'

Yeah, of course he has, that's what we pay him for.

'I'm just checking; you never know, his boss could be on his case or something.'

Do you know anything about this court case where the Cardboy is challenging the littering charge?

'Yeah, that was me. It got thrown out of court. They couldn't stick the littering charge on me because it's inside of four walls, so the judge threw it out.'

What, so we can't get done anymore?

'Looks like it. All the Cardboys can thank me now. There's fuck all the police can do.'

My first thought is that something doesn't sit right with that result, but we'll see. I carry on all around the backstreets, hitting every box I come to. There's plenty of time to think while doing this job, and now I don't mind being up at this time in the morning on a quick march. The whole round goes really smoothly, it's six-thirty and the round is done. I jump in the car and get home at seven-fifteen. What a fucking result! I have an hour workout on my rollerblades, a nice bit of breakfast, and go to sleep for three hours, waking up naturally just before midday. That seems to be the emerging pattern, and it suits me for now. I've got the top-up to do in a few hours, so I don't venture out too far. One of the girls I put cards out for has a dominatrix day on Wednesdays. She'll dress accordingly in tight leather gear, maybe a mask too. I've not seen her dressed like it yet. She has a room, or as she calls it, 'The Dungeon,' where all sorts take place. That, I am interested in seeing. I've got to pick up some cards from her tonight, so I'll see it then.

TOP-UP

Another beautiful sunny day of about twenty-four degrees, and most of the cards in Tottenham Court Road are still up, so I breeze down there in under twenty minutes. The backstreets are all up still, just how I like it. Fuck all work to do this afternoon, and it feels like I'm just going for a nice West End walk. I get to Oxford Circus, and there's only one of the main four boxes needing a top-up. The window cards are up, together with every other Cardboy's cards. They don't come out as early as me in the mornings. The respect is there, as no one has moved my window cards so they could get theirs in a better position.

I like it that the windows are caked in cards and will be hiding me inside from the police as I work. I open the door and I'm in. Bosh, six cards up, and out. I make my way to Soho to get the red phone boxes there; I know they'll be patchy. Then through to Cambridge Circus, always waiting for people to finish using the phones in those ones. Then I walk back up Charing Cross Road, but I'm going straight through as I don't do this road.

As I stroll up, I can see a fellow Cardboy. He's got the obligatory multi-pocketed black waistcoat on, and I'm sure I've seen him before putting up cards a few times around Oxford Street. Big old fucking lump, I know that. Look at the fucking muscles he's got. They call him 'The Major' for some reason, and he's quickly marching towards a phone box, where there's a policeman in there ripping down all the cards, and it looks like he's gonna have a pop at him. What the fuck is The Major going to do here? I've gotta see this, so I stop and cross the road to get a closer look. The Major, who obviously was pissed off at the copper for taking down all the cards he probably just put up, pulled the door open and proceeded to tell off the policeman.

'Oi! What're you doing?'

'*They're disgusting!*' the policeman said.

'*They may be, but they don't look better all over the pavement do they? I mean, look at the mess you're making. That's littering.*'

'*Well, I'm gonna pick them up,*'

'*Go on then.*'

I couldn't believe what I was seeing and hearing, a complete role reversal. I'm standing here watching a policeman get on his hands and knees and pick up every single card he threw on the ground. The Major then said to him,

'*That's better. Don't do things like that,*' and walked off.

I've gotta catch up to him.

Excuse me mate, I just want to say something to ya. I can see you're a Cardboy; I'm one too.

'*Yeah, I know. I can tell by your waistcoat.*'

Well, I've got to say that was brilliant, what you just did with that policeman. I've never seen anything like it.

'*Yeah, well, they piss me off. I've got stacks of fines, stacks I tell ya. I just done that box, and there's him ripping them all down. What's your name mate?*'

Tony. You're The Major, right?

'*The Major, yeah right. That's not my real name though, obviously, but yeah.*'

Well, it's nice to meet ya.

'*Yeah, likewise. Call me Tommy. That's my real name*'.

Well, you were shouting at that policeman like a fucking sergeant major. Okay, Tommy, I'll see ya later.

I walk off back to Tottenham Court Road station and make my way to The Dungeon. The train is going slowly through the tunnels somewhere beneath the streets of the Metropol-eye. I'm loving the beat of the wheels going this slow; it sounds like the beat of Elvis's track Bossa Nova: ba-doom-doom, bossa nova, ba-doom-doom. I jump off the train at Gloucester Road and walk up Cromwell Road. It stinks around here like something I don't even know of. The ground looks like it's not been deep cleaned for decades, and to think that I don't take my shoes off when I go into my own home. Mind you, my carpet ain't that much better. Right, here I am, number thirty-three A. It's a flat above a carpet shop funny enough, and the state of that doorbell. What is that shit on it? Fuck that, I'll use my key to press it. The intercom clanks on, and first I hear a cough before I hear the maid say,

'Hello,'

Then I hear the girl's voice in the background shouting,

'We ain't ready!'

I make my introductions, and the maid shouts back to the girl,

'It's alright, it's Tony the Cardboy. Come up, pet,'

and she buzzes me in.

These must be the narrowest stairs I have ever walked up. I can put my hands in my pockets, and both elbows can touch the walls at the same time. The carpet's in better shape than mine though, and it's freshly painted in here. I get to the top of the first flight of stairs, and there's a beautiful stained glass arched window, and the next flight of wider stairs opens up to a much larger space with ornate Victorian detailing of the finest quality that is stunning to look at. I love seeing all this architectural stuff; it puts me in a good mood. I walk comfortably up the next flight. The carpet on these stairs is floral and old-looking but in near-perfect condition. I make my way to the front door of the flat and stand there waiting for them to open it. I hear two locks quietly unlocking before the door opens, and Rose, the maid, wearing one rubber glove covered in blood, says,

'Quick, come in love, we've had a right palaver.'

What's happened?

'She might tell ya. She's in the kitchen. I'll be just a minute; I just need to take these gloves off.'

She pushes open the door to The Dungeon and goes in. I get a short glimpse of what's inside: a lot of red and black decor with a cage and straps, whips and paddles hanging up on a wall. There's a white table in the middle of the room that's splattered in blood, and then the door closes. I carry on walking along the corridor into the kitchen, where Francesca is sitting at the table wearing an all-in-one skin-tight black shiny rubber bodysuit, nervously smoking a cigarette. I can smell the rubber from her suit fill the air around me. It reminds me of fixing the puncture on my bike when I was a kid. It doesn't seem like a good time to see The Dungeon properly today. I'm not sure if I should ask her what happened, but I do anyway.

What's happened?

'Oh you won't believe what some punter just came in and asked for.'

She's telling me what happened, but clearly she's a bit shaken, so I'll finish off explaining. A client came in and said to her, 'I want you to put a nail through my balls.' He had even brought his own hammer and nail. Francesca then sat the man on the white table in The Dungeon, opened his legs, pulled his sack skin out, held the nail to it, and whack! Banged the nail through the skin, and into the table beneath. Even though the man growled in pain and delight, he wasn't happy. He wanted the nail through his actual bollock and not just the skin. Now, I don't know how much one would charge for such a thing, but it was enough to make her agree to do it, and so she continued. She held the ball steady with the pinky edge of her clenched fist at the same time as holding the nail straight. She said she counted to three and whacked this nail in, piercing the ball and through to the other side. She said the man screamed in agony and then started crying and saying, 'Yes! Yes! YES!' she said the blood squirted everywhere, all over the walls and ceiling too. I stand there with my poker face on as she's trying to tell me more, but fuck that shit. I'm tempted to ask her how much she charged for that but refrain from doing so. She wants to go home now, and I don't blame her. People in this world are fucking crazy. I mean, a man can bleed to death doing that kind of torture surely? Francesca is in a bad way, as pale as a packet of mozzarella and she hasn't stopped shaking.

'The cards are there for the rest of the week, Tony.'

Will you be alright Francesca?

'I'll be okay, I've got to. Rose is in there cleaning up all the blood, I can't go in there until it's all gone. Never again am I doing anything like that. I'll just be whipping and stuff in the future, that was too freaky for me. Here's your money for the three days so far, it's been good this week, obviously doing a good job.'

I do my best Francesca.

'Yeah well, we're getting a ton of calls from your round, so well done.'

She hands me over one hundred and eighty pounds, and I leave to go to the rest of the flats.

6:15PM

I've collected money from five flats for the work I've done up until today, which comes to nine hundred pounds. There's one flat left to go to: Trilly's flat, that sexy woman that quite frankly knocked me for six. I'm standing outside her flat, ringing the bell, and I'm starting to get a hard-on as I wait for her to answer.

The maid opens up and lets me in. I walk the corridor to the kitchen and Trilly is just lifting a tea bag from a mug.

'Do you want a cup?'

Nah, thanks Trilly, not for me.

She's gorgeous, she's had her hair and nails done and wants to show off to me.

'I've just had my nails done.'

Let me see.

I grab her hands to inspect her nails.

They look alright Trilly. A lot of work has gone into those. They did a good job.

She beams a smile at me and strokes my cheek. There's something about this woman, I want to know more about her. I find myself setting up another date with her.

When are you free again to meet up for drinks?

'I'm free this weekend.'

Okay, Saturday at seven-thirty. Meet me at,

Before I had a chance to say where, she said,

'I'll come to you, we can have a drink around your area.'

This suits me fine. Close to mine at the end of the night. I definitely ain't going back to no working flat. The date has been set, and I picked up one hundred and eighty pounds from her. I'll be spending that on her anyway on our date, on cocktails and whatever else takes my fancy. I leave her flat with a total of just over a thousand pounds in my pocket, or 'sky rocket' as my Cockney pals would say. Not bad for three days' work and only four-hour working days. I'll pick up another seven hundred and twenty quid for Thursday and Friday. That's eighteen hundred pounds for the week.

I make my way to Baker Street train station and jump on the Jubilee line.

FRIDAY AFTERNOON

I'm getting a bit tired coming out in the afternoon to do the top-up when I've been out since four. It's easy, but it would be better for me to get someone else to do it. Three-hundred quid a week it would cost me. I can afford that; I've just gotta find someone who's right for me. I'm coming up to the last two phone boxes on Tottenham Court Road on the left outside McDonald's, and the cards are down in the first one. There's a man in there on the phone, so I stand next to the wall of the building behind me and wait. There's another man standing next to me on crutches, leaning up against the building with a stookie on his leg and one of those, 'here's a boot to fit your stookie jobbies.' A pal dropped a bench on my arm and broke it when I was in school, and the Scottish doctor who treated me said,

'Aye, ye'll be alright with a wee stookie on ya pal.'

Everyone else I know calls it a plaster cast, but stookie has always stuck with me. I better ask him.

Are you waiting to use the box, mate?

'Yes, I am.'

That's okay because my plan is to just slip in there before him and whack six cards up, well twelve including the window. All done very politely, of course. Gotta be polite when I need to slip into a box before someone needs to use the phone, that goes without saying. The man in the box puts the phone down and starts to collect his belongings from the little metal shelf under the phone. At this point, the man waiting to use the phone before me steadies his crutches and hobbles his way over to the box as the other man opens the door and leaves. The man on crutches is just about to enter, and I have to seize my chance.

Excuse me mate, can I just put a couple of these cards in before you go in there please?

He is halfway in the box but agrees.

'Go on then, but hurry up.'

There's just six,

and quickly start to put them up.

You said a couple.'

I know, and just six more on the window and I'll be out.

As I'm doing the window, the man is holding the door wide open for me and standing half in and half out of the box. As I put my last card on the window, he says to me,

'I shouldn't let you do this really.'

I look at him, and he's holding up a police badge and smirking at me, so I say to him,

Ah mate, I'd never have known you were police, that's good undercover you've got there, but what happened to your leg? That's not part of your cover, is it?

He laughed and said,

'No, I was chasing a burglar, and as I jumped a wall, I broke my leg.'

Ooh, nasty. Well, you get better soon.

And off I walk. Fuck that shit. That was crazy. Holding the fucking door open for me. A copper!

I walk past Warren Street station and turn left onto Euston Road to check the first two boxes there; all cards are up, so I carry on to the next two. Again, all cards are up. It's just like an afternoon walk again with the odd box needing a top-up, but I still would rather have someone else do it for me. There is someone I know who might be up for it. I'll ask Billy. I brought my car in today because I have to pick up all of next week's cards from a couple of girls; that's six thousand cards in total. I'll be damned if I'm taking that on the train, so I parked in a little spot, not too expensive, at the back of Euston station while I did my whole round, passing Oxford Street and all around the backstreets there, Soho, Cambridge Circus, and I even hit a few of the boxes on Marylebone High Street and around the British Broadcasting television centre before heading back to my car.

I got to the car just before the metre ran out. I'm driving along Eversholt Street, coming up slowly to the traffic lights outside Euston Station when a man decides to cross the road in front of me. It's fine if someone crosses the road properly; walking straight across the road takes roughly seven seconds. But you get some people who don't do that; some people walk at an angle across it, which takes about eleven seconds. But this guy took at least fifteen seconds to get just halfway across the road at the angle he was walking. I was going slow, but he was forcing me to go even slower. As I passed him, still in the road, I muttered out the window at him,

Get out of the fucking road.

And I slowly pulled up at the traffic lights. I sat there looking at the bright red light in front of me when the guy who was faffing across the road came up to the car. Well, I didn't see him coming, but I certainly felt the punch he threw at me through the window. Bit of a shock. He was ranting something or another at me and approaching the window to do it again. Now, I could have and probably should have driven away, but the lights were red, and so was my temper at this point, so I decided to step out of the car and challenge him. I hit him twice with right jabs to the face, which only served to make him more mad and come at me again. I swerved his punch and jabbed him in the face once more. His friend then approached from nowhere with an empty vodka bottle in his hand, screaming at me,

'C'mon then, let's have it.'

He chased me around my car, swinging this bottle around. How was I supposed to defend myself from this? At that moment, I saw a bin close by. I pulled out the metal inner and held it in front of me as the man with the bottle ran towards me and took a swing. I raised the bin as the bottle came down towards my head, and it crashed loudly against the metal. The first guy was then running towards me for his attack, so I decided perhaps I shouldn't hang around here much longer. I had no other choice at this point but to run. I ran up Euston Road towards King's Cross, leaving my car with the engine running at Eversholt Street traffic lights. By the time I got to St Pancras train station and looked behind me, the guys were nowhere to be seen. They had stopped the chase, but how was I gonna get back to my car? I stood at St Pancras, thinking hard about the consequences of going back to my car in case they were waiting for me. Obviously they know I have to come back, so they could be just laying in wait for me. What the fuck am I gonna do now? Bollocks to this. I don't wanna, but I think I'm gonna have to call the police. It's odd calling the police for a punch-up, something I've never done, so it doesn't feel right, but I've got no choice at this point if I wanna get to my motor intact.

I'm standing outside King's Cross station, waiting for the police to turn up. I feel like a pussy. I feel like my masculinity has been tamed because I had to call the big, strong policeman to save me from a fight, and it makes me feel weak. I stand there, listening to the sound of the police siren far in the distance, feeling more and more like a pussy, and then the police call me on my phone.

'Hello, this is the police. Where are you exactly?'

I'm standing outside King's Cross and St Pancras on the pavement.

'Okay, stay there. We're on our way.'

As the sirens become louder and louder and I begin to see the neon blue lights, I'm sheepishly walking towards the edge of the curb to flag them down, feeling like the biggest pussy ever at this point, feeling I've let myself down, especially when I come from the area that I come from. Calling the police because you get into a fight is unheard of. This is embarrassing now. I mean, I've been in a few scraps over the years, and the police were only involved once. I didn't call them, but I remember that particular time because I had to think extremely quickly. I was attacked in a pub one afternoon. Someone called the police because the guy had me in a headlock for ages under his sweaty armpit.

It wasn't easy to get out of the fucker, but I still managed to duck the police when they rocked up. I was at the pub with my girlfriend at the time, Debbie. We met another couple there and were all chatting nicely. My girlfriend went to the bar to buy a drink, and the girl's boyfriend went to the piss hole. So I'm there chatting with his girlfriend, and we are continuing to have a laugh about whatever bollocks we were talking about. As her boyfriend came out of the toilet and came towards us, I stood up to go to the toilet myself. His girlfriend was still laughing. The guy just walked up to me and punched me full on the nose. I immediately punched him back. As I'm fighting him, I'm thinking, you jealous, needy, insecure fucker. You can't bear to see another man making your girlfriend smile.

I guess I'm gonna have to just beat you up then if you keep coming at me like this. I was calm and doing rather well at defending myself in a violent kind of way until the fucker got me in that headlock. I fucking hate headlocks. I've never headlocked anybody. What's the point in that? I'd rather say to the guy, 'Leave it out, mate. I don't want any agro,' than hold his fucking neck and time how long I could keep it there. If you're gonna fight, then fucking fight. Leave the wrestling shit out. But I could not get out of this fucking grip; it was so boring. And it's no fun trying to defend yourself when all you can see is the floor that's 4 inches away and the possibility that one extra twist from him could end my life. Well, I had to tread carefully. No matter how hard I was trying to punch him off of me, he would not let go. And it was so hard trying to hit a target that I couldn't see; swinging punches behind my head was not an easy thing to do. Oh, and I was kind of upside down in that headlock too. Very technical to get a punch away from that position, but I tried all the same until he finally let me go.

Unfortunately for me, the guy followed me outside and wanted more trouble. About thirty other people came out too, all shouting and wanting ringside seats. I didn't wanna be there. He was fuming and trying his hardest to get back at me but was being held back in the car park by three or four guys while he was ranting on about fighting me and all the shouting and palaver from everyone else. What a mess, and I was stuck there. Pacing from side to side slowly like Mike Tyson in his corner, waiting to come out for round one, I looked at Debbie and winked at her.

Stay out the way Debbie.

She smiled at me. And all of a sudden, four or five police cars screeched up. They all jumped out of the cars. They were all looking for someone to arrest, so I had to think fast. I had Debbie, who was out with me for a nice time before all of this nonsense. She behaved impeccably throughout this escapade.

Debb', quick, come here.

She came over, I put my arm around her shoulder, and putting the biggest smile on my face and looking directly in her eyes, we walked through the crowd of people scattering and shouting, with police running in between them like dodgem cars, bumping into them with outstretched arms. One copper came running straight up to me and stood there like a goalkeeper waiting for a penalty to be taken, looking for the panic in my face, I guess. But

I had thought of this already, and with that big beaming smile and looking like I'm in love, all cuddled up with my arm around my lady's shoulder, of course he's gonna think I'm not causing any trouble, and off he ran, looking for someone else that looked guilty. The desired effect had worked, and we walked calmly, and straight through the middle of the chaos and mayhem that I guess I created, back to the car, and drove out of there.

But this scenario was nothing like the time back then. Two police cars screeched to a halt, and a policeman wearing a baseball cap jumped out with a gun pointing at me and shouting,

'GET BACK! PUT YOUR HANDS UP AND STEP BACK.'

But I called you!

'PUT YOUR HANDS UP AND STEP BACK.'

I'd better do what he tells me and explain later. I look down on my chest, and I can see one, and now two, red laser dots moving around. At that moment, the whole noise of traffic and people everywhere came to a dramatic audio sensory shutdown. It's as if I am in space looking at the world. Or in the movies when the action goes into slow motion very silently. I'm thinking, wow. I'm gonna go out like this? Those fuckers are happy to kill me; look at where their lasers are. What's wrong with aiming at the leg? How trigger-happy are these fuckers anyway?

Hold on Tony, you've done nothing wrong. Just keep your hands up and communicate with them.

Hold up. I called you! I got attacked and called you. I called you because I left my car there at the traffic lights in Eversholt Street, and I need to get back to it.

After realising my story checked out right, they got me in the car to go back to Euston Station to get my car. The copper then says to me,

'We had reports that there was gunfire at this incident.'

No, that was me pulling out the inner metal bin liner in the street and using it to defend myself. He had a bottle, and it was crashing down on the bin. That's probably why someone would think it was a gun because they heard that.

They drove to another police car that was parked opposite Euston Station in Grafton Place, where they had got hold of the two other guys that were in the fracas. With a bit of back-and-forth walking, the copper came back to me, flipping the pages open of his little notepad and said,

'So you wanna press charges against these two, right?'

No, I'm not.

'What? You're not gonna press charges?'

No, I'm not.

'But we've got them here.'

I don't care; let them go.

There was a bit more up and down between the police before he walked over to the two musketeers and said,

'You're lucky, he doesn't wanna press charges. You're free to go.'

The two guys looked at me as if to say, 'Thanks man for not getting us nicked'. The policeman seemed pissed off that I didn't press charges, but I didn't care, I just wanted my car back. Of course I was not going to press charges. I was embarrassed to call them in the first place for these two urchins. I got in my car and drove off.

SATURDAY, 3.15PM

I'm counting money at home when I get a phone call from Trilly.

'Hello, Tony, it's me.'

Hello you.

'I hadn't heard from you, made me wonder if you had remembered tonight.'

Yes, of course I remember. I look forward to seeing you at seven-thirty.

'Ah, that's good. Well, I just wanted to check. What are we gonna do anyway? Where are you taking me?'

That's for me to know and you to find out.

'What! You're not gonna tell me?'

Er, no.

'Ooh, don't do this to me, I wanna know.'

And you will know, all in good time.

'But I wanna know before we get there.'

I promise you, you will know what and where it is two seconds before we get there. I'm a little bit busy right now Trilly, and I've got to go, but I'll see you at seven-thirty tonight.

'OK, see you then.'

I carry on counting the money: two thousand, eight hundred and seventy-five pounds. That's it. Surely I've got enough. I know that's enough. That's the central heating money right there. After all these years of freezing in the house, I can finally afford to get the house warm for my mum. We're so used to it being so cold, I just can't imagine what it will be like to have it all warm and cosy. I don't want to waste another second. I'll call the plumber right now and arrange a start. I feel very excited and proud.

7:28PM

I hear the rumble of the little sports car pulling up on my driveway, It's Trilly. I watch her from the upstairs window as she gets out of the car, and she looks so sexy. She's wearing a pink and white floral dress and white high-heel shoes. I'm looking forward to fucking her again as she strolls over to the front door and knocks three times, bang on seven-thirty. I really shouldn't encourage this. I have to remind myself she's a working girl, and I won't get too involved with a working girl. I'm just going to have a bit of fun with her, and that's it.

Derricks has two cabs sitting outside. Fuck me, that's rare for them on a Saturday night. I get allocated one of them, and I whisk her off to a little cocktail bar in Essex, around the Woodford area, called 'Ted's,' a very posh-looking place with mirrors on the ceiling and on the bar area, very comfortable sofas with some of them tucked away in their own little booths. The lighting in here is spot on, and the music is that sweet soul stuff. Trilly orders a Coconut Quencher, a sweet cocktail with a shot of Remy Martin VSOP, a drop of agave syrup, and topped up with coconut water over ice with a twist of orange and a bit of orange zest to finish, while I went for the Brandy Snap. There's hot water in this fucking drink, Drambuie, Angostura bitters, whatever the fuck that is. Even a fucking small knob of butter in this bad boy, some double cream, and brown sugar. I don't think I'm gonna like it, but it's so far out there I have to try it. There's a well-appointed Italian garden there, again with nice lighting up against the white walls and structures, with healthy big plants and bushes in various places and a very ornate pergola in the corner with a comfortable round sofa. This is where Trilly and I are sitting. We are laughing and joking and having fun.

I'm teasing her and having a good time. She has a very infectious laugh and even had a couple of other people in the garden laughing just by hearing her.

My guts are hurting a bit from all the laughing. Very witty, she's a funny girl. I like that quality in her. Just then, the drum roll and intro of '**Don't It Drive You Crazy**' comes on by the Pointer Sisters. A wicked tune, and Trilly turns to me and, bang on point with her air drums, she sings,

'Don't it drive you craaazyy, I love this song.'

She pulls my hand to dance.

'C'mon, let's dance.'

Fuck yeah, I wanna dance.

I love this track too, and we stand up in the beautiful Italian garden where most people are sitting around. I moved a small round table out of the way in the middle and created a dance floor, which she eagerly runs onto. She's looking at me dead in the eyes as she wiggles and moves to the music ever so slowly and provocatively. Her figure is amazing, plus those deep, gorgeous looks. Although we are out to have fun, I also want to fuck her right now as she slowly shimmers towards me in an even more hypnotic dance state than she was when she first hit our little dance floor. Now my cock is growing stiffly down my left leg. She moves in closer still and slowly raises her arms up, and around my neck as I start to dance with her. She shifts her left leg between my legs and, with a perfect fit, gently pushes her vagina onto my cock as we slowly dance together, getting away with heavy petting in public. There was only ever going to be one outcome. I whispered in her ear,

I smell you.

We continued to dance, writhing to the music in perfect unison, legs, arms, touching and feeling in every possible way that could be disguised as dancing and then parting again to dance facing each other. She's not taking her eyes off mine for a second, and here she comes again. She's coming in so tight, and I won't resist her wanting to rub herself against me like this. I'm loving the way she dances with me so perfectly, ensuring we stay connected down there in the dimly lit garden. Now there are five other couples dancing here, perfect for hiding amongst. This is a long song, over six minutes, and Trilly is getting extremely steamy. She's trying to pull me in even closer as we continue to slowly rub against each other in a game where the only rule is that we do not get discovered. Still looking at me dead in the eyes as we do this magical dance together, I rub my cock up and down her clit. Looks like she's loving this and moving beautifully along with me. This song is perfect for us right now. She's pulling me in closer, and I can feel her starting to shudder. Here comes that groan in my ear as she pulls me in closer still and cums right there on the dimly lit garden dance floor.

We went inside to get another cocktail and took them to one of the secluded booths they have in there to make ourselves comfortable. There are thick, deep red, velvet curtains on this booth, and Trilly wastes no time in closing them. We're alone, but I don't trust it because someone can still walk in here. Trilly's walking over to me, she sits on my lap, and slowly moves around in a dance while holding onto my arms. I think I know where this is going as she says to me,

'That's the first time that's ever happened to me, out on a dance floor.'

Just then, a Luther Vandross song came on called **She's So Good To Me**. Trilly is moving around more and more on my lap as she dances to the music. She lifts up her dress and sits back down on my lap. At this point, I have a raging hard-on which she feels out with her butt. I'm thinking about cutting the night out short and getting her back to my house so we can get busy, but Trilly has other plans. She reaches behind her and undoes my belt and trousers, grabs and strokes my cock before pulling it towards her and guiding it deep into her vagina and begins to dance in such a sexy way over it. I'm just gonna lean right back and spread my arms and legs out like a fucking starfish. I am...in...pure bliss. I'm lapping up the whole of this song in this position. She then stands up, turns around, and straddles me again as the next song starts.

'You Can't Turn Me Off' by High Energy, and Trilly is showing a lot of high energy in a very slow rhythmic motion as she looks deep into my eyes. Shit, she's really into me. We kiss passionately as she holds me tight and rides me in one of the sexiest ways I've ever been ridden. Just as the end of the song came, so did she. And after she jolted her last jolt, she looked at me and said,

'I don't know why, or what it is, but I just feel really drawn to you.'

Well, let's just enjoy how you feel right now.

She then got off my cock, got on her knees, and sucked on my dick like she loved doing it. I again assumed the starfish position and enjoyed every single moment of it. Just then, the waiter flung open the curtain. I quickly pulled the tablecloth over Trilly as the waiter said.

'Hi there, do you have any empties?'

I then said to Trilly,

Did you find it?

Only then does she stop sucking my cock and, while still gripping it, she says,

'Yeah, I found it alright.'

The waiter grabs the empty cocktail glasses and asks,

'Do you want another?'

Nah thanks, we're going now.

And he leaves, closing the curtain behind him. Trilly continues to suck my cock and I can hold it no longer and explode in her mouth and as she vigorously wanks me off, I continue to squirt the rest of my baby gravy all up on the underside of the table. I'd better move to avoid the drip. Where's that fucking table napkin?

It's so dark in here I can't see a fucking thing. I sort myself out and do my trousers up. Grabbing her hand I led her out of the booth.

'Where are we going?'

We're off to see the wizard.

She's laughing as I lead her through the bar.

'Ooh, the Tin Man, I hope I meet him on the way. He's my favourite.'

We're both feeling hungry at this point, but we don't do the traditional restaurant date. Instead, we hit the local chip shop where we can sit inside to eat. The man asks us what we fancy, and we both say exactly the same thing at exactly the same time.

'Just a chip roll for me.'

Just a chip roll for me

Trilly laughs at our synchronicity, and we both say exactly the same thing at the same time again but to each other.

'I fancy fish with that.'

I fancy fish with that.

Trilly laughs again as the waiter asks us what fish we want. We look into each other's eyes, and again we say exactly the same thing to each other at exactly the same time.

'Cod roe.'

Cod roe

I wonder if we will order the same drink. I grab a pen and invite Trilly to write on a napkin in secret what she wants to drink, and I do the same.

Right then, after three, we both turn the napkin over at the same time. One, two, three.

Exactly the same thing! RIBENA. We both laugh at our choices. Now that the food's here, it's fucking horrible. The chips are rock hard and look like they've been fried five times, and this chip has got moving oil in it. Looks like a fucking spirit level, and the state of this fish—I'm worried about my teeth. But we were hungry, so we picked at it anyway. We are having fun; she's making me laugh tonight. She turns to me and says,

'I've had so much fun tonight Tony, thank you.'

It's not over yet, c'mon.

'Where are we going?'

You'll find out.

I led her out of the chip shop, into a cab, and onto a lovely pub called the Horse and Well. I'm coughing as soon as I walk into this cigar and cigarette smoke-filled pub. They have live music and show sports events here, but I ain't here for that. I plan to whoop her at darts. I should say play her at darts, but I'm so fucking good that I just know I'm gonna whoop her, and of course, there will be penalties for the loser. After fanning a clear pathway through the smoke to get to the bar, I get us both a drink and grab the darts. It's game on.

Trilly seems really happy to have three darts in her hand, and with a beaming smile, she says to me.

'I love darts; reminds me of my dad. When I was a little girl, he used to play darts and would get me to play too.'

How old were you when he did that?

'Four, maybe. I got pretty okay at it too at one point. He taught me the right way to stand and how to guide the dart to where I want it to go.'

Well, it sounds like your dad was a bit of a professional.

'Oh, he was. My dad was a big shot darts player back in the day and bagged himself a fortune in prize money. He got loads of spinoff television work and advertising from it too.'

Where is he now?

'He's in a place that he shouldn't be. He hurt someone whilst trying to protect me. I've always been close to dad. He's my rock. A proper man who always made me feel protected and safe. When the boyfriends I had as a teenager used to come round, although my dad was always polite and nice to them, he used to somehow scare the shit out of them and then I'd notice a difference in them before we finished. I think it's just how masculine my dad is. It seemed to show me how weak they were around him. It kind of put me off. Probably why I stayed without while a lot of my mates were riding the cock carousel. They keep trying to get me out with them but I don't want to put myself in that club environment where it's full of thirsty men just wanting to have sex. That's all men go there hoping to find, and the women go there just for the attention, and a lot of the girls I know go ahead and bang them just for the validation. I went once for my girlfriend's birthday and had ten men hitting on me in two hours. By the tenth one I'm sure I was as rude as hell to him just to get him away from me, I don't want to be like that either. The nightclub is not the best place for a bloke to go to find a decent girl. Some of the girls I know who're into that scene have boyfriends at home and they constantly get up to all sorts of shit in the clubs with the random hot guys that approach them. You remind me of my dad a bit.'

I remind you of your dad. Like how?

'Oh I don't know, you just make me feel a certain way. I feel very feminine around you'

So I make you feel that way, eh. And your dad's in prison right?

'Yes. He is, unfortunately. The next door neighbour. Dad used to get him round every couple of weeks or so to play darts. He found out what I did a little while ago, and because he knows that the neighbour used to run a couple of brothels, somehow he was convinced that it was him who got me into the game. But he never did. It was a woman whom I used to work for, looking after her horses that got me into it. Anyhow, he must have confronted him and the neighbour ended up getting stabbed in the neck with a dart and died there in dads house. He called the ambulance, and tried to revive him, but by the time the ambulance came, it was too late to save him. Dad got charged with manslaughter and he's on remand waiting for sentencing. My dad's not dangerous. I don't know what happened but he didn't mean to kill him, I've not seen him in almost a year, I'm having such a good time tonight I just want to forget about it for now.'

Yeah, of course Trilly.

I then announce the start of the game.

I'll go first.

I raised my first dart, and as Trilly's dad put it, I guided the dart to where I wanted it to go. Boom! Treble twenty. Second dart, boom! Treble twenty. Third dart, boom! Straight twenty. My score, one hundred and forty. Trilly smiles as she says,

'What are we playing for?'

I hadn't thought of that yet, so I said to her,

The loser has to cook breakfast and do the washing up with nothing on. You can wear an apron for the washing up if you like.

And I give her a wink.

Trilly is smiling as she steps up to the line, bowing her head and slowly raising it in unison with her hand, and steadies the dart. Boom! Treble twenty. Next dart, boom! Treble twenty. Trilly lifts the third dart and boom. Treble twenty. She raises her arms in triumphant glory and lets rip in true Bruce Spendley darts-commentator style,

'ONE HUUUNDRED AND EIGH-TYYYY!'

I'm standing here aghast as she walks over to me, squeezes my cheeks with her fingers and thumb, and says,

'Mine's with a double egg in the morning,'

before turning and walking back to retrieve her perfectly placed darts from the board. But now it's my turn to throw.

10AM SUNDAY

I'm standing there doing the washing up with nothing on but an apron. Naturally, Trilly decides to tease me, and I can't blame her. I was so cocksure of myself that I was gonna whoop her.

'Thanks for the breakfast honey. You look good in that apron too.'

She puts on her clothes, fixes her hair, and puts nothing on her face but lip balm, and still looks so fucking hot. I could fuck her again right now, but a man must let the pussy cat go.

We have a four-second snog before she's out of the door.

'Bye, handsome.'

Go on. Get out of here.

I watch her from the window as she walks to her car, gets in, starts the engine, and out comes that familiar sound of the electric guitar intro to Chuck Berry's song from her stereo

Johnny B. Goode.

Hearing that puts a smile on my face. Could she be a Rock 'n' Roller? I eat some more breakfast, roll a joint, grab the guitar, and strut around the living room playing that very song.

MONDAY, 3:15AM

I'm having my coffee and checking my money. I've gotta be back by seven to sort my shit out before the plumber comes at eight to start work on the central heating. About fucking time too. All these years in the cold, and now finally my mum and I will be able to keep warm in our own house. I just can't imagine the difference it's gonna make. Right, here we go: waistcoat, blue tack, and out the door. All the cards are already mixed and in my waistcoat pocket.

No music on the drive this morning.

I think it's because I'm still trying to imagine how nice a warm house will be, but it's still hard to imagine. Empty roads are a joy to drive on, but I find myself sitting at this massive junction with the traffic lights on red. I can see for miles in all directions and there's not another car in sight, and yet I'm sitting here waiting for some fucker that ain't even there to pass in front of me.

I feel ridiculous.

The length of time I'm waiting for these lights is ridiculous too. C'mon, man, I've got shit to do. Fuck it, I'm going.

I drive through the red lights, and straight away there's a "Whoop whoop!" behind me. Police sirens. Shit, that's some points on my licence and a fine, and I pull over. I'm not gonna sit here like a guilty driver waiting for the policeman to take his time to walk over to me, so I get out and walk over to their car instead and say,

Is everything OK officer?

I can see that getting out of the car has thrown them a bit because they don't usually get that response.

'Er, wait there.'

They both get out of the car and put their hats on.

'Do you know why we've stopped you this morning?'

Well, after taking extreme caution, I proceeded past a red traffic light because there were empty roads and not a car for miles around.

The policeman looked at his colleague, then said to me,

'Yes, that is why we stopped you. Have you been drinking at all?'

No I haven't.

He then gets out his machine and proceeds to breathalyse me and says to his colleague,

'Do you know, in Sicily, they turn off the traffic lights by 11 pm if the streets are empty? Well, they leave them on amber so drivers can go on empty junctions but just do it cautiously. That's a much better system. I can't stand sitting at red lights in the early hours when nothing is around.'

The test comes back negative, so the copper says to me,

'OK sir, you can go.'

OK, I'll be off then.

I jump back in my car and drive off.

I got to Tottenham Court Road at four-fourteen, parked my car on Great Russell Street, and walked back to the eight boxes outside the Dominion Theatre where the cleaner is washing the last box. He wants his money.

'Where's my money?'

Alright, alright Tim, fucking 'ell.

'And you owe me a fiver for that bit of blue tack.'

Fucking 'ell Tim, I've got a new name for you: Timmy Tight Pants.

'Call me what you want when you pay me, darling.'

I give him fifty quid for the round and a fiver for the blue tack, then I go into the first box to decorate it with my cards. A quick look around for police and go! Six on the back, and one two three four five Six on the window, quick quick and out that box. Seven more boxes like that, and I catch up to Timmy Tight Pants.

I'm inside the last box there, putting my cards up while Timmy is using the squeegee on the outside of it. He shouts out to me,

'When you go down the road, just leave the old cards on the little shelf in the box and I'll take them when I get there.'

Alright Timmy.

And I'm off down Tottenham Court Road. The first set of four boxes down there are caked in yesterday's cards, and I wanna get away quickly, so with no hesitation, I swing open the door and pick the cards off from inside as fast as a kid would pick up cookies from a plate at a party and start to put my cards up. The cleaner pulls up to do this one and says to me,

'Pass those old cards, I'll get the blue tack off of those.'

How long have you been doing this job then?

'Couple of years. This is the fifth job I've had since I came out of prison as part of a reintegration programme.'

How long have you been out?

'Five years. I did ten years for robbery.'

What did you rob?

'It was a post office.'

Bloody 'ell Timmy. Did you have a slow getaway driver?

'I got the money, but the old bill was everywhere, and I was running over the flyover footbridge over the busy Newham Way Road in East London trying to get away.'

That's where I come from. Hold on. You did it on foot?

'The driver took off when he heard the old bill and left me, and the old bill came at me from both ends of the bridge. I knew that was it. I was not going to get away, so I just threw all the money over the bridge and the wind took it everywhere. It was raining cash and that was it. I got ten years.'

I paused as I remembered something that happened when I was a kid.

So it was you! I remember that. Everyone was grabbing scattered money every-where. So it was you who chucked it. All my mates were telling me it was raining money. I was gutted that I was not there for the big scramble, but I still found three one-pound notes two days later when I was walking home through the park near that road. I was only about ten years old.

Scramble. Reminds me of being in school. We used to throw a handful of change up in the air and shout, SCRAMBLE! Just to watch the other kids going mad trying to grab it all. There'd be kids getting their fingers stamped on just as they were about to pick up a stray ten-pence piece they saw. It was crazy but good fun to watch.

So after ripping yesterday's cards from the phone box and leaving them on the shelf, I neatly and quickly whack my cards above the phone, with another six on the window, and I'm out, sweeping into the next box at speed. I do this all the way down Tottenham Court Road until I get to the McDonald's at Warren Street train station. But oh shit! I've just put my cards up in the prime space, the space where D puts cards up. I dunno what I'm thinking. I'm not even working for D. What am I gonna fucking do here? Shall I go back and move all my cards over to the side a little bit so D has space, or just leave them there for one day? It's only one day for fuck's sake, and I've got this plumber coming at eight this morning. This is what I've worked for, and I ain't going back to rearrange the cards just to be late in getting back. Bollocks to it, and I carried on with the route. I'm coming up to the entrance of Warren Street train station. There's a man standing on the step there facing the street, he's holding a bottle of Lucozade, and he's tipping a white powder from a sachet into it on the sly.

As I walk past him, I'm looking him directly in the face. He hasn't got a clue that I just saw what he did. It's still dark, but I fucking did, and now he's all smiley as he turns around to help the young, hopelessly drunk lady he was with, struggling to navigate her way through the ticket barriers. I can't believe I just walked right past this man without saying anything. I know what you're up to, you fucking bastard, drugging her to rape her. This shit doesn't stick on my conscience too well. They're probably gone now. I had a chance to do something, but I let her down. All I had to do was shout out,

DON'T DRINK THE LUCOZADE! and I could have stopped her from whatever fate he has in mind for her. Or even just knocked or snatched the bottle out of his hand. I was that close to him as I walked past. You fucking bastard.

I make my way to the Oxford Circus phone boxes after completing all of the ones in the backstreets, and they are all bare as the cleaner has just been through. I hit the first box with a familiar speed: one two three four five six, all on the back in under six seconds, six on the window, and out! Bang, straight onto the next one. I'll mix it up a bit, start on the window: three four five… I'm just about to put the sixth card up, and right there, stepping up to the window, is a policeman. Bollocks! Bang to rights.

Can you come out of the box, please?'

Oh, fucking hell. What was I fucking thinking? What a fucking prick I am; I can't believe I didn't notice him coming. He's so slow, taking all the time he wants to get my details. I haven't got this time to waste; that plumber is gonna be there. I've gotta be there before him. I gotta butter this copper up. I've gotta go. At least make him hurry up.

Have you had a busy morning officer?

'Just stand there for a minute.'

Well that didn't bloody work. Go on then, you prick, find your fucking pen. I'll try again.

Nice and quiet this time of the morning, eh? I like this time of the day.

'Is this your job then?'

I can tell he's not gonna fucking bend.

Job? Nah, it's not a job.

'How much do you get paid for this then?'

Paid? I don't get paid.

I wish he'd stop asking me all these fucking questions and get on with it.

'What's your name?'

He's taking down my name and address, and then he said the worst thing I could hear him say.

'Right then, give me all your cards.'

Shit! I can't have him taking these.

You've got my details; why don't you just leave me with the cards? I'm still gonna hear from the court. What do you want to take the cards for?

'Just empty out your pockets, c'mon, give 'em here.'

I can't believe I'm giving him all my cards, it's a fucking joke.

'Is that all of 'em?'

Well, yeah.

'What else have you got on you?'

Nothing, just blue tack.

'Give us it here then.'

Are you really gonna take my blue tack?

'Yep, give us it here.'

Keep calm Tony, I've gotta keep calm, this fucking prick. Reaching into my pocket to pull out the ball of blue tack a little smaller than a tennis ball, I'm looking him straight in the eyes. He's loving the fact that I'm pissed off. But shit! I can't pull it away from his hand now. Any second now he's gonna see it, and that's a big enough chunk of hash stuck to the side of that blue tack to get me carted off.

'Actually, you can take this back.'

He's now unknowingly handing me back over a lump of the finest Himalayan hashish that I couldn't find earlier, presumed lost. But I've got no cards. I can do no more. Fuck this, I'm going home.

I got home at eight-thirty, just as the plumber had pulled up. Today is the day. Central heating in this house is an amazing achievement. One thousand, four hundred and ninety-five pounds it's costing me. This plumber is a lovely man, and I like the way he gets to work on it straight away. The noise of those fucking floorboards being ripped up and carpets being torn; I've gotta get out. It's a bit too loud and messy for Mum too, but she's definitely happy that it's being done. So, while she's shut herself off in her bedroom, I think I'll go and get an oil change on the car. The mechanic in this garage is noisier than the plumber. Let's have a look underneath the car while it's up there. It's so loud in here I can just about hear my phone ringing.

HELLO?

'Hello, Tony, it's the plumber. It's your mum. She was making me a cup of tea, and she collapsed. She's sitting down now, but I'm not sure what to do.'

Alright, thanks, I'll call an ambulance, and I'm coming back.

I left my car at the garage, and I've never had such a quick cab service from Derricks, but the ambulance has already taken Mum to the hospital. I got the cab driver to take me there.

It turns out that Mum had a mild stroke. I'm so grateful she can still talk and laugh and stuff. I think she'll be alright after a few days' observation there. I'll get some bits for her and bring 'em later after I check on the plumber. Thank fuck he was there to help her.

Bloody hell, he's going so fast, and he tells me that it's going to take three days to finish it. Fine with me. It's just after lunchtime, and I get a phone call from Terry.

'D's not happy with you mate. I'd call if I was you.'

Look, I'm not having a good day today. I'll ring D later.

'Well, it's up to you. You're taking the piss. I wouldn't leave it too long if I were you.'

I put the phone down on Terry, but I ain't got time to ring D now. I've got my mum to sort out and the plumber to think about.

It's obvious what D's pissed about anyway—using that space in the phone box. Big deal. I made a mistake and had no time to correct it. I'll explain that later. D will be fine.

I'll put the cards right when I go back out there today on the top-up. That's if D is that bothered about 'em. It's only for one day.

I grabbed some bits for Mum and went to the hospital. It's so nice to see that she's in good spirits and ready to come home already. It's best she stays in there though, for a day or two for observations. We chatted and laughed a lot during my visit. She is funny.

After that, I jumped on a train and headed for the West End to do the top-up.

There were a few cards still up in the places I put them in the morning, but a few boxes were down as well. Did D rip 'em down today? Who knows. But halfway through the top-up, I get a call from my brother.

'Hello, Tony. I've got some bad news. Mum has had another stroke. It's a lot worse this time. She can't move her left side at all. Her face has all dropped, and she can't talk to anyone. I'm at the hospital now with her.'

I don't want to do the cards anymore today. I just want to be with Mum. Fuck the rest of this route; I'm getting my arse up to the hospital.

Mum isn't looking so good. Her face is swollen, and her eyes seem sunken into her face. Look how slowly she turns her head to look at me. I can see she wants to smile, but she can't. Don't cry Tony. I mustn't cry.

'Give me your hand Mum. It's alright Mum. I'm here. I love you Mum.'

It's not nice seeing Mum like this. Not a word out of her, and I've run out of things to say. I'll just sit here with her.

These chairs ain't very comfortable when you sit in them for this amount of time.

I feel like staying here all night with her, but I've got to go home. Ah, that's good. I'm glad Sis has turned up. She can take over sitting with her. I need food and a shower. Oh, and I'll have to get around to calling D.

The plumber has left the house in a decent state considering all the floor-boards he was ripping up today. He's put the walkway ones back for safety. He's done a lot. There are wobbly pipes sticking out everywhere, and that boiler looks like the top of its league. Not much food in the cupboards that I fancy doing tonight, so I'll pop out to Bamish, the large family-run corner shop and get some supplies. There's one white girl named Sandy that I know who works there among a family of Indians, and here comes the mum now.

Hello Mrs Patel.

'Hello hello.'

She always looks nice in her saree, sitting there behind the till. She moves so slowly.

Where's Sandy, Mrs Patel?

'Who, Sandra? She's there somewhere working. I don't know.'

Oh, here she comes now.

'Hi Tony, how are ya? Not seen you in a while. What ya doing in here?'

Well I've gotta eat ain't I?

'Yeah, sorry. I meant, what are you after?'

Just a bit of dinner Sandy. Mum's in the hospital.

'Oh no Tony, what happened?'

Ah, she had a bit of a stroke.

'A bit of a stroke? That's serious, no?'

She'll be alright Sandy. I don't wanna talk too much about it now.

'OK, but let me know if I can do anything, will ya?'

Yeah, 'course Sandy. Thanks."

'Are you sure you're OK?'

Yeah, I'm OK Sandy. Let's just change the subject. Don't worry about me.

'You're the only person who ever calls me Sandy.'

What do you want me to call ya, Sandra?

'No, I like Sandy. It's different. Do you remember when we used to go carol singing as kids?'

How could I forget that? We made a fortune.

'We were good, that's why.'

I know we were. None of this, 'We Wish You a Merry Christmas bollocks. We opened up with 'The First Noel or 'Silent Night'.

"Yeah, in perfect harmony we were. We had that big chocolate tin with us, full of money."

I think Mrs Patel is calling you.

Yes, Mrs Patel?

'Pay-pa-bag.'

What did she ask for?

'Oh, she wants a paper bag. I've gotta go Tony. I'll see ya later.'

OK Sandy, I'll catch ya later.

Sandy comes back seconds later with the bag and hands it to Mrs Patel, and I can't believe what she wants it for. She opened it up, brought up a big hacking greeny from deep in her throat, and gobbed in it. Sandy's face is in shock and horror. I'm not too impressed either. Fuck doing that as part of a job.

I've got myself a half-decent munch from Bamish, but I'll have a little walk first to clear my head and get some air. I'm praying that Mum recovers well. It's a nice evening, so I'm in no rush to get back home. I'm slowly walking along the small rear car park of Bamish, where there are short bollards all around it. I think I'll just sit here on one of 'em for just a minute.

I don't know how long Mum will be in the hospital. Ouch, itchy leg. I lean over an inch to the left to scratch my left shin, and at the very second that I move, I feel a massive blow of something or another come down right on my neck and slide down hitting my shoulder. What the fuck is that! I can't run; I'm falling. What is happening to me? Have I been hit by a car? It feels like a car. This fucking hurts so much.

I'm falling forward, and then I hear a voice shouting,

'YOU CUUUNT!'

I look back as I'm still struggling to find my balance to run, and it's fucking D holding a baseball bat high up in the air and about to swing it down on me again. Seeing this danger has made me come to my senses quickly, and I swiftly have it away on my toes, across the main road and down a side street, and I am not stopping until I am well clear of this fucking nutter.

After running a while, I look around. I don't think I'm being followed, so I slow down a bit.

I can't believe that just happened. I've got to go back home, but I'll sit it out here and wait for things to calm down a bit. Get my fucking breath back. My neck really hurts; I can't move my shoulder very well. That could have been the end of me. I didn't even hear D creeping up behind me. And if I never got that itch in the first place, if it wasn't so strong and made me wait for one second longer before I scratched it, that baseball bat would have hit me in the middle of my head for sure. That was so hard that there's no way my skull could have taken that.

Shit! That would have fucking killed me. D tried to kill me. Just like that. Divine intervention or the universe saw its way to give me that itch right at that very moment. Someone's looking out for me. It's just not my time to go yet. This is crazy. Why am I still here? It's scary thinking of what could have happened to me. I could be dead now.

Fuck that shit.

I sit there a little while longer before walking home, cooking myself some dinner, and then going to bed. I'm so thankful for that itch.

TUESDAY, 4AM

I'm up sorting myself out for the round this morning, but I've gotta be on my guard if D comes running at me again with a fucking baseball bat. Maybe I should have rung when Terry was telling me to. Might have been able to avoid that altogether. Well, I'm gonna have to face D today if I'm to earn any money, so I finish my coffee and jump in my car at four-thirty. Empty roads on the way to Tottenham Court Road, and I reach there by four-fifty. Pulling into my normal parking spot and walking round to do the first eight boxes outside the Dominion, I am not only looking out for police but looking out for D too. Timmy Tight Pants the cleaner has been and gone. Terry has been and gone. But there are none of D's cards up, and there's all of that space just above the phone left empty by Terry and soon to be left empty by me. I am standing here outside the boxes just having a good slow look around for D first. I don't wanna be trapped inside a phone box with D in the same mood as yesterday. I'm a little scared, but I mustn't show it. How am I going to do this first box? I've gotta just do it fast and get the fuck out. This reminds me of when I was a kid, scared to turn the lights off before sprinting to get into bed. I pull the door open, and it squeaks loudly. Fucking done my ears in that did. Right then, cards out of the pocket, quick quick.

I'm not gonna put my cards in D's space, but I'd better keep looking around in case that nutter comes running at me with that bat. I put my cards up off to the side, one two three four five six, quick look around for D, six on the window and out! Why am I breathing so deeply? I've gotta calm down; this is bollocks. I look around for D as I walk to the next box, door open and in, one to six, all on the back. Window, fucking road runner speed, one two three four five six and out! Where's D? That fucker's gotta be around somewhere. Gotta get these last six done, too many boxes together in one place for my liking.

I go from one box to another, but I don't think I'm being discreet enough. Stop being paranoid Tony, just keep a lookout for D. Next box, one two, all the way to six. The rest are done in record speed, and I'm out and walking up Tottenham Court Road to the next set of four. I put my cards up to the side while I look about for D and the police before making my way to the next four boxes where Terry is just walking into the last one of the four. He likes to take his time putting cards up. Fucking slow, I smash the other three boxes, again keeping well clear of D's space. The fucker's out to kill me, and I catch up with Terry on the last one. He'll know where D is.

Morning Terry, where's D?

'I dunno. Not been seen. Didn't you get in touch yesterday?'

Kind of, yeah.

'Wasn't happy with you yesterday for putting your cards up in the space. That's D's space. You should have seen the face.'

I did.

'Nah, I mean when your cards were up in the prime space. Looked like D wanted to hurt ya. You're lucky.'

I know.

I make my way to the next set of two opposite Goodge Street train stations. There's a car parked close by with two men in it drinking coffee. The window cleaner who does the shop windows is also there working, and the newspaper guy is setting up his stall. A few other people are mulling about, no biggie, so I stroll into the phone box and quickly put my cards up, one two three four five six. As I'm walking out of the box, the two men are getting out of the car. Turns out they're two coppers, undercover in a Volkswagen Passat.

Sitting there on a break, watching me go in there and put all my cards up. *"Hold up a minute."*

He takes another sip of his coffee and places it on the roof of the car before getting out his notepad and pen.

'Police. What's your name?'

Tony.

'Tony what?'

After giving him my name and address, he says,

'How many girls are you working for?'

He then walks into the phone box, takes down the six cards that I just put up, and then proceeds to make a note of all the telephone numbers before saying to me,

'These are getting more explicit as time goes on. How would you like your kid sister to see these while she's walking down the street? Something's gonna be done about this. You've got women with their legs spread wide open these days. Have you got any ID on you?'

That's another thing you have to make sure you do as a Cardboy: you always have to have your ID with you. Basically, it just prevents you from being taken away by the police, provided you haven't got anything else you shouldn't have on ya. They know where you are; they let you go, which is what they did.

'Alright, you can go now.'

Still bollocks though. That's another fine on the way. I carried on quickly to do the rest of Tottenham Court Road, knowing that those two would be driving down the road soon. I don't want 'em stopping me twice. There's no sign of D today. I kept away from the space, and it is a bit dodgy that the cards are still not up, but nevertheless, my eyes are wide open for that piece of shit. Once is enough being crept up on from behind. I did all the boxes in the backstreets off Tottenham Court Road, then the usual Oxford Street, the mega shopping street with all the brands squashed together. Soho, the seedy side of London with peep shows advertised by neon lights. Cambridge Circus, with the theatres and posh, early, elegant looking bars. Euston, well nothing much happens there but it's just got one of the busiest main train stations in London and King's Cross. A major train station. Beautifully structured building built in eighteen fifty-two , before jumping in my car at Euston and heading home by eight.

I had a bit of breakfast and went straight to bed for a three-hour kip. I woke up at midday, and I'm feeling pretty good, until I think of Mum. I hope she's improved today. The plumber is working away, and he's called in two other plumbers to help him, so the heating will apparently be done by today now. That is quick. I went to see Mum. It's sad for me to see her like this. I can't see much improvement today if any. The day was moving along at some pace, and before I had a chance to do anything else, I was back out there to start the top-up at four. D's cards have not been up all day, and luckily for me, the whole of Tottenham Court Road's cards are still up, and I haven't got to do a single box. These are the sweet days that I love. I'm getting paid for strolling around the West End. I'm on the lookout for D of course But apart from that, it's quite relaxed. I put cards up in the couple of boxes that are down in Oxford Street and head off to Soho to check those messy boxes, and sure enough, they are fucking messy, cards all crooked and all over the place. I put a few of mine up, keeping them all nice and neat amongst all the shitty ways the other Cardboys work, and head on through Charing Cross Road. I jump on the train from Tottenham Court Road station to Euston station to grab those last few boxes around there and King's Cross before jumping on the train at Euston to head home by five-thirty. A quick round today.

Wednesday morning at four forty-five is the same. I mean, D's cards are not up. Terry has been and gone and left D's spot again, and I still have to be on my toes. Fuck knows what's happened to D. I put my cards up clear of the prime spot and move on up to each box down Tottenham Court Road. I'm not enjoying being out here today; I'm not feeling it. Not only do I have to look out for D at work, I've got the same shit when I get home, but I complete the round without any aggravation.

I got home this evening, and people are talking about D going off the trolley and smashing everything up with a baseball bat. Turns out, on Monday night with a friend, D and this friend took a load of ecstasy tablets. Fuck knows what else people put in that shit. But instead of getting all lovey-dovey, D went the other way and started smashing the house up, then ran outside and smashed the windscreens of neighbours' cars for the pettiest of long-held grudges with 'em. Those neighbours didn't even know why their motors got smashed up, so of course when the nutter saw me sitting on the bollards, and thought of me taking that money, well, I was bound to be the next target. Makes me shudder again as I think of what would have happened if I never got that itch. Thank fuck for that. Anyway, after I ran off that night, D went home and proceeded to take more of these shitty pills, according to the friend. And of course, all those drugs made the heartbeat so fast that it just stopped working after a massive heart attack, and she died right there on the spot. Fucking pills. Overdose. Went do-lally. I can't believe she's dead. D is dead. I can't get my head around it. Dennon is dead. Well, she tried to kill me with that fucking baseball bat, so I shouldn't be gutted for her.

It's a warm evening tonight, and I decided to get a Chinese takeaway from the best takeaway around called Tade House, run by a Chinese family and headed by the eldest son named Ping. I say it's the best one, but it's the only one I ever go to. Actually, once I did go to another one in a town called The Abbey Arms. Made me throw up. It had the longest hair I've ever found in a food item, about eight inches.

Tade House is safer and better. I'd have chicken chow mein that would come in a little white plastic bag, and I'd get a curry sauce which I'd pour straight into the bag and then tie a knot in the top to close it. Then, I'd turn it upside down and bite the corner off so it resembled one of those cake icers. Then continue to squirt, suck, and eat the chicken curry and chow mein through the hole that I made with my teeth. The ribs from there are delicious, and I can't forget the pancake rolls. But tonight, I'm gonna go for the chicken and noodle soup for starters, and you can't beat a bit of egg-fried rice. They do chunky chips here, but you do get a choice.

'*Chunky or normal?*' Ping says.

Chunky please, and can I have sesame seed prawn toast, please? Oh, go on then, I'll have some spare ribs and a sweet and sour sauce as well, and another curry sauce, please.

'*Nine pound forty please.*'

There you go, keep the change.

There's no table in the place, just a bench built into the wall on two sides for waiting customers. A good place to hang out when there are a few people in there. You always know someone who's standing there waiting for their treat. The seat on top of the benches is made of black, vegetarian leather, and the entire walls are covered in that flat, dodgy sheet of plywood that's made to look like logs pushed together but is so thin you could snap it in half like a biscuit. The counter spans the width of the shop, and there's one door behind Ping with a little square hole in it. The hole has a shelf that's on the kitchen side of the door, and that's where every meal gets put on and dragged through the square by Ping at the counter. I stand there and peek through the square door hole to see a marvellous spectacle of wok tossing on the stove with flames shooting four feet in the air. The magical calmness of the chefs, who have done it a million times before, natter in their native tongue that has to be loud enough for them to hear each other over the sizzling of the meat and veg in the pans while it's all bagged up and contained, and out comes your food on the little shelf.

There's a flat above the takeaway which they live in, and the door to get access to this is a door close to the shop entrance, basically side by side. Right there outside of those is a bus stop. I remember once, I was walking up to the shop to buy some milk. I turned the corner, and I was in the middle of a war zone. There were a good few lads from the area that I recognized running around wielding golf clubs and pieces of wood, and the usual find-what-you-can-get weaponry that's close by. I didn't recognize another group of men who also had inventive weaponry and were running around in the same fashion. There were punches being thrown at people who were hitting the ground and bouncing back up again just as fast. I remember hearing someone shout,

'It's the Greeko's. The Greeko's are in town.'

A rival gang had entered the area, not something that most outside gangs dared to do because this area has a reputation for some of the hardest and most villainous men in London. A strange face around here is a face in danger. I stood in the bus stop watching the carnage, thinking, perhaps I shouldn't be here. There was an old lady next to me, so I felt that I had a duty to stand there and protect her. And maybe I wouldn't get attacked by the Greeko's if I was standing close enough to her. A Scottish bloke, who is one of the known faces around here called Stefan McKinley, came running up to the shop with a bloody nose, carrying a piece of wood. He was trying to get away from an imminent thrashing by one of these 'Greeko's' carrying whatever weapon that he had. I didn't know which one was after him, but he obviously did. He went running into the Chinese takeaway shouting,

'Quick quick, you gotta hide me!' to which Ping replied,

'OK, I've got a secret passage.'

So Stefan jumped over the counter, ran into the kitchen, and disappeared into the yard. The next second, he came running out of the side door to the flat before realising he was standing in the same place outside the Chinese restaurant. Of course the bloke who was after him caught up, and Stefan just continued to leg it down the road. I never found out if he caught up with him or what happened, but the fighting all seemed to be over very quickly.

This food smells lovely.

Is that mine Ping?

He grabs the white carrier bag of food and checks the ticket on it.

'Chicken noodle soup, egg fried rice, spare ribs.'

Yeah, that's mine, thanks.

There's always enough to leave some for the next day. I'll eat this and go and see Mum.

At the hospital, Mum is not looking very well at all. In fact, it looks like she's rapidly going downhill. Her eyes have sunken into her head; she's not the same Mum that I saw just a few days ago. I think she is on her way out. She turned her head to look at me, but there was no smiling at all from her. Maybe it's the drugs they are giving her which are making her all docile. I don't like seeing her like this, and I want to cry, but I won't, I can't. I'll grab her hand and just... Well, just chat to her.

They're putting in the central heating Mum, It'll be all nice and warm for you when you come out. Heat at last for the first time in how many years? Thirty? Forty?

By the time I was getting kicked out by the nurse, it was ten-fifteen. Mum was already asleep at this point, and I had to sort of wake myself up to leave too. When I got home, all the floorboards had been put back, and there was a nice little note left by the plumber that read:

'All finished. Thank you very much. I hope Mum gets better soon, and I'm glad I was there. Just press the 'ON' button for a quick hour boost, just like I showed you, and the timer is quite easy to work out too. It all fired up nicely. Any problems, just call me. Mick.'

Lovely. All done and sorted, but I'm knackered and need to sleep, so I won't test it now. Fuck it, I can't even be bothered to brush my teeth tonight. Flop! Lights out, I'm gone.

THURSDAY, 3:15AM

It's a little chilly this morning, but I'm thinking of the brand new central heating, all fitted and primed for its first use. I power up the 'ON' button, and it all fires up in sync. I can see the little flame through the boiler window. It's three twenty-five, and I can already feel the difference in temperature in the whole house. All of a sudden, the house has become cosy for the first time ever. Fucking brilliant. I walk into the coldest rooms in the house, which are the bathroom and the toilet, and they are snug and warm too. Mum should be here to experience this. She bought this house in the sixties, and it's never had any heating in it apart from those two gas fires. It's transformed the house completely. Maybe I'll fit a new kitchen next, but right now I'd better get out there to earn the money for it. I'm thinking of D as I drive into the West End at four o'clock. Pulling into and parking on the side street off Tottenham Court Road, I walk back to the eight boxes at the Dominion Theatre where the cleaner is. Terry is putting his cards up in the boxes the cleaner has already cleaned. He's so fucking slow; he puts his cards up like he hasn't got a single worry in the world. He's also leaving D's space again. I go into the end box and proceed to put my cards up, but now, for the first time ever, I'm going as slow as Terry. It's because I'm thinking of D, and I'm putting my cards up in her old space. Terry sees me doing this and comes over to start all that shit up again.

'Oi, what ya doing? You can't do that. D's gonna put her cards up there.'

I don't think she'll be putting 'em up today Terry.

'Why, have you seen her?'

No one's gonna see her again. She's dead mate.

'What ya talking about? You're kidding, right? What happened?'

Overdose mate.

'Nah, really?'

Really. A bunch of dodgy E's she ate, dropped down dead with a heart attack on Monday night.

'Fuck that. So you ain't wasting any time using her space are ya? What about her girls?'

I dunno, are you doing 'em?

'Nah, not me. I've got enough. I don't need any more, bloody headache. You ring 'em up. I don't wanna, I don't like having lots of cards.'

Cor, I could imagine you having more cards. That would take you all day to finish at the speed you go at.

If Terry doesn't want the work, maybe I should step in before someone else does. More cards mean more money, so why not? I'll call some tonight. I proceeded down Tottenham Court Road, but because the cleaner was still at the Dominion, I had to strip down all of yesterday's cards. This time the cleaner asked me to leave the discarded cards on the little shelf in the box, and he'll get 'em and bag 'em up when he comes through to clean 'em. He's gonna pick off the little bits of blue tack on the back of each one to sell it back to us as one big lump.

I carry on putting my cards up in D's space for the rest of the route: backstreets, Oxford Street, Soho, Euston, the usual spots, and finish the route by seven-thirty. I jump in my car, which is parked in Euston, Eversholt Street. There's a couple of flats of D's down this street. Gonna ring those ones for sure. Luckily they know me already from when I did the cards that day for D.

SEPTEMBER 9TH, 4AM

It's Monday, and I'm driving into the West End with the weight of my waist-coat considerably more due to the extra cards I have in my pockets. Over the Friday weekend when I rang D's girls to explain what happened, they've all been desperate over the last few days to get their cards up. They all jumped at the chance to have me take over. Each of 'em gave me five hundred cards to put up each day, so all of a sudden I've gone from two hundred and forty pounds per day to five hundred and ninety pounds per day. Two thousand nine hundred and fifty pounds per week.

I have a lot more cards to mix and pockets to fill, but I'm up for it. I've got thirteen girls all mixed up into seven pockets, and I've still got three empty pockets to use on this waistcoat, so I'm doing OK. I'm listening to '**I Ain't Mad At Cha**' by Tupac Shakur. I love that song. It's all over the radio because he got shot on Saturday. Gunned down in a drive-by shooting in Las Vegas. He's not dead, but in a bad way in the hospital. He's too important to die. I don't see him as just a rapper. I see him as a kind of messenger, a civil rights leader.

His song '**Dear Mama**' is another great track from him. Makes me think of my mum. A time-lapse in my head. From the early memories of being with her to seeing her lying where she is today. I find myself crying now as I drive. No one can see me now, on my own in my car, and thank fuck for that because I can't stop these tears pouring out of my eyes now. I'm approaching the Limehouse Link tunnel, a series of interlinked tunnels that connect with Canary Wharf, the newly built central business district of London, but I can't see where I'm driving properly, and I cannot stop myself as I bawl out loud. I just wanna give love to her and have her home in the warmth, but I'm scared she's not gonna make it. I have to pull the car over to find a tissue. Fucking state of me. Crying and blubbering uncontrollably like this. A police car pulls up slowly beside me and the window slides down. I quickly try to straighten my face up but it's obvious I've been crying. The copper then speaks to me.

'You alright?'

Yeah, thanks. It's my mum. She's had a bad stroke, and she's in the hospital. I just got a bit tearful and couldn't see the road properly, so I stopped for a tissue. I'm OK.

'I'm sorry about that. You take care.'

He saluted me, and the car drove off. I dried my eyes with a tissue, and after blowing the sadness gunk from my nose, I regained my composure and drove off through the tunnel, getting to Tottenham Court Road at four-twenty.

I'm standing in the first of the eight boxes outside the Dominion Theatre with thirteen cards to put up on the back and thirteen on the window. Let's go! Smash! Up they go. Same on the window quick quick, bish bosh, thirteen and out! That took about twenty-three seconds. Next box, do it quicker, one, two, right up to thirteen. Window, super speed and out. Six more boxes here to do and with a quick look around for police, I'm in and out of the remaining boxes in a minute and a half. That's good going, and off I go to the next set of four boxes. There's a total of a hundred and four cards that I'm going to put in just these four boxes. The cleaner has been and gone, and Terry is not here yet, so off I go and I smash my cards up in all four boxes in record time and make it to the next set of four on the same side of the road. The cleaner is sitting in his van picking blue tack from the old cards he took down, which is handy for me because I forgot to buy more and I have a shitload of cards to put up. I didn't even have to ask old Timmy Tight Pants before he pipes up.

'Do you wanna buy this blue tack?'

And with that, he pulls out a massive ball of it that was mostly white tack with only a little bit of blue squashed into it. It looks like a planet.

'Fifteen quid.'

What! Fucking 'ell Tim, fifteen quid for that! I'll give you a tenner.

'Oh alright, go on then, a tenner.'

I thought I heard you say that.

'Have you got my money for going in front? And where's D? She owes me money too, fifty quid for last week.'

D's not gonna be around anymore Tim. I'm doing her cards from now on.

'Why, what's happened to her?'

She's retired.

'Well, if I'm gonna let you put all your cards up and her cards up, I'll have to get more money from you.'

Yeah yeah, don't worry Timmy Tight Pants, I'll give you more.

I take out some money, count out one hundred pounds, and give it to him.

I'll give you this each week.

'Wicked, thanks Tony. If you're going to take down yesterday's cards, don't throw them, leave them on the little shelf in there.'

Yeah yeah I know.

I enter the box, and at lightning speed, I take down all of yesterday's cards and then pepper that phone box with twenty-six of my fresh ones. I'm getting so fast at this. Just as I finish these four boxes, Terry rocks up wearing an Arsenal shirt under his waistcoat. Perfect opportunity to have a bit of fun with him. I do like to wind people up about their football shirts. So I asked him,

What happened? Did you have absolutely fuck all to wear so someone lent you that?

'Very funny. I was at the game on Saturday. Good game.'

What was the score?

'It was a draw. Two-two, against Aston Villa. We were two nil down coming into the second half, then Paul Merson scored a wicked goal in the seventieth minute before Andy Linighan scored a goal in the ninetieth minute.'

Terry and I continue down Tottenham Court Road, tearing down all of yesterday's cards and putting up ours. It doesn't take that much longer for me to put up the extra cards, and I can feel my pockets getting lighter and lighter as I go. I do have an extra route though because D's cards go into Holborn. That's London's historic law district. It's a bustling mix of legal buildings and offices and includes the Royal Courts of Justice which serves high profile civil cases, and a museum, which was the home of one of the greatest British architects, John Soane who built and lived in it until his death in eighteen thirty-seven. It displays all of his collections of antiques, furniture, sculptures and architectural models and paintings. Hatton Gardens diamond dealers are a short walking distance away. There's a very busy cafe culture there catering for the office workers and tourists alike. There's a closed train station there, where The Prodigy filmed the video for that **'Firestarter'** song, with a little bit of an area called The Strand thrown in. That place became known for its coffee shops, pubs, and restaurants for the aristocracy when they first moved into the West End during the seventeenth century. It was a hub for theatres and music halls during the nineteenth century. There are still a few theatres there to this day. I finish all the backstreets, Oxford Street, Euston, and King's Cross. I check the time and it's seven o'clock. I would like to be out of the West End by eight, so I speed-walk in my Adidas convertibles back to the car parked in Euston. I drive and park at the bottom of Grays Inn Road. After quickly sorting out the cards in my pockets, I make my way on foot to the two phone boxes at the junction at High Holborn. The sun bursts out as I walk into the phone box. I have a good look around for police while I pretend I'm using the phone. Then I hit it. Bang bang! Three, four, five, six, seven all on the backboard, then same again on the window and out the box in a flash. Into the next box, cards out, one two... my phone rings... I look at it and it's my brother. I instantly know what this call is about. I know it's Mum. I think she's dead.

Hello.

'Hi, it's me.'

Yeah, I know.

'She's gone.'

My eyes well up with tears and I try to hold my blinking back to stop them from falling but it's no use, and my sniffing and blinking sets me off.

'Where are you?'

I'm in the West End.

'Are you coming home?'

I'll be over this morning, see you in a bit.

After putting the phone down, I make the sign of the cross.

Bye Mum, I love you.

I wipe my tears dry and continued to put the cards up in this box as quickly as I could. Mum has passed forward now and there's nothing I can do about it. I feel like just stopping what I am doing right now and going home. I'm gonna cry again, I can't focus on going home, that makes me sad. I'll focus on these cards. That'll take my mind off it for now. Five more on the back, three four five six seven. Same seven on the window and out! Doing the last ten boxes around this area feels different after getting that news. I don't give a fuck who sees me or anything; I just put my cards up blatantly. It's only a silly fine anyway. I should be like this all the time, especially with the money

I'm on now. Why should I give a shit when they're giving out thirty pound fines with no record? What the fuck should I be worried about?

I'm gonna make some fucking money.

SEPTEMBER 13TH, FRIDAY AFTERNOON

I'm getting ready to go and do the top up, and it's all over the news about Tupac Shakur who has died in hospital. He held on for a few days but that was it. Who the fuck would want to kill him? I guess everyone's got someone who doesn't like them. He seemed like a decent bloke, a big loss there. Very talented too. As I walk downstairs to leave the house, I can see there's a brown envelope with a red magistrate's court stamp on it. I know it's a fine for the cards, so I stand there and quickly flick it open.

I was expecting the usual thirty or forty pound fine, so it was a bit of a shock to see this one: two hundred and seventy-five pounds! For illegal advertising! What happened to the fucking littering charge we all got? I'll deal with that later, but right now I've got the top up to concentrate on before going around to thirteen flats to pick up my money. Payday.

Sitting in my car on the way to Tottenham Court Road, I'm thinking of Mum; I have her funeral to sort out.

The top-up sees me with one hundred cards for each flat, one thousand three hundred in total.

I bring the car in as I'm picking up cards from all the flats for the whole week; that'll be a good few boxes full. The waistcoat is bulging out, and the police know how to spot a Cardboy just because we wear these fishing jackets, but it's a little chilly, so I have a jacket over the top of it, incognito style. Same old Tottenham Court Road start, Dominion Theatre and the eight boxes there.

I'm a bit tired today and don't really feel like doing the top-up at all, so it was a result to see all eight boxes still up and intact from this morning. Sweet.

I stroll down to the first set of four boxes and I can see the first box completely bare. I open the door all casual and slower than normal to put up twenty-six cards, but then I hit the speed button and GO! Sliding out cards at a rate of two at a time while doing the double pinch of blue tack, top pockets, two from the front and two from the back. I put one on the back and a duplicate on the window, bish bash bosh, nice and neat, double quick. All of them up, and out! Twenty-six cards up in twenty-three seconds. I turn to walk out of the box, and a plainclothes policeman with his ID badge on his hip is gently and slowly opening the door for me to get out. I didn't even notice that copper standing there, nicking another Cardboy he's caught doing these same boxes.

'Erm, come over here for a minute.'

He guided me over to one side, close to the other Cardboy.

'That's a lot of cards you've got there. Have you got any ID on you?'

I hand him my driving licence, which he studies.

'Right then Tony. You will have to make a court appearance for this.'

I'm thinking, like fuck I will. I'll pay the fine and save my time. He did all the usual bollocks and didn't take my cards which was a result. And off I went. I walked into the sandwich bar at the next set of four boxes and ordered a coffee so I could give myself a bit of time for the copper to go. I ain't in any rush, and those quiche slices look nice, so one of those too.

After coming out of there, it was a quick look around and into the first of that set of four. Only two of the cards were down, but it's a bit fucking confusing because I don't know yet what fucking pocket I've put 'em in. It feels like I'm playing Higher or Lower, just like the Bruce Forsyth game. I pulled one card from every side of every pocket before I found the right ones.

All the girls told me that they had a good day when I rang 'em, so there's no worry there for pay. Looking down and scanning the inside of my pockets,

I familiarise myself with what pocket's got what cards in as I make my way to the next set of two boxes outside of the furniture shop. Step up the pace, Tony, c'mon, four down in here so in I go.

I scan the next boxes as I'm approaching from twenty feet away. I'll know if I have to use my thumb to slide out a card or my finger and from what pocket I'll go to. As smooth as that, I swiftly make my way up the rest of Tottenham Court Road, checking and patching up in a few boxes. Same in the backstreets, patchy in parts, but most of 'em stayed up.

Oxford Street is busy as fuck; there are people everywhere. You can't see the scenery, just bodies bumping into each other and making me walk slowly.

I feel like I'm in a queue. There's a bloke here with a little guitar amplifier and a microphone singing Johnny B. Goode. He's really good; I think I'll slip him a folded-up fiver when I get out of this box.

For the first time I'm enjoying doing these main boxes, and I know it's because I can hear live Rock'n'Roll just outside. Go Tony, go, go. I smash a few cards up and take great delight in folding up a fiver, dropping it in his guitar case, and moving on.

Ah, bollocks! Here comes mister Policeman Plod to spoil all the fun he's having.

Well, that's that then. Fuck knows why he's closing him down. He was bringing good cheer to the street.

It's six-thirty when I finish the top up, so it's back to the car to start the flat runs. Fucking traffic everywhere; it's moving, but very slowly. And that pepperoni quiche I ate is really making me grunt, fucking stinks, a rotten pungent smell that I kind of like.

I drive slowly towards Jenny's flat on Eversholt Street. Jenny is the maid. It's starting to rain so I close all the windows and fart out that warm, pepperoni mist some more. If it were someone else's fart in the car that smelt like this, I would be hanging out the window by now. So as I sit there floating on the pepperoni cloud in silence, I hear someone calling me.

'Tony, Tony!'

I look to my left and it's Jenny. She has a massive smile on her face. It looks like she's just had her hair done, so as it's just started to rain, I know she wants a lift. She's got a big shopping bag with her too. She comes right up to the door. I put my hands up as if to say, don't open the door, I did a fart, and it stinks in here, but it was too late. This is awful; there's no way out of this; she's coming in. She grabs the handle, opens the door, and gets in with her beaming smile.

'Ooh, it's so nice to get a lift. Are you coming to see…'

She closes the door and immediately stops talking. I know she was gonna say 'me,' but I also know the pepperoni delight has given her a fright. First, she looked at the door handle as she thought of getting out and walking, but her hair getting wet in the rain made her change her mind. Weighing up the odds, she slowly turned to look at me with lowered eyebrows and said,

'Where's the button for the window?'

I opened both windows, and she looked straight ahead and never said another word to me for the four minutes she was in the car. I picked up two and a half thousand cards from her for next week and two hundred and fifty quid in cash.

After collecting from here first, I go to all seven of her flats and pick up cards and money from them all, totaling seventeen thousand cards and one thousand seven hundred and fifty pounds in cash. I then go on to collect more cards and one thousand, two hundred quid in cash from my flats. That's two thousand, nine hundred and fifty pounds for one week's work, not too bad.

8:45PM

Home at last. This is the latest I've ever got back home from work. I'm fucking knackered but still find the staying power to knock up a quick sea bass fish dinner on the grill with some rice, salad, a dumpy bottle of beer, and a nice joint after, which gives me the giggles. But now I'm looking at this brown court envelope on the table as I suck on my long spliff, this soon straightens up my face as I think of the two hundred and seventy-five I have to pay. Along with looking at all the money I also have on the table in front of me, I guess it evens itself out as tax on my earnings.

I read it properly and learnt that because of that fucking dickhead arguing the littering charge on the grounds that it was not littering because the box has four walls, and that littering can only be littering if it is done outside in the public with no walls. That, of course, was a silly fine, and now that the charge is illegal advertising, fuck knows the limit that these fines can go up to. The copper who nicked me for it is named here as P.C. Farquhar. This puts the smile back on my face; I misread it as 'fucker'!

So instead of just paying the fine, I decided to write a self-representative letter to the court in my defence. I wanted to imagine this letter being read out in court and perhaps even get a chuckle from the judge, so as I wrote the letter, I included his name as many times as I could. The letter was only half a sheet, and yet I included 'Farquar' a total of twenty-five times. It was P.C. Farquar this and P.C. Farquar that. Farquhar, Farquhar, everywhere. I wouldn't find out what effect it was gonna have, but it was funny to me as I wrote it.

10:00PM

The late-night telephone call. It's Trilly. I'm now thinking about Mum, so I don't really want to answer, but I've not spoken to her for a few days. Let's see what she's up to.

Hello Trilly, how are ya?

'Hello Tony, fine. I was just thinking of you and just wanted to say hi.'

Well it's good to hear your voice, Trilly.

'I've been missing you.'

Well, why don't you bring your hot self over with a bottle of wine and we'll cook dinner together. When are you free?

'I'm free all weekend.'

Come over Sunday at six-thirty. Does that work for you?

'Yes. Sunday is perfect, but wait, can I tell you a story?'

I'd love to hear what you've gotta say Trilly, but I'm really knackered. I'll see you on Sunday, then I can properly give you all my attention. You can tell me all about it then, but I've really gotta go now. See you Sunday, yeah. Bye.

I put the phone down and then got my head down on that pillow.

SUNDAY EVENING, 6:29PM

My doorbell is ringing. I open the door and Trilly is standing there, bang on time and looking stunning. She took my breath away. She's wearing a short, red dress with white polka dots that has an open neck down to her cleavage, sock tights, and shiny black shoes with tiny white polka dots. She looks like she has just come out of the hairdresser's with flowing hair stroking across her shoulders. She has made such an effort for me and she's done a fantastic job. I have to let her know.

You take my breath away! You look stunning, Trilly.

'Aah, thank you Tony. Here's a gorgeous bottle of wine but I want a cuppa first.'

As she strolls in, I kiss her on the lips and she walks into the kitchen to fill the kettle up.

'Are you having a cup?'

Yeah, I'll have one.

'What are we cooking then?'

We're cooking ravioli with creamy mushrooms and asparagus.

'Ooh, sounds delicious, something I've not done before.'

Well, there are two of us making it, so it better be nice. If it comes out shitty I won't be too harsh on ya, being it's your first time.

'Is that a picture of your mum up there?'

I stop myself from welling up again. I was hoping she might help to take my mind off Mum, but here she is, bringing her up.

Yeah, that's Mum.

'Is she still alive?'

She died a few days ago.

'Oh my God, so recently Tony. I'm so sorry. Are you alright?'

Well, it's Mum ain't it. I'm alright.

'But you look sad now.'

I'm okay Trilly. It's just fresh, that's all.

'Lay on your back, I wanna do something to you.'

I lay down, and she knelt on the floor above my head and reached for my neck. As she started to push her fingers and thumbs around places on my neck, and then began a slight pulling action, I could feel a magical electrical sensation that travelled from my head top all the way to my toes and back up again. A feeling of pure bliss and relaxation, she does this for about five minutes, and by this time I am melting. It's the next best feeling to an orgasm and reminds me of what I'll be experiencing with this sexy woman before me in due time. I'm getting hungry now and I want an early dinner, so it's time to get cracking on that.

Dinner is looking like a success. I mean, I did a bit, cut the asparagus up and shit, but Trilly took to my kitchen like a Michelin star chef. She said to me,

'I'm doing this but with a twist.'

She has such a sexy accent, and I want to get to know her a little more. I have to remind myself though that she's a working girl, and I'm just here having a bit of fun with her, but damn she's hot. She's Spanish and comes from Cordoba. She has silky smooth dark hair and cat-like dark brown eyes. We ate dinner and made our way to the sofa.

'Did you like the food?'

I loved the food, thank you.

'Good, my mother taught me well.'

What was it like as a kid growing up in Spain?

'Oh, during the summer, we would all sit in the garden, and my mum has a kitchen in the garden. And oh my gosh, the food that we would all eat, with my grandmother cooking too and my aunties there, it was wonderful. We used to play in the garden all the time. My mum and dad built a big house and they have dogs and chickens, they grow olives there.'

That sounds idyllic.

'Oh it is. You'd love my country. You should come there one day.'

You never know, maybe one day. What's your fondest memory growing up as a kid?

'I remember we would sometimes all go camping in the summer. It was so hot, and sleeping outside was the best place to cool down. That was fun, sleeping under the stars, wonderful. I've been having a wonderful time with you Tony. I really dig your whole vibe.'

Well I'm glad you're having a wonderful time.

I'm sitting next to her on the sofa, and she wastes no time sliding over to kiss me while at the same time grabbing my crotch. She's so responsive to my touch, and these moaning sounds she makes are incredibly sexy, it really fires me up. Her attraction to me seems a suppressed ten, which is incredible to feel from her, and she's so easy to be with. I feel like I need to know more about her. I'm curious as to why she started working in this game. I can't imagine how a good, healthy upbringing could amount to becoming a working girl. Maybe there's some traumatic childhood situation that put her on this path, but at the same time, after spending time with her, she seems so together. I don't sense any trauma with her at all. She's beautiful. She's studying business. I wanna ask her how she got into this game, but at the same time, I don't want to discuss it with her. And if I do, it has to at least be in a fun and playful way, but being able to chat with fun and playfulness about how she got into this is not something I want to risk right now. And as with all women, I know she is emotional and will always come from that place. If she's had some bad experience about it all, then for sure I will put her in that place if I bring it up. I ain't prepared to spoil this moment for her.

She pushes me to lean back on my sofa, stands up, and lets her red dress fall to the ground before stepping out of it. She really does have the most incredible body. Her tits are the perfect size, the perfect shape, and they sit on her chest just perfectly. Her nipples have grown to a size that is sending me crazy as I lean forward to stroke them. She pushes me back onto the sofa and slowly goes down on her knees. She wants my trousers off and slowly makes her way up from my knees, touching all the way up my thighs until she gets to my belt. All this without breaking eye contact once. Slowly undoing my belt, she slides my trousers and boxer shorts off, releasing my rock-hard cock in a spring-like action. I lean back and close my eyes to feel her nipples touching my knees and slowly moving halfway up my thighs. I'm loving feeling her hair gently tickling my legs, and then I feel the warm moisture of her mouth gently clamping down onto my cock. This is sheer bliss. She's sucking, licking, and stroking my cock in a manner that is sending me to a place of pure ecstasy, and she is enjoying sending me there. I can't help but think that she is so good at giving blow jobs on account of her doing it on a regular basis for money, but at this point, even though she is doing it to me for free, it keeps creeping into my head, the fact that she is indeed sharing her body and this experience with other men, which would normally be a no-go for me. Or so I thought. Not that I'm trying to make her mine or anything. I'm loving the sex I'm having with her, and she really is quite sweet and likes some of the things that I like: darts, Rock'n'Roll, and she even plays the drums. I could really jam with her but I'll keep my distance and not get too involved.

It's been at least fifteen minutes that I've been having my dick sucked. It's fucking great, and as she senses more and more of the electricity running through my body, she just goes faster and faster until I cannot sit still on my sofa any longer. With a sudden jolt, I'm exploding every part of my energy out of my cock and into her mouth. This is the best feeling in the world; nothing beats it. My cock stays solid as she continues to suck on it like she's just started. As she looks up and smiles at me, she's taking off her knickers. She stands up, turns around, lifts up her red dress, and from between her legs, she grabs my cock and gently guides it to her soaking, swollen vagina.

Ah ah. Not without a Dunky my darling. I stretch over to reach my jacket pocket and get out a box of three, wasting no time putting the love jacket on my cock. Now I'm ready and she is just as eager. She slides herself slowly onto my cock as deep inside her as it will go. I'm caressing her back like I'm shuffling and spreading out a deck of cards on a poker table, exploring every muscle and contour that I can as she fully enjoys writhing around on it. As she slowly lays back to rest her back on my chest with my cock still inside her, I feel her start to shake. I slide my hands very slowly and gently all around her perfectly shaped tits and very erect nipples. Right then, she groans the sexiest groan that turns me on even further. She cums and shakes, which sends me over the edge, and I begin to orgasm too. After we both cum, I take off the Dunky, wipe my erect cock dry, then put another one on for another round. She straddles me again, but this time with her tits slapping tantalisingly onto my face while my hands are all over her very well-formed arse as she rides me with great enthusiasm. There's something about Trilly that makes me want to explore more and more with her. I sense a pureness, but I know I'm deluding myself to think that a working girl has pureness about her. I mean, all of the girls I work for are cool, fun, and sensible in all their conversations. They all seem nice enough. I can't believe one of 'em said to me she'd buy me a flash car if I'd be her boyfriend.

An afterthought would have got me what I would have preferred: a Mercedes one-ninety, but the deal was already off. If I can't stand the thought of other men fucking the same women as I am, why the fuck am I doing it anyway? A working girl is definitely not pure enough for me, but why the fuck do I feel this one is different? Could it be just because she's easygoing? That's great she is like that. She goes with the flow, she's fun to be around. But it's not just that; there's something there, a lot deeper. She's smart, and by the way she is behaving, she has a very high attraction level to me. And she's about to cum again right now as she rides me faster. Here she cums. As she's shaking and groaning even louder than the first time, it's that sound she makes that sends me into orbit. Her Spanish accent in that groan is so fucking hot. She squirts her love juice over me as I continue to fuck her. I can feel myself about to cum again, so I hold onto her tight as I shoot my load once more. My thrusts slow down as I feel the need to withdraw to remove the Dunky. I stood up and took it off to wipe myself dry, but Trilly grabbed my cock and again slid her tongue down the underside of it, taking it deep into her mouth, sucking it to rock-solid status again. I grabbed the last Dunky and wanted to put it on, but she insisted that she suck my cock for longer. I wasn't about to take this lead away from her. You do your thing Trilly, go ahead and do your thing.

Before long, I'm feeling the strong urge to fuck her, but I take my time putting the Dunky on, slowly opening the packet with my teeth as I get gently cock-tugged by this gorgeous woman's mouth and hands. She looks up when she hears the packet opening and smiles at me before turning around, suggesting that I fuck her doggy style, all while not breaking eye contact with me. I slide the Dunky on and slide into her. She lets off that gorgeous Spanish groan as I fuck her gently but firmly from behind.

OCTOBER

Another month, and more news about a death. This time it's René Lacoste, the black tennis player. A fiery, fiesty player who was known to snap most of his opponents up on that court. "Rip and shake them apart," was said to describe him. Through that style, he picked up the nickname of 'The Crocodile,' and being the sharp business-minded man that he was, he jumped all over that and started a clothing brand putting his nickname as a logo on all his shirts. That fiery crocodile. Rest in peace René. I never had one of his shirts when I was younger like the other fashionable kids did. Mum couldn't afford them; they were quite expensive. I had the Fred Perry and Ben Sherman shirts, they had class and were a little more affordable too. They were the uniform of the 'Rude Boy,' the 'Skinhead,' and even the Mods come to think of it, wearing them under their two-tone suits.

After my round this morning I was knackered, so I got in, and went straight to bed. I think it was eight-thirty when I got my head down. I really needed it. I didn't wake up till twelve-thirty and I'm so hungry now.

There are two brown envelopes on the floor by the front door. I know they're court letters, but I wasn't expecting two of 'em. I open the first one, and it's the verdict from my piss-taking letter I wrote to the courts about Farquhar. This is okay. I've gone from a fine of two hundred and seventy-five pounds and being told to shut my mouth, to it now being reduced to less than fifty percent—all the way down to eighty quid! Now for the other letter. I open that one, and it's a new fine, and they want three hundred and ninety-five pounds from me. I don't want to write another letter. I'm going to turn up in court for this one. It's next week. I want to have my say. These fines are just getting bigger and bigger. Just like the Spice Girls. They're everywhere.

They've just brought out another song called '**Say You'll Be There**.' Not quite Rock 'n' Roll, but I like it still. I'm feeling very awake and ready for the top-up so I decided to go in earlier than normal. Same old Tottenham Court Road start. Outside the Dominion Theatre and working my way up the street. First set of four boxes are all down as I approach, and there's a man in a suit in the first box. He's not using the phone but instead, he is holding a small square piece of tin foil and burning a lighter on the underside of it. Is he on the gear? Chasing the dragon? I think they call it that. He's definitely not the archetypal heroin junkie; he looks quite smart. I guess you could call him a functioning junkie, one that still goes to work every day. Fuck that shit. I'll just stick to my weed thank you very much. I ain't going into that box after him either. I don't want to breathe any of that shit in.

So it's into the first box which is empty. A blank canvas for my twenty-six cards. GO! First the backboard. One to thirteen, Ooh I'm so quick now. I smash the window with the same amount and out. Into the next box. Peppering the box with my twenty-six cards on the backboard and window, repeating the same in the next box and off to the further set of two. But who's this guy standing there? I mean, I know he's a Cardboy. He's got the waistcoat on and blue tack in his hand. He's waiting for the woman to come out of the box, but I've never seen him down here before. I go to the adjacent box which is empty too, apart from this guy's two cards. He has not put them up in the prime spot. In D's spot. My spot. His cards are down the side. A quick look around for police, and I smash my thirteen cards on the back and thirteen on the window. I come out, and he is standing there looking at me and says,

'Oh so you're doing D's cards. How is she doing?'

Not very well.

'Really, what's the matter with her?'

She's dead.

'Fuck off! Really?'

Yeah, really.

'What did she die of?'

Oh, I dunno, it's not come out yet.

I wasn't about to tell this guy what happened to D. I've not got a good vibe about him really. So there we are, both standing there, waiting for the woman to come out of the other phone box.

What's your name? I've not seen you around here before.

'My name is Michael. I don't normally come up this end. I just do around the Baker Street area, but one of the girls wanted her cards down here. I'm just here for the day that's all. What's your name?

Tony.

I didn't offer my hand to shake his hand. I don't like or trust him for some reason. We are both standing there, chatting while we wait for the woman to come out of the phone box. When she did eventually come out, I casually walked in and noticed the woman had left her purse on the shelf. I immediately came out of the box to call the woman back.

Excuse me, you've left your purse.

As soon as I shouted that out, this fucking Michael prick grabs the purse from the shelf and says, *'Shhh, don't say anything.'*

I can't believe he's out to steal this woman's purse. The woman heard me calling out and was walking back saying,

'Oh my purse is there?'

I said yeah, but this Michael twat says,

'No, we haven't got it.'

I'm thinking, don't you fucking dare nick her purse before she says,

'But I heard you say you had my purse, and I did leave it in there, I know I did.'

That fucking prick. If I don't do something now, he'll have that, so I said to her,

Yeah, yeah, we've got it.

Then I turned to that prick and said,

'Pass it to her.'

He looked at me as if to say, 'Why did you bloody say something?' and I looked at him as if to say, 'You cunt, you can fuck off away from me.' I mean, the amount of money us Cardboys make, he must have had at least seven girls he was working for, and still, he wants to steal someone's purse. 'Scum'ite' we call those kinds of people. I want fuck all to do with him, and my hunches were right. I walked away from him without even saying goodbye. Prick.

The rest of Tottenham Court Road was very patchy because a good few cards had been taken down. Time to get busy. When I got to Oxford Circus, there was not a single card in the box, which puts me on edge a little bit. Is someone watching these boxes? Is someone just waiting for me to go in there to catch me red-handed? I shouldn't be so worried about this victimless activity, but I still don't need the fine. These four boxes need to be done, so I'm going in. I put just over one hundred cards in these boxes, thirteen on the backboard and thirteen on the window, then continued to walk down Oxford Street. The whole of Oxford Street has been taken down. What is going on? I enter the next set of two empty boxes, and I'm very alert at this point, looking left and right more times than I usually do before putting up the cards. The problem is, the police are always plain-clothed down here, so I ain't got a fucking clue who's who. I might as well just close my eyes and do it. It is a fucking cat-and-mouse game out here. There's a group of five people at the next set of two boxes with big black bin liners. They are collecting all the cards from the boxes. They don't look like police, but I don't feel like approaching them to stop it, so I hang back a little and just watch what's going on. I'll just go in there after and whack 'em all up when they've gone. Just then, my phone rings, and it's Mandy from Grafton Mews.

Hello Tony, don't put those cards up you've got of mine. Come round and get some new ones.'

It's too late; I'm already putting them up.

As she's explaining, it turns out that there has been some bother or complaint about how explicit the pictures on her cards are. They were getting raunchier, I can't deny that. They seem to have gone from bikini and sarong photos to legs spread apart and the vag' being pulled open by two fingers. It's not right for kids to see all that shit really. One woman has gone into a box and seen her picture on one of the cards. That must have been really freaky for her. The police head of vice has ordered the girls to tone down their cards immediately or face having no cards in the box at all. So throughout the day, all the girls have been in overdrive ordering new cards with just writing on them and calling me to come and pick them up. But I haven't got my car with me, so I won't be picking any up until tomorrow. And that works out to about twenty-seven thousand cards. I'd better clear the boot. This also means that I won't be working tomorrow, just collecting cards.

NOVEMBER 1ST, FRIDAY

It's the day of the court case where I had the chance to pay that three hundred and ninety-five-pound fine or attend the hearing. I dressed up smartly and went to Clerkenwell Court to argue my case. Not that I had a case to argue—they caught me red-handed. I had to go to prevent a warrant from being issued. With all the formalities in the courtroom, paperwork, and the judge swatting up on what was what, they called me up to stick it to me. Maybe coming was a bad idea. Maybe I should have just paid the fine. That would have been a lot easier, that's for sure. It's not as if I couldn't afford it. I'm on nearly three grand a week, and it's not as if I get these fines regularly. They are getting larger and larger though. A big jump from the twenty to thirty-pound fines we used to get for littering. So, one guy stands up. I guess he's the prosecutor, but this is not a criminal offence, just a civil one. Nonetheless, he's standing there and asking me these fucking questions.

'Are you Tony Hemming, of forty-two King Regents Lane, Bustom House, London?'

Yeah, that's me.

'On Tuesday the 15th of October, you were seen placing prostitutes' cards in a telephone box on Tottenham Court Road. You were stopped by PC Mullard, who found a number of cards on your person. Let me put this to you, Mr. Hemming. Is this your form of full-time employment?'

Now, I had to think fast about how I was going to answer this question. Obviously, I was not going to say yes; that would render you liable for up to seven years in prison. I wasn't about to fess up to immoral earnings, no fucking way, so I told him straight.

No.

'Are you saying this is just your part-time work?'

No, I'm not.

'Then why are you doing this, Mr Hemming?'

Well, it's not that I get paid or anything like that. I just—I like blow jobs, and I get blow jobs from 'em.

I looked at the judge, and he had a little smirk on his face. I made sure I looked a bit embarrassed and a bit shy when I said this to make it believable.

'So you do not receive any monetary payment at all for this service?'

No, I said no. Can I just add that I didn't think there was anything wrong with what I was doing? In fact, if I may say, I think the girls are doing a really good service for society, and I'm happy to be a part of it. There's a lot of men out there who cannot get a girlfriend for one reason or another. They may be extremely shy at approaching women, or they might be severely disfigured, or even just very ugly, with no woman attracted to them. I've seen a man with a condition that left hideous lumps and bumps all over his face and body. How is he going to get a girlfriend? He needs love and intimacy too, but he may not be able to get anyone. I just don't think that's very fair, so these girls can help a man in those situations. I think it's a beautiful thing—everyone needs love, everyone deserves someone to hold, kiss, and have sex with. Not only that, but there are also men out there who will prey on women for their sexual gratification. There are a lot of women who have been raped by desperate men who cannot find a woman for one reason or another. These girls, in turn, help to keep other women safer on the streets. If the girls keep providing this service, then maybe the urge to rape our women will disappear.

I looked at the judge, and he had this smile on his face as he stared at me and said, '

*Alright, okay. I've heard enough. Mr Hemming, regrettably, you will still be
receiving a fine. Can you pay this fine?'*

Well, Your Honour, it won't be easy but I'll manage.

'Okay. I'm setting this fine to forty pounds. The case is now dismissed.'

And with a swift close of his files, he said with a smile,

'You are free to go, Mr Hemming.'

And that was it! Was it worth attending? Fuck yeah. I saved myself three
hundred and forty-five quid for that trip. He probably goes to see the girls
himself. Chefs, politicians, policemen, lawyers, actors, and musicians— people from all walks of life visit these girls. I don't ask the girls which men come
to see 'em. Men who are married see the girls behind their wives' backs. They
are in these situations where they are not intimate with the women they have
been married to for ten, twenty, thirty years. All attraction is gone, and they
are just staying with who they used to be crazy about but no longer work on
their relationship.

I remember one day going to a flat to pick up some cards for D. The flat had a
little cafe next door with one or two tables outside, and one of the tables was
literally one step away from the girl's front door. Sitting at that table sipping
coffee was a famous singer whom I had actually met before on about four or
five occasions. I first met him at a party I was invited to. Lovely bloke, and we
chatted for about thirty minutes back then. He had a massive hit in the late
seventies and went on to more success with a few more hits in the eighties. I
had seen him around the British Broadcasting television company building
in London while I was on my round, and we'd greet each other, which to
me was very cool. Anyway, I said hello to him as I approached the door, and
we exchanged pleasantries for a couple of minutes. Then I rang the bell just
above his head to the flat where the working girl was. I noticed a slight unease
when he saw me press the button as he sipped his coffee, I felt that he was

just waiting for his appointment time to go and see the girl there. I was only at the flat for twenty seconds. I walked up two steps at a time to the front door, and the girl who was in a rush said to me,

'I gotta go. All the cards are there; I've got a client. Thanks.'

She closed the door, and I was off down the stairs. By the time I got out the front door, the singer was gone. But it's none of my business what a gentleman does. I guess at this point I should tell you who he is.

MONDAY

There's been a drastic and rapid change in the cards. As quickly as that, all the pictures on all the cards have been removed, leaving nothing but text on them. I've got to go and pick up the new cards from everyone. The police head of vice, Jake Regan, wanted this change instantly, and the girls obeyed. None of them want to get shut down, that's for sure, so at ten o'clock in the morning, I'm driving my car into London to grab them. There's a lot of traffic out here at this time, but I'm part of it, so I can't complain. I'm sitting in my car on Gower Street, moving four feet every so often. I look to my left, and I can see the famous magician Larno Wenner strolling along the road. I loved him when I was a kid growing up, and my first thought was to say hello, but I'm in my car, and he's strolling along. I move twenty feet this time before coming to a halt in more traffic, and Mr. Wenner is catching up with me. Instinct took hold as I grabbed a pen and a scrap bit of paper, jumped out of my car, ran around the front of it, and straight up to him, which did put him on high alert a bit. So I quickly smiled and said, *Hello, Larno. Can I have your autograph please?*

'Oh, sure.'

He looks at me as if I'm going to do something to him but signs the piece of paper for me.

'Thanks Larno.'

I quickly run and jump back into my car, back to sitting still in the traffic. I'm not feeling good sitting here, and I want to get out as soon as possible. I'm embarrassed that I made such a fuss to get Larno Wenners' autograph. And look at all these people around me—what must they be thinking, watching me make a fool of myself? But I loved him when I was a kid. I still like him, but I'm a grown man now, and performing an act like that was definitely a kid's instinct. I've got enough of those that come out now and again; I don't need any more. Even Larno himself was looking at me funny. That was embarrassing. I'll never do something like that again. It's not as if I've not met anyone famous before—I have! I've just never asked for their autographs before. Thank God this traffic is moving, but here I am again, catching up to and driving slowly past Larno Wenner for the second time. He's still looking at me funny as he walks side by side at the same speed as I'm driving. He looks embarrassed for me. Fix up Tony. Put it behind you—that ain't you at all. Shake it off. No one in all these cars is ever going to see me again, so what have I got to feel embarrassed about? The traffic lights are green; I'll feel better when I'm out of here. I chuck a left into Grafton Way and I'm gone. I head to Mandy's flat to pick up her cards and as usual, she's pleased to see me.

'Hi Tony, it's good to see you.'

Hello Mandy, how are ya?

'I'm fine now I've seen you. Come in.'

Cor, you're murder. Ain't you married?

'Married? No, fuck that. I had one piece of shit hanging around me for way too long. Fucking deadbeat he was. You're not married are you?'

I'm not married Mandy. Just dating and having fun.

'What? A good-looking man like you and you've not found 'the one' yet?'

Mandy, every woman I meet has the chance to be the one and win me over. When I meet the woman who pushes all the right buttons, then maybe she'll qualify to earn my attention and be the one. But until then, I'm just having fun.

'She's gonna be a lucky girl, whoever that is. I can just tell.'

Well, they're out there somewhere, but I'm not focusing on that. I'm focusing on work and pushing forward towards life's goals.

'Oh yeah? And what are they then?'

We can save that for another time Mandy. My car's outside and I don't wanna get a ticket.

'Right then, the cards. I'll go and get them. They're all writing and no pictures. Everyone has to do it, or they'll stop us altogether.'

Yeah, I know.

I grabbed the cards from Mandy and quickly made my way back to the car before driving to Grafton Mews to pick up some cards from the flat there. I parked around the corner and walked back to the small porch entrance of the four-story building and pressed the number eighty-eight on the shiny gold intercom panel. And waited casually with my hands in my pockets for an answer. I slowly turned around, took two slow steps to the pavement, and glanced to the left. To my shock, and his, by the look on his face, there was Larno Wenner again, walking towards me. Oh for fuck's sake, he's gonna think I'm stalking him. I can't handle this. I've never felt so embarrassed. Don't worry Mr Wenner, I was just going to this flat anyway. I'm not stalking you, I promise. I'll even give you your autograph back. I turned and walked back to the doorbell, pressing it in quick succession in my desperation to escape from him walking past and seeing me. My mind's going crazy! Open the fucking door! Open the fucking door! I can't face Larno Wenner again, and he'll be walking right past this doorway any second now. Do I turn around to see if he saw me? Of course he fucking saw me; I saw the look of horror on his face. The poor bloke might be thinking I wanna hurt him. I'm still waiting outside the block of flats for an answer and can't resist the urge to have a slowish look around to see, only to have it confirmed. Of course he fucking saw ya. I'm gutted, but there's nothing I can do at this point. The door finally opened, and I went in feeling defeated. I picked up more text cards from there and made my way to the next flat, and onward until I collected from all thirteen flats.

I got home at eight-thirty and started to mix the cards. This presents itself as a visual trip; a lot of 'em have the same text font and some even have the same layout. By the time I ate my oven chips in a bap, 'cause that's all the effort I could be bothered to put into cooking tonight, and mixed all the cards, it was nine-thirty, and my bed was calling me big time.

TUESDAY, 4AM

I'm up. I've got my waistcoat already loaded up with cards. Nourishment-wise, all I have is a cup of coffee and a packet of malted milk biscuits to dip in, but it's enough to keep me going till the end of the round. By four-fifteen I'm in my car and driving up the West End. Parking up at Great Russell Street, I do the same walk around the corner to the first set of eight boxes outside the Dominion. I think I'll time myself on these boxes; it's four thirty-six, and I've got to put up two hundred and eight cards in all of 'em. Go! I swing the first door open, and I'm in. I go to the top-right outside breast pocket first, pull out two cards from the front, and quickly whack those up on the backboard. Down to the hip pocket with two cards from there as quick as I can—three, four bosh, and they're up. Next two from the further outer hip pocket—five six. Then, with controlled speed, I reach for the parallel pockets on the other side of the jacket, and just as fast as the first side, I whip the remaining cards up on the backboard. Thirteen of 'em. I repeat the same thing all over again. Go! Super quick, like Bruce Lee with nunchaku. I pepper the side glass with the same combination as I did on the backboard. One to six, quick quick, seven to thirteen, and out. Same again with the next seven boxes, and I hit the stopwatch button at two minutes and twenty-nine seconds! Not bad at all.

I continue the walk up Tottenham Court Road to the next set of boxes. A quick look around, and I'm in. The cleaner has been and gone before me, so the boxes are bare of any cards and smelling of disinfectant. A nice disinfectant smell, but it takes a while to dry on the backboard, and of course, the blue tack will just not stick to a wet surface. Luckily, I have my cloth, and not just any cloth—it's a chamois leather cloth, which means it's much quicker to get dry, but it does get mucky easily. An old, sweaty, manky, dirty rag in my pocket is off-putting, so I've cut my chamois into twenty-three small pieces. That way, I can use one for a week and chuck it after. That's making one chamois leather last for nearly six months. Just two wipes with this cloth get the backboard dry, and I start to whack the cards up—one, two, three—police!

I pick up the phone quickly and bluff, holding it to my ear, pretending I'm talking to someone. A smile on the phone is always a good bluff, so I make sure I'm smiling nicely on the phone as they drive past me. Down with the phone, and I'm off again quick time—eleven twelve thirteen. Window, quick wipe, and go. Another thirteen cards up, and I'm out! Next box, same again, and out. Off I go, quickly pacing up Tottenham Court Road to the next set of two. Bosh! Quick as I can, I do those two, and off again to the next set of four. As I'm walking along, the same police car that passed me earlier drives past me again, with the copper in the passenger seat having a right good old stare at me. I act confident and continue my walk to the next set of four, and in I go. The police cannot see me in there at this angle, but they may drive around again, so I must act fast.

The backboard in this one is dry already, so I can be quicker. Thirteen cards on the back and out. I look up the road for the police car, and it's in the far distance but still driving slow, so I quickly go into the box at the same angle in case they are looking back. I smash that box too before coming out to notice that they have gone. As fast as humanly possible, I set about the other two boxes like Edward Scissorhands—yeah, that fucker, that's me—thirteen cards up in one box, two boxes, and out. As I walked across the road to the next set of two boxes, I had a good look up and down the road for police and to my relief, saw none, so it was business as usual. I completed the whole of Tottenham Court Road without any hiccups. There are two boxes to do on the Euston Road just around the corner from Warren Street Tube Station before cutting back in to do the backstreet boxes off Tottenham Court Road around Mandy's flat. At this time of the morning, I know the cleaner has already been to Oxford Circus, so I head on down there, hitting all the other boxes on the way.

It's coming into daylight as I get to Oxford Circus. The main four boxes are all bare. There's the obligatory glance about for the old bill before I slide into the first box like Jeffrey Daniels. That man can dance. When he moves his body to music, fucking magic happens. I mean, to come up with the moonwalk! Well, we all learned it from him. I was fifteen then, body popping and all kinds of shit on the dance floor. I just loved body popping to Herbie Hancock's **Rockit**. We used to get down to that big time. OK Tony, focus. No police. Go! Thirteen cards up, nice and neat, all over the backboard.

I'm feeling more confident as I do this. They can see me out here, and basically, I think they don't really care about us. They know we're harmless, they know where we are. We don't cause any agro, but they will still have a purge now and again. I do the rest of Oxford Street without a hitch or a sniff of police, plastering cards up in the backstreets from there and then into Soho for the few boxes in that area. By the time I made my way round to Cambridge Circus and walked up Charing Cross Road, it was fully light out, and the other Cardboys had been down the road. I think I'll take another walk up Tottenham Court Road just to check. Dominion Theatre boxes seem fine. I'll just check the first set of four; it's only a short distance from the Dominion. Wow! Look at these boxes. About five Cardboys have been along after me and Terry, each with a few girls to do, and I have never seen the boxes look so different. There must be fifty odd cards on that backboard now and not one with a picture of a naked girl on it. Every one of 'em is just text. It looks quite artful. All just black and white text. Anyway, they're all up, so it's back to the car and off to Kings Cross. I park in nearby Euston and walk the rest of the way. Parking is a lot easier at Euston. I walk along Euston Road, stopping to do a few boxes along the way.

But I'm getting that dodgy vibe again. I always get this vibe when I come to Kings Cross, especially when I'm at this cluster of four boxes opposite the station. I won't do the side windows of these; I'll do the backboard only. Here goes. I look once for the police, and I'm in the first box. This should be quick—thirteen cards up in no time and out! Next box, another thirteen. Onto the next, and the next, then one more set of thirteen and done! Four boxes all up nice and neat in forty seconds. I know I'm being watched; there are cameras over there, but I don't think the police will deploy their men out to a Cardboy passing through. Not the Metropolitan Police anyway. The British Transport Police can be crafty though; they hide behind pillars and stuff. Once these boxes were done, I headed back to my car at Euston for the drive home. It's seven forty-five. This is my favourite time of the grafting day, driving home when everyone else is just going into work. I've afforded myself a nice four-day trip to see my friend Nile in France for his surprise twenty-fifth birthday party. His mother has been living out there for years, and he's out there visiting her. She organised for a good few of his pals to go out there for this party. I fly out on Friday.=

Terry has agreed to take over just four of my flats for Friday and Monday. He's a good Cardboy, so I'm a bit gutted that I can't get him to do all thirteen flats for me, but I have got someone else to do the rest. He's right up for it. The Major. I've only met him properly the one time when he made that copper crawl on his hands and knees, so I don't know if I can trust him with my cards, but there was no one else I could ask. I've gotta give him four and a half thousand cards on Thursday. I'll be paying him nine hundred pounds, and it's on his route already. Only thing is, he has to get there early if he's to secure the best position in the boxes. I'll be cringing if he gets there late and has to put my cards up high on the backboard or, worse still, the roof! I can't expect the other Cardboys coming through to leave a massive gap in the middle of the phone box just so my cards can go in there late. Part of going into town earlier means that they don't even bother trying to compete with me. I'll have to tell him about that. I can't have him fucking up.

THURSDAY

I brought my car in today for the top-up because of the thirteen thousand cards in the boot to give out to the boys. I've had a good couple of days out here, but it will be nice to get away from it all for a few days. I've not been able to afford to go anywhere on a plane since the first time I flew on my ninety-nine-pound bargain holiday to Spain, Majorca when I was twenty-one.

I met Terry on Tottenham Court Road at the junction of Percy Street at five o'clock.

'How many cards have you got for me Tony?'

I told ya Terry, four thousand.

'Well, I've gotta carry 'em about, that's all. I wanna make sure you're not slipping me any extra. Just as well I've finished my round. I'll do it for two days but that's it. I don't want loads of cards to do.'

Cor, you don't half moan a lot don't ya. I've never heard anything like it. You're getting an extra four hundred quid for going the same route as you do anyway.

'I don't care about the money, I've got plenty of money, I don't need more.'

Alright, moany bollocks. But thanks for stepping up for me, you moany old bollock ache.

I give Terry the cards and off he goes. Now, where's the Major? I said I'd meet him here too, but he's nowhere to be seen. Just as I'm about to call him on the phone, he spots me standing at the junction and shouts out.

'EYE EYE, what's happening? I just got nicked down Charing Cross Road, fucking plain clothes copper, crept up behind me he did, the fucker. He said to me, 'you will be fined for this.' I said really? just pile 'em up with the rest. I tell ya Tony,

I've got so many fines from this game it's a joke. Hang on, I worked out that at the rate I pay 'em, I won't have 'em paid until twenty twenty-three! That's ridiculous! I wanna get 'em squashed, this can't continue like this, it's giving me palpitations. What you got for me then?'

Nine thousand cards for ya.

And I get him the cards from the boot of my car.

'Cor, fuck me, they're heavy.'

Have you got your motor with ya?

'Yeah, yeah, I've got it parked up around the corner. That's a fucking joke too, a pound for fifteen minutes on that meter in Oxford Street, and that's the cheapest one! Four quid I put in that so I'd better be quick. Right, so you want these out tomorrow and Monday right?'

Yeah, is that cool?

'Yeah, sorted, leave it with me, I'll take care of 'em.'

The Major walked off without saying goodbye.

That's it. I'm free. I'm fucking off home to get sorted for the trip. I jump in my car and drive through the mishmash of traffic before leaving the West End for the clear run home. As I'm driving near the Canary Wharf, which is a massive, new city development right in the heart of the East End of London, my phone starts to ring. It's Trilly.

Hello Trilly, how are ya?

'Hi Tony, I'm good, I was just thinking about you and wanted to say hi. I was thinking about the last time we were together and how much of a great time I had.'

Ah, well that's nice of you to call to tell me you're thinking about me Trilly, and I'm glad you're good. Well then, let's get together again if you liked it so much. When's the next time you're free?

'Ooh, I'm free this weekend.'

I'm busy all weekend Trilly.

'Oh, okay, well, I'm free on Wednesday and Thursday night.'

Cool, well let's meet on Wednesday at seven-thirty at…

'Can we just cook dinner at yours? I'd really like that.'

Sure, we can do that Trilly, I look forward to it.

'Ah, you never guess what happened to me today.'

Babe, I'd love to hear it, but tell me all about it over dinner next week. I'm driving and I need to concentrate. You can have my undivided attention next week. Catch ya later.

'Oh, okay Tony, see ya next week.'

Bye Trilly.

This is so dangerous, getting involved with a working girl. And I definitely don't wanna chit-chat on the phone to women anymore if I'm just dating 'em. I've watched a pal of mine make that mistake before. His problem was he'd fucking tell everything and the world about himself on the phone. And then he'd run out of things to say when he'd see her in person. She'd then know everything about him and there'd be nothing to dig and discover for herself about him, and women do like to dig. Nah. Set a date and get off the phone is my motto when you're dating. You can't seduce 'em over the phone anyway. At least this way, she'll be looking forward to seeing me so she can tell me all this stuff that she just wanted to say over the phone.

FRIDAY MORNING

A well-deserved break from all these cards. I'm off to see my mate Nile in France, in a little town called Civray. His parents have a beautiful country house out there, so he's gone out for his birthday, and they organised a surprise party for him with all his mates from here flying over. Should be good; there's a bunch of really great musicians going. With a drum kit set up and everything. Maybe I'll get to play a bit of Rock'n'Roll there. I'm flying out from the small City Airport, which is about a twelve-minute car journey from my house, maybe not even that. It's a small plane, and this pilot seems like he's having loads of fun. He's flying straight towards the Canary Wharf Tower and ascending quite aggressively. It's obvious he's going for a close shave just across the top of the building, but I don't mind. I'm quite enjoying it. He flies over the very top of the building and slowly banks to the right. The top of this building looks great, we're gliding seeming like twenty feet from the pointed top.

It reminded me of another job I had not too long ago, concrete pouring. I might have been about sixteen or seventeen at the time, I can't remember which, but they were pouring out a car park as part of the whole of Canary Wharf building site, very close to the Canary Wharf Tower. I was there as a labourer doing whatever jobs. The Wharf was coming to an impressive end. The stonemasonry work there is very duplicative of the old City of London's architecture. There was an external caged lift that ran the entire length of the main building from bottom to the very top so the workmen could use it to work on any one of the fifty floors. I kept looking at these workmen from where I was working, flying up in the lift and thinking, I'd love to go up there. It looked a bit scary. One lunchtime I'd had enough of just wanting to go in it. I already had a high-visibility vest and boots on, so I could easily mix with the workmen who worked on any site in that area. I walked the short distance to the tower. There was a gatekeeper to the lift, opening and closing it to let the workers in and out, so I just casually walked up to him and said,

Top floor please.

He opened the gate and I stepped in. Closing the gate, he sent me up.

So there I was, being hoisted up the outside of the tallest building in England in a rickety lift shaft that was open to the elements. It rapidly got higher and higher. The higher it got, the more the wind was gushing through the gated mesh that made up the walls of the lift. I wasn't even halfway up before I was feeling a little scared. The wind was beginning to make a loud noise and got stronger the further up I went. At this point, I could see for miles; it was an amazing view, and as I approached the last top three floors, the wind started to howl and blow my clothes all around me in multiple directions. I got to the top floor, hair was blowing everywhere, I opened the shutter gates of the lift, and then the gates to the entrance of the building. I stepped over a small gap between the lift and the building and I could see down the side of the entire building. The fear and the thought of falling from this great height through the gap while knowing it was safe to step over it is a bit exhilarating. I stepped into the dusty building where the sound of the wind calmed down. It was one big expansive floor with windows all around from floor to ceiling. The sun shone into the numerous windows and lit up the few workmen's tools and materials lying around on the floor. I was the only person there. I unwrapped my sandwiches and just walked around looking out at London from all angles. The winding curves of the River Thames were very visible, and I could see West Ham United's football ground at Upton Park. I found my school, my house. It was a great place to have lunch. There was scaffolding all along one side of the wall to the apex of the building. It has a pyramid-style roof on top, but whatever they were gonna put on the inside of the roof, they hadn't done it yet, so I went up the ladders at the top of the scaffold, all the way to the very innermost top point of the building. At the very needle point of that building on the inside is a square plate of metal. It's not that big; I remember it being about the size of a twelve-inch vinyl album cover. Jimi Hendrix's album **Electric Ladyland** springs to mind.

I walked along the top platform and reached up to touch that plate. I wanted the plate to not be there so I would have been able to put my finger right into the top point, but it still felt like I had conquered the tallest building in England. And here I am now, flying feet above it with a big overall achievement of conquering it all over again. I thought of King Kong from the film, sitting on top of the building, and I was the pilot who was trying to gun him down. I flew over West Ham United's football ground, and before long, I was landing in Poitiers Airport, and my four-day rest had begun. The party was that night in the adjacent barn to the house that was very cosy, and as Nile had been whisked away for the day, it was perfect for all the friend arrivals. When he returned, he clearly didn't have a clue what was about to happen when he was asked to fetch something from the barn. I'll never forget the look on his face. What a great surprise. We had a great night.

People were on the guitars and the drum kit, everyone having a go, all jamming along and having fun. I could hold back no more. I grabbed a guitar, strapped it to my neck, and started playing the opening riff to Chuck Berry's **Memphis Tennessee**. The drummer that was there started drumming along in time with me, and I was off with the opening lines,

loooong distance information give me Memphis Tennessee...

I just love Rock'n'Roll. I sang the song and it felt like magic.

SATURDAY MORNING

My head hurts. I don't normally drink that much. I kinda like the buzz of two or three beers better than the amount I shoved down my throat last night. Such a good night though. It's nice sitting out here in a French country garden with the sun on my face. There's a breakfast being prepared now by Niles' mum and sister, but I've got my eyes on this fruit-filled croissant in a closed see-through box on the veranda table I'm sitting at. It's the last one. I can still eat breakfast after that so I go for it. It's so bloody nice, rhubarb I think. I'm halfway through it when my drummer pal Tom pipes up and shouts,

'Don't eat that!'

It's too fucking late, I've eaten half of it.

'The amount of flies that were on that.'

The packet was closed. I just opened it.

'Nah, it was last night. I was sitting here, looking at it and thinking, the amount of flies on that, looked like there was an army of at least a hundred of 'em. I scared 'em all off and closed the box.'

Now you tell me. I feel sick, gimme that water.

'Don't drink that water!'

Why, what's up with the water?

'It ain't safe.'

For fuck's sake. What's that?

'Wine. Rosé.'

Gimme that then.

I glugged that wine from the bottle. The hair of the dog and the puke of a hundred flies. I'm really grossed out by this, but I guess I won't die from it. But I can't stop gagging.

Breakfast has done the trick though, helping me take my mind off it, and no more gagging. Bob, who is Niles' mum's partner, decided to take us out for a little drive. There's a village he wants to show us. It's called Oradour he said. Oradour-sur-Glane is the full name of it, so off we went. Bob puts a Beatles song on as we drive through the country lanes that I've never heard before. It's a beautiful sounding song. He tells me it's called **Blackbird.** It's the perfect setting to be listening to this song. We arrive at this village, and as I get out of the car, Bob starts to tell me about it.

'During the war in nineteen forty-four, SS troops were retreating through France when they came across this little village. The majority of the men from here were at work at the time, and about two hundred of these troops started causing havoc. Not just any old havoc. They rounded the women and kids up, shot and killed them. Others were herded into the church, shot, and set on fire. In fact, they burnt the whole village down. Every shop, every house, the church didn't escape the flames either, and with all the people burning inside. They held the doors shut while they listened to the screams from the outside.'

I stood in the church and had an eerie feeling come over me as I continued to learn the history of the place. The only thing that didn't burn was the confession box. And there it stood, still in the corner after all these years. I guess the troops didn't enjoy conducting such a wicked act, so the box was probably left for them to confess the sinful crimes they had just done, or were about to do. Nothing else escaped the flames. There's an old burnt, rusty shell of a beetle car over there. The wheels have sunken halfway into the ground now. It was left exactly as it was found fifty-two years ago. The whole town was left exactly as it was found. There are bullet holes in the walls everywhere, black, charred wood around the shop windows that are broken, with bits of glass still sticking out in various places. I can almost smell the burnt wood and other materials as I walk through the town, which resembles a cowboy Western place like the ones they showed us in the movies, but with everything destroyed. I'm standing in front of a barber shop right now, looking through the smashed and burnt window frame.

On the inside window ledge, right there is an old Brown's hair clipper. It's all burnt and rusty but still lying there, just as it was found all those years ago. Inside, the burnt chairs and accessories are still in place. I'm starting to feel like I was there all those years ago, but I mustn't cry. I need to walk away from this barber shop—it's so sad to see. There's a big stone wall with all the names of the people who were killed here on it. As I stand here reading the names, knowing that there were kids here too, my eyes well up with tears a little, enough to blur my vision but not enough to roll down my face. I don't want anyone to see me wiping my eyes, so I man up to try to prevent the inevitable tear, which rolls off my cheek and lands on the toe of my right shoe.

Bob, of course, has already noticed my sadness and hands me a tissue. Fuck it, I've been busted.

'You alright mate?'

Yeah Bob, thanks. Sad isn't it?

'Yeah, it is sad. Shall we go?'

Yeah, I've seen enough of this.

'And they've built a whole new town right next to it. Do you wanna go and see that?'

Nah thanks Bob, I've seen enough.

There are four of us in the car driving back to the cottage, and neither I nor anyone else is saying a word. I'm not talking because I'm still trying to get over what I just saw and can't stop thinking about the victims. A terrible thing to have happened. Imagine all the men coming home from work that day to see that shit. I'm thinking of that song I heard from the Beatles on the way there.

Can you play that song again please Bob?

'Yeah, I can do that Tony.'

And he puts the song on again

This song seems like the perfect one, and in my mind, I'm dedicating it to all the victims of this atrocity. We get all the way back to the house without another word being said by anyone. It was a nice day, so I decided to go for a little stroll into the local town to clear my head. I'm walking along the streets of Civray. There are a few old buildings around here. There's a very old and ornate church here on my left—the Church of Saint Nicholas. I cross the street and turn right to the gorgeous smell of bread and cakes being baked. Up ahead is a patisserie, which I'm guessing is where that gorgeous smell is coming from, and it's making me hungry. I'm walking towards it and—what the fuck! It's fucking Larno Wenner! He's walking towards me and shit, he's seen me. He looks frightened. I don't fucking blame him! What are the fucking chances of that? He's stopped walking and is looking from left to right for an escape. If only I could tell him, it's not what you think Larno! I'm not a stalker, honest.

Fuck this shit. I've gotta walk past him now. I can't look at him. I'm strolling past, looking the other way, but I catch his reflection in the glass window, and he's nervously fixated on me as I embarrassingly walk closer to him. His hands are almost up in a defensive position. Just walk past him Tony, and don't fucking look. Bollocks to it. You know the truth. How fucking embarrassing. As we're passing each other, my body temperature is going up. Well, he's certainly gonna have a story to tell about the stalker he keeps seeing.

The remaining two days at the cottage were nice and relaxing. There was a big pot of weed to smoke in the middle of the table with the written instructions, 'Help yourself'. The food was delicious, the weed was good, and the company was spot on. I flew back to City Airport on Monday evening at six-forty.

There's no time to fuck about; I've got shitloads of cards to mix tonight for the morning. I should have taken another day off to recover from that little break. By the time I mix all the cards, make my dinner, and eat it, it's ten fifteen, well late for me. Especially with the times I get up in the morning, I'm knackered and need to sleep right now. I can't even be bothered to floss my teeth tonight. I can't even be bothered to brush them. It won't hurt for one night, or at least that's the story I tell myself. When I was a kid, I hated brushing my teeth. Fuck knows why I haven't got a single filling today. Mum used to scream at me constantly.

'Tony! Tony! Go and brush your teeth!'

I'd go into the bathroom and use the nails on two of my fingers to scrape the plaque from the two front teeth only, and that was it. I did develop sensitive teeth later on in life though, and funny enough, that stopped being sensitive the minute I started to floss.

If I'm lucky, I'll get five hours of sleep tonight.

TUESDAY, 4AM

No time for any reflection this morning, and I whack the kettle on for my obligatory coffee. Cards are already mixed and hanging up in my waistcoat. Blue tack is on the new radiator—I've got it on low heat just to take the edge off the chill a bit, but I need my blue tack soft. I'll whack it on the car heaters too on the way in. I jump in my car at four twenty. It's been raining all morning, which is not good for the cards staying up. There'll be condensation all over the surfaces, so I'd better prepare to really rub 'em dry before I put them up. I've gotta be quick though, because six seconds later it'll be wet again with more condensation. I drive into Tottenham Court Road at four forty-five. and park up in the side turning for the short walk to the Dominion boxes. Terry has just started too—he's just finishing his second box and comes out to greet me.

'Oi, who's that geezer you 'ad doing the cards for ya?'

The Major.

'I dunno about no Major, this was another fella. I've seen the Major; he's about six foot. Nah, this was another geezer, didn't have a clue, he shit himself.'

What do you mean?

'Like I said, he didn't have a clue. He was like… you know when you see a cat trying to cross the road but it's shitting itself and holds back from running? Well, that was what this bloke was like in every box. He grabbed the phone box handle, and an ambulance drove past with the sirens on, so he let it go and ran off round the corner. I couldn't believe it—he took ages looking all around before he put one card up. He was dropping 'em all over the floor. He bent down to pick 'em up and whacked his head on the shelf there. It was like watching Laurel and Hardy. Where did you get him from? He told me he's never done the cards before.'

I gave the cards to the Major to do.

'Well, he obviously got someone else to do it, but he's got someone who's never done it before. I'd have words I would.'

For fuck's sake, I'm gonna fucking have to.

I enter the first box and I'm off. One two three—floor. Fuck it, I forgot to wipe the back. This is gonna take ages like this. I speed-wipe the backboard and try again. One to thirteen cards up, wipe the window down, hit that with thirteen cards too, and out! Next box, quick look around, and the same again. Wipe, cards, and out! And again, and again, and again until all eight Dominion boxes are done, and I'm off to the first set of four on Tottenham Court Road. Weather's getting no better—doesn't look like it's gonna stop anytime soon either. Terry's looking in a right state, his trousers hanging down round his arse. I've gotta say something to him about that. Can't have him walking around with me like that.

Pull your trousers up!

He pulls his trousers up, but they immediately fall down again, and he doesn't give a shit about it.

Listen, Terry, I know you're a Gooner, but I don't wanna see your arse'n'all. Why do they call you Arsenal supporters Gooners?

'Go on then, take the piss. It's a badge of honour. At least we've got a team. We're fourth in the table; where's West Ham? Fourteenth. Your players are playing like that bloke you had putting your cards out. They're a disgrace—you're only four points away from the relegation zone. We even sold you Hartson for three mill' and you still can't beat us. He's the most expensive player West Ham have ever bought.'

I suppose I can't argue with that. Terry and I both systematically complete the whole of Tottenham Court Road with the usual banter, taking the piss out of each other, with not a copper in sight. But I better still keep my guard up—I don't wanna start getting complacent just because the day goes as smoothly as this. There's not much looking around for police as I walk into the boxes, and most times, I just watch 'em drive straight past me anyway. Eight times out of ten, they don't really care about us Cardboys. They look at me as they drive past, and I just look at them and smile sometimes. I just kinda know they're not gonna stop and just carry on whacking the cards up. They know who I am and can come and get me anytime. These fines are getting bigger though, so I've gotta be a bit careful. Money's good, but I don't wanna keep paying it out in fines.

There's a couple of girls in these backstreet boxes who have started putting pictures up again. They're not explicit, but they are titillating. No nipples out, but I can see them poking through the nightdresses they're wearing, and she's sitting rather provocatively. I hope this doesn't fuck it up for everyone else trying to make a bit of money. There was talk of it all coming to an end if the picture cards went up again, but they've been threatening to stop it for years apparently. For all sorts of reasons, but they've never gone through with it. Obviously there's someone in power that doesn't want it stopped; otherwise, that would've been it. And with the head of vice looking after 'em, I just don't see it. I better milk it while I can.

I get to Oxford Circus first, and the only cards up are two of these picture cards. They're not in the space that I normally put my cards up in. No one's out here moving my cards, but I wonder who's getting out here this early putting these out? Could be that Indian Cardboy Prem. I've seen him about a few times this early but doesn't normally come till just after Terry and me. Right, let's get this bollocks box done. I open the door, and in! One to thirteen, quick as I can, all on the back, and then… tap tap tap on the window—shit! A fucking copper! Standing there smiling at me, holding up that fucking badge.

'Can you come out here for a second please? Empty out your pockets.'

As I begin to hand over my cards, blue tack, keys, he stops me and says,

'I just want to have a look at the cards.'

After having a look at them, he handed them back and said,

'Off you go.'

And just like that, I was off. Didn't take my name or address, and didn't wanna look at my ID. I reckon he was probably just trying to find out who's putting the picture cards out again. I carried on doing the whole of Oxford Street without any more hassle, and then onto Soho, Cambridge Circus, Euston, and King's Cross. By eight o'clock I was on my way home. Not a bad day considering I should've gotten nicked.

There's a saying amongst working girls, which is **money on the floor, money to the door**, and sure enough, if you go to any of the girls' flats, you'll always see a few bits of loose change around the front door, in a corner or by the wall on the floor near it. So I do it myself now. Not a lot, about one pound fifty's worth of scratch. I'm not superstitious, but I like the idea of it bringing in money through my door, so it's worth a go for me. I like that it rhymes too. Actually, come to think about it, there's another thing I do about money— maybe I'm just superstitious around money. I remember one day, I was reading a feng shui article in a book somewhere, and it said you should never leave your toilet seat open. It said if you do, it invites the flushing away of any wealth. Well, I was in between one of my many dead-end jobs, so I was a bit skint at that time, so I thought I'd just jump up and close the fucker, just in case, and as soon as I done it, my phone rang with someone offering me two piss-easy days of work on a building site. It fucking wasn't easy by a long stretch, but work was work, and I got two hundred quid for it. I don't think I've ever left the toilet lid open again.

I'm home now, but I'm not the only one. Two pigeons are perched in my living room on the mantelpiece.

Fuck off!

Here they go, flapping all around my living room, trying to fly out of a closed window, but where's the key to that fucking window? I go into the kitchen to open that window, but of course, it's still open from when they got in. So it's back in the living room, and walking in there fast has scared the crap out of 'em, and they're off in a panic again, trying to find the way out. There are feathers dropping off 'em both as they bash into the telly, the picture on the wall. Shit, I'm struggling to get these out of here. *Aargh!*

Fuck that! I hate it when they fly at me like that—they're on the attack. How can I let a fucking pigeon put the frighteners up me like this? Fuck that. What can I use to get it out? The vacuum handle. That'll do. Come on, out you fly. Go to the kitchen.

C'mon little bird.

This is taking ages. I'll have to try the charmed approach.

C'mon. I'm not gonna hurt ya, get on the end of this and I'll take you out. C'mon.

I'm moving it closer and closer to the bird that's now sitting on the telly. I think the charming approach is working 'cause it's not flying off anymore.

Come on, jump on.

I've got the handle right up close, and it's not moving, just standing there. I push the vacuum head so close that I touch its chest and push a little—still no movement. Hold up! He's getting on! He's jumped on the vacuum!

There you go little fella. C'mon, I won't hurt ya. Just hang on tight to that pole.

I can't believe I've calmed this bird down enough to get on the end of it, let alone let me walk it out. I feel like Dr. Dolittle. Fucking Noah's Ark. But just then, my phone rings and scares the bird off the perch.

Bollocks. Hello.

'Hello Tony, it's me. I was just thinking of you and thought I'd call to say hi. What'cha doing?'

Oh...allo Trilly.

'You OK? You sound a bit different.'

Yeah, I'm fine Trilly. I've just got a couple of birds in here I'm trying to get out.

'Oh, right. You've, uh, got a few girls you're dating then?'

Oh, no Trilly, haha, that's so funny. They're birds of the feathered kind. They flew in the window, and I can't get 'em out.

'Oh Tony, that is funny.'

Yeah, none of these two birds I've got here are as hot as you Trilly. They're standing here with no clothes on, but I'm still gonna kick 'em out.

'Ha ha, Very funny.'

It'd be great to see ya. When are ya free to get together?

'Well, I'm free Saturday and Sunday.'

OK then, Saturday night, seven-thirty, meet at mine—how's that sound?

'Sounds perfect Tony.'

Well alright then, I'll see ya seven-thirty at mine. I gotta go deal with these birds now. Catch ya later.

Right then,

C'mon you, jump on.

The bird jumped straight onto the vacuum handle, and I carried it out of the kitchen window. The other bird sees how safe it is and gives me no hassle as it jumps onto the vacuum head too and lets me walk it out the kitchen window.

I feel like I'm on autopilot with Trilly. I always find myself setting up dates with her when she calls. She's so horny. I love fucking her. As dangerous as it is, with all the blokes fucking her on a daily basis, I still want to fuck her. I know I must stop, but I can't. This attraction won't let me stop seeing her. She could have any kind of disease. What the fuck am I playing at? What a fucking mug.

FRIDAY

The police are at two of the flats I work for—Sergeant Ferguson or something. He's the head of vice in London, so I can't go round there right now to pick up any cards or money. There's been a robbery. Some geezer's running around, robbing a couple of the girls at knifepoint. He pretends to be a punter, and when he's round there, he pulls a knife and nicks all their money. The thing is, he doesn't realise the head of vice is there to protect the girls, not prosecute 'em. He figures that because what the girls do is illegal, they wouldn't dare go to the police. He thinks he's got an easy target, but he's so wrong. While he's walking around thinking he's gotten away with it, piss-free, he's really being hunted for armed robbery.

So that's five hundred quid I'm down this week. I might even have to write that money off altogether. I can't ask for it—they got robbed for fuck's sake. So much for the picture cards toning down. Seven of the girls I work for have gone straight back to putting them up. There are a few others in the box too, from flats I don't work for. All putting pictures back up again, but fuck it—I'll put up whatever they give me to put up.

I'm looking forward to taking off these fucking shoes when I get through this door. New shoes are never comfy for me. My weekend starts right now—seven-thirty, Friday night. I roll myself a nice joint, and I have half a bottle of decent wine there, which is probably off by now 'cause I opened it a week ago, but I do have my Vimto trick. I grab a glass from the cupboard, and that wine does taste rank and foul. A little splash of Vimto in the bottom of the glass, wine on top, and ooh, that wine now tastes like one of the best wines in the world. The perfect Friday night. Now, I need to be playing some good old Rock'n'Roll, and '**Johnny B. Goode**' is on my mind, so I grab my guitar and let out the opening riff. I just looove Rock'n'Roll. And even though my phone is now ringing, there's no way I'm stopping to answer it. They can bloody well wait till I've finished my song.

Go go… Go, Johnny go, go.

My missed call was Trilly, and now she's calling back again.

Hello Trilly, how's it going?

'Oh, just great Tony. Sorry I couldn't come to see ya to give you the cards—I was busy. You heard about all that's been going on?'

What, the robberies? Yeah, he's robbed two flats.

'Four flats, and he's got a knife.'

Four! Fuck me, and he's not been caught yet?

'Nope, still roaming the streets, the fucker. I'm a bit scared to carry on working while he's still on the loose to be honest. Can I come over to see ya?'

What, tonight?

'Yeah, if that's alright. I don't really wanna be alone tonight. That's if you're not going out or anything.'

Well actually Trilly, I just feel like chilling out indoors, so if you fancy coming over to just do that, I'd love to see ya.

'I'm on my way.'

See ya soon.

What the fuck is going on with this fucking Trilly? So sexy, she fucking blows me away with that special something she's got, but I still can't put my finger on it. One thing's for sure—she definitely makes me wanna keep at it to discover more about her, at least until the time comes when I know I'll have to part ways with her. It's such a shame she does that job because I could definitely see her hanging around for a bit. I finish my joint and another glass of wine before jumping in the shower to be ready for when she comes round. By eight-fifteen, she's at my door, and I've not even finished in the shower yet. I grab a towel and wrap it around my waist to open the door. Now, Trilly is standing there with a long beige Burberry mac on, with one side of her long dark hair draped down the front of her right shoulder. She looks stunning. She pulls the towel from my waist to reveal my solid hard-on and swings it behind her head. I hold onto the two ends of the towel in front of her, slowly pulling her in the front door and gently guiding her down by the towel ends. With her head cradled in the middle of the hammock-like towel, I guide it over to my cock as she opens up and welcomes it into her mouth. She groans as she sucks hard and deep—I've never known a woman to appear to enjoy sucking cock as much as Trilly is. I want to get more comfortable, so I lead her into the living room and sit back on the sofa with my arms and legs stretched out wide as she kneels on the sofa beside me. Now my face is gurning with the technique she's got for sucking my cock. What a fucking blowjob. I reach over and place my hand over her pussy, which by this time is dripping wet. There goes that sexy moan she does, which sends me over the edge, and I explode my cum deep into her mouth. She's drinking up every drop of it as she continues to lick and suck my cock, keeping it solid hard. She's dripping all down my hand as I thrust my fingers in and out of this beautifully tight vagina.

She then lifts up her leg, grabs my cock, and slides herself down onto it. I'm inside of her, with no dunky on. She's so tight. I've always wanted to feel her like this, but fuck! What a risk. I'm now going against everything I would never allow myself to do. And it feels so right but I know it's wrong. She's a working girl. Trilly is writhing and sliding up and down on my cock. It's just too good to ever want to stop. Mother Nature has hooked me with the best feeling in the world, as from deep within me, I feel the start of my orgasm coming on. I hold back while Trilly rides me, and she goes into this deep groaning. She's boiling up to climax too. She opens her eyes and mouth wide as she momentarily goes silent before letting out this loud groan. She's shuddering on me and claws at my chest, and I feel powerful squirts of her juices up my cock and over my body. I feel her contracting all around my cock, and I don't hold back any longer, but I don't pull out. I shoot my cum deep into her, which sends her into a speed frenzy of fucking me even harder. She collapses on top of me after another orgasm. This is fantastic, but I know what I shouldn't have done. I should have pulled out. We're both covered in sweat and out of breath as we lay back recovering. I sip on the champagne that she brought over. She then says to me,

'First you took my virginity. And now, I think you have my heart.'

What!? Did I hear her right? Did she just say she was a virgin before me? But what about all the guys she sees every day?

But what about all the guys that come to see ya?

'You mean the punters?'

Yeah, the punters. Doesn't that count or something?

'I don't fuck them.'

What? You fuck none of 'em Trilly?

'No Tony, not one.'

Well. Why do they come then?

'I just beat them up Tony. Well, I say beat them up, I slap them about a bit, kick them, and stamp my stilettos into them sometimes, but just abuse them really.'

And you've never had sex with any of 'em?

'I've never had sex with anyone Tony, apart from you.'

I can't believe I'm the first person she's had sex with. Maybe that explains why I felt she was special. I knew there was something, but this is the last thing I expected it to be. Fancy Trilly being a virgin. I feel very privileged to be the first man to be inside of her. I shouldn't have cum inside her though. I order an Indian meal of the typical English order: chicken korma, pilau rice, onion bhajees, Bombay potatoes, and naan. I used to ask for 'naan bread' until I found out that the word 'naan' means bread, so all along I've been asking for 'bread bread.' Fucking delicious it was. We ate that, drank more champagne, and smoked a few joints before more sex way into the early hours. My new knowledge of Trilly having no other man's cock inside her makes me wanna let loose and give her an experience, so I gladly go down on her—another first for her, she tells me—and I ate her fanny out like it was a fucking lemon meringue pie, and I love meringue pie. It was so pleasurable to be the first man to go down on this woman, so I made sure she had multiple orgasms with that service. We fucked some more until we just collapsed in a tired heap of sweat and both fell asleep with my cock still inside her.

A fucking virgin. I should keep away before I fall in love with this woman. I've never thought about a woman like this, and Trilly is certainly winning me over.

SATURDAY, 9:15AM

There's a beautiful birdsong from my garden every morning, and we both wake up to the sound of it. This morning's birds sound like the song '**Love is a Stranger**' by the Eurythmics. It's bang in tune with the part of the song where she sings, '**and I want you, and I want you**'. There's also a pear tree in the back garden. Well, it's in the woman's garden who lives next door who's not friendly with me, and it hangs all over my garden wall, and every year I eat the pears from it. Lovely they are, and I must get to eat at least fifty of 'em. Not this year though, because the sound of the birdsong is quickly snuffed out by the sound of a chainsaw hacking its way into the trunk. She's had enough of it, and it's coming down. I shouted to her to stop, but she never heard me, and at the end of the day, it is her tree and in her garden, such a shame as I've eaten from that tree for years. I almost felt like it was mine. There's a lesson for me there—don't get attached to anything.

I make Trilly and me a cup of coffee and whack a couple of scones in the oven. She looks gorgeous first thing in the morning too. We have sex again before she has a quick shower, gets dressed, and leaves me to fall back to sleep again.

By midday I was up. I had a dream about people calling Trilly's name—first a woman's voice, then a man's voice, then a loud, worrying scream of her name, "Trilly!" Then a flash image of Trilly on a hospital trolley in a hospital gown, and then someone running down a corridor—all a bit bizarre, but it did put the mockers up on me a little bit.

I can't let myself get soft. I think I'll pull back a bit from Trilly.

It's nice having the dough to go out on a Saturday afternoon and get myself a nice bit of clobber. I love to look sharp—it makes me feel good, and when I feel good, I act good, and when I act good, I get good back. I've got myself a nice jacket, "one of a kind," the bloke tells me. Yeah right. Is that why you charged me a hundred and eighty quid for it? There's under-shelter shopping at Stratford, and on a rainy day like this, it's perfect. There are lots of little cafes dotted about, so I drop by one to grab a coffee—a busy little noisy place, and all the windows are steamed up. Can't see fuck all out of 'em, but the coffee's good. My phone rings, and it's Tamara—she's a hot friend of mine. I met her at a party through a little group of mutual friends ages ago. I wanted to fuck her then, and of course, she knew that, but she did have a boyfriend, and I don't wanna be on the receiving end of a butthurt, raging boyfriend just 'coz she couldn't control her hypergamous nature and I couldn't control my urges. And there's always the saying,

"Never mow another man's lawn."

We've been out together a good few times though, just the two of us as friends, and she's a cool friend, but I like the sexual tension between us. She'd sit on my lap at gatherings and fuck around with me, as a "friend." My cock would get stiff between the crack of her arse, and I would not try to hide it. She would then wiggle around on it and mold it into the most comfortable position for her. It was such a turn-on for her to be doing that to me in open events.

If I had a very attractive woman I loved, who had male friends like me that she went out with, I'd be concerned. What bloke has an attractive lady friend that he doesn't wanna fuck? Whether she has a boyfriend or married.

I don't think there's a time that I've spent with her that I've not had a flash thought about fucking her, and that can be very dangerous, so no. The woman I choose to have a relationship with, will not have a gang of male friends or "orbiters" hoping to get their balls in with her the first chance they get, hanging onto her every word. Do-boys—they all wanna fuck ya bird. I'll never trust a bunch of blokes who're supposed to be "friends" around my girlfriend, and no bloke should.

They ain't fucking fooling me. Friend. I mean, I can't imagine if my mum and dad were happily married for thirty-three years and mum wanted to go out with a small group of men she calls friends every Friday night. She wouldn't do it. Not without my dad being there too.

Nevertheless, she's calling because she wants to spend time with me. She wants to go out for a drink.

She's got a new boyfriend and is living with him.

I value loyalty in a relationship—in fact, I'd go as far as to say that the number one thing that any man values above anything else is loyalty in his woman. Your girlfriend cheating on you has gotta be the worst thing that a woman can do whilst in a relationship with you.

I won't cross the line and respond to Tamara's subtle advances, especially while she has a boyfriend. I wouldn't wanna be the bloke wrapped up in that bollocks. Fuck that.

There've been do-or-die moments though. I remember one time when I had a girlfriend, and Tamara was seeing a different boyfriend. She rang and invited me to pop in for a coffee on my way home. I agreed to that and got there at around seven that evening. Her boyfriend was away somewhere for a couple of days. We chatted, had a laugh, and drank coffee, which turned into a glass of wine. A big, fat, bulbous bottle it was, with a very rich, ruby taste. I can taste it again right now just thinking about it—lovely. We got into a little bit of play fighting, which turned into her getting a little bit of a back strain that she wanted to stretch out, so she asked me to support her back while she made an arch shape, bending backward with her hands and feet still on the floor. I was standing above her with one of my legs between her super long legs and the other just on the outside while I reached with both of my arms underneath her waist. She stretched out to the max until she let out a little groan of satisfaction. That was enough to trigger a hard-on and, of course, made me want to fuck her right there, but I resisted the temptation. The girlfriend I had at the time was sweet to me and super hot, so as much as the invitation was there to stray off course with Tamara, my morals kicked in and I just didn't do it.

I could feel that Tamara was ready to indulge in any activity that we were naturally heading toward, so at that moment, I thought it was best to leave. I told her that I'd better be going, but she insisted I stay for a "cleansing," or so she put it. She told me to sit back on the sofa and relax while she held her hand six inches from my forehead, then told me to close my eyes. I could feel the heat of her hand slowly moving down my face, down my neck, and onto my chest. Ever so slowly and without her touching me, I could feel her hand moving down my stomach and then hovering six inches over my fully erect cock, which I didn't try to hide—I couldn't hide it. I had trousers on that made it impossible to hide. My eyes were still closed and the sexual tension was as strong as ever, but still, my morals were kicking in so I pulled the plug, said I had to go, and left with my stonking hard-on. I had a hot chick of my own that I was serious with. And even hotter than hot Tamara. We'll meet for coffee.

MONDAY, 4:44AM

I'm driving into Tottenham Court Road when the phone rings. It's Terry.

'Yeah, where the fuck are ya?'

I'm driving in right now.

'Well you should have been here by now. The Baker Street boys have been.'

What do you mean?

'They've come and put all their cards up in our spaces.'

Well fucking take 'em down then!

'Nah, you don't understand. They've come to take over Tottenham Court Road. That's what they said.'

Just wait there. I'll be ten minutes.

I got off the phone and carried on driving at the pace I was before the phone call. I don't like speeding—not since my mate got killed by a speeding car down a side street when we were playing football at eight years old.

Getting to the Dominion Theatre boxes, there's no sign of Terry. But in the boxes, there are eight or so Baker Street cards all on the backboard. I quickly swiped 'em all down and proceeded to put my own cards up before walking to the next set of four.

They've been here too, and from here, looking down. It looks like they've done the whole of Tottenham Court Road.

I'm in the first of the four boxes taking the cards down and putting mine up when all of a sudden, the side window of it smashes. At first, I thought it was a car crashing into the telephone box, so I quickly tried to jump up as high as I possibly could to prevent my legs from being crushed, but now the other window is getting smashed.

There are two blokes standing outside. Now, I'm presuming they're the Baker Street boys wanting to know why I'm taking down their cards. One swings a baseball bat again smashing the door glass, and continues to beat around the box with me still in it. Definitely a worrying time, and I've gotta think quick before I get my head smashed in. My secondary thought is that I've got to protect the empire. That's what D used to say. And with that, I grew some balls and shouted at the top of my lungs,

Aaagh!

I then ran out of the box straight into the bloke with the bat. He lifted the bat to take a swing at me, but I got to him first and hit him with a peach of a punch, so hard on his chin that his feet lifted a little off the ground before he came crashing down with his arms straight beside him. His head bashed on the ground, and he just lay there. I turned, expecting to now face the other one, and he just took three steps backward before turning around and running away. I calmed down a bit, but I'm worried about what I've done to this bloke. I hope he's just knocked out. His stomach is moving up and down, so he's alive.

I must give him an image of me besides just that. I can't have them taking over. I grab the bat off the ground and poke him in the chest with it until he wakes up. With the fat end of the bat an inch away from his nose, I say to him,

Now, Fuck Off!

With not much hesitation, he gets up, picks up his baseball cap, and slowly walks away. Fuck, that was scary. I'm shaken up, but I've got a feeling the Baker Street boys won't be back anytime soon. I continue down Tottenham

Court Road, taking down all their cards and putting mine up. I get to the last box at Warren Street Station, and Terry appears.

Where 'ave you fucking been?

'*I went to get back up.*'

Back up! Where are they?

'*Well, I couldn't find anyone.*'

You were supposed to be bloody back up; I could have died back there.

'*Why, what happened?*'

With Terry deciding to join me for the rest of the round, we hit the back-streets together. Then Oxford Street, Soho, Euston, King's Cross, and then onto Russell Square. We finish the round by seven-thirty, and the car is on a metre for a change, so no need to rush back for it. We decided to stop off at Carlo's Cafe at Euston for a spot of breakfast. I normally go for a sweet breakfast to get me going in the morning, but today was the complete opposite: sausages, chips, and beans. I just want to lay down and sleep after eating that. Great, left me not wanting to move anywhere, and we just sat there chatting for a bit. By the time I felt ready and able to move, it was nine fifteen. My phone rings, and it's the Major.

'*You best get down here; all your cards are coming down as we speak.*'

C'mon Terry, the cards are coming down again; they've fucking come back.
Shitting myself a bit as we run back to Tottenham Court Road, I say to Terry,

You better not disappear this time.

'*I won't, I'm here ain't I?*'

We get back to see the Major standing there while two cleaners strip the box. They are not the usual cleaners.

What do you know about these then Major?

'Well, I spoke to one of 'em; they're from Westminster Council. That bloke over there told me that the council have had enough of the complaints they keep getting about the cards everywhere, so they're going to do something about it. He said they're clamping down on us. He said they're coming out twice a day for a week, but we don't know the times, he said they're sending out different cleaners all the time.'

The rest of that week was a fucking nightmare. The worst week I've had out here. I'd be up at my normal time, put all the cards up, and because I knew the cleaners would also start down Tottenham Court Road, I'd have to stand there loitering. Even though all my cards were up, I'd then just wait there for them to come down again so I could put them straight back up. They normally came between half nine and half ten, but on Thursday they came at eleven twenty! I was so pissed off. It's not as if I could go up and pay these cleaners to leave 'em up either. Fucking paying out for Timmy Tightpants to leave 'em up, and they're coming straight down afterwards. I hope it is only a week.

FRIDAY, 8.30AM

I'm in the Soho box that someone shat in. It's permanently known to me now as the shit box. One, two, three, four, five, six. I can just about get these cards to stay up today; it's pissing down with rain and cold. And these red boxes with the black wooden backboard are even harder to get the cards to stay up than the metal ones. I've still got to go back to Tottenham Court Road to replace the cards that I know will be coming down soon. I'm not standing there this time in the rain waiting for them to turn up today, no way. I'll fuck off to do more of the route before I go back. Fucking ball ache. As I get to Cambridge Circus, I can see the Major getting frisked by a plainclothes policeman. As I'm walking past him, he's going through his pockets and taking stacks of cards out. The Major sees me and, like a mug, says,

'Hello Tony.'

I nod hello to him, and the policeman immediately focuses his attention on me.

'Erm, can you come back here a minute?'

Fucking 'el, what does he want?

'Are you together?'

No, we're not together.

'Well, he obviously knows you; are you putting out the cards yourself then?'

What cards?

'What have you got in your pockets?'

He goes into my pockets and pulls out a stack of cards.

'Well, what are these then? You're lying to me.'

But I wasn't putting them out.

He smiles and continues to clean out every single one of the cards from my pockets, smirks at me, and says,

'You can go now,'

and flicks his fingers at me, which really pisses me off. Fancy saying hello to me when the cozzers are going through your pockets.

So, as Benjamin Franklin once said, "Failing to prepare is preparing to fail." I have prepared for stuff like this, so I head back to the beginning of the route to the Dominion. Right on the corner of Oxford Street, outside Tottenham Court Road Station, there's a bloke named Gregory who rents a piece of land from Westminster Council. He sells newspapers from it. He has a very well-put-together stall that folds away in the evenings. They all call him 'Gregory the Bakery' for some reason—fuck knows why, and I ain't gonna ask him either. To me, he's Greg Baker. You never see him not looking sharp. Nice clothes, nice watch, about forty-two years old, lovely bloke. Always says hello to me every day, and I've always been able to have time for a quick chat with him.

'Allo Tony, you okay? You don't look right.'

Ah, I just lost all the cards I had on me. You got those cards I asked you to hold onto for me in the orange carrier bag?

'I've got 'em right here Tony. Let me grab 'em for ya.'

He opens up one of many little trap doors at the side of his stall and pulls out the orange bag of cards. I've only got ten of the thirteen girls I should have in there, but it's better than nothing, and just in time because those second cleaners have been out and already stripped bare Tottenham Court Road. I breeze down there at record speed. Ten on the back and ten on the right side window. Same old routine, no hassle. They're only taking down the cards on this road before they go straight to the Baker Street area, which I don't do anyway. I go for a shit in Macky D's and grab myself a sausage and egg muffin while I'm there before going home for the day. Job done.

FRIDAY, 12:35PM

I woke up in a panic for a brief moment, thinking I'm a bit late to put the cards out. Fancy forgetting that I'd already done 'em! I've had four hours of deep sleep. I dreamt that there were two of me running around—another one of me. I was dreaming of all sorts of other weird shit. My phone rings and stops, rings and stops again, and by the third time I think I'd better get out of bed and answer it. It's Trilly.

Hello Trilly, how are ya?

'Well, I'm all right, sort of. Are you sitting down?'

As soon as she said that, I knew she was pregnant. She's pregnant. She wants to meet to discuss things, but by the tone of her voice, I know she's looking forward to it. I shouldn't be thinking of the choice of keeping it or not. It's her body. And it's a baby. My baby. We arranged to meet the next day at seven in the evening. She's coming to mine.

SUNDAY, 10AM

Well, that's that then. She's serious about the baby. I knew she was gonna say that, but I couldn't show her that I wasn't too happy about it. I mean, I'm not ready for a baby. I'm fucking shitting myself. What's gonna happen to that kid? I deserve to be happy with Trilly, but fuck me, can we even do this together? She seemed happy about it this morning before she left. How could I spoil that feeling for her with a display of me not being ready? She said she's gonna carry on working for a few months. I guess it won't hurt. It'll hurt the guys that pay for the beatings from her. Especially with all those hormones she'll have flying about now that she's preggers. There's no telling what she'll do to 'em.

But I do love her, and I don't know what I'm gonna do with this baby. Guess I'll just go along to see where it takes me.

Trilly seems easy-going enough to want to do this together. But she could be thinking completely differently from me, so I can't get carried away. She told me she wanted the baby, and that's it. She didn't say she wanted to be with me.

I need to perk up a bit, so I put the radio on, and the song that is playing has a kicking piano stab in it. I've not heard it before, but it's got me rocking till the end until the DJ announces it's by an American R&B band called Blackstreet. '**No Diggity**' is the title; it's got Dr Dre on it, and it's a banging little tune that got me dancing. I got the taste for it now and cooked myself a breakfast of bacon, sausage, tomatoes, mushrooms, hash browns, eggs, beans, toast, and a fried slice of bread. Never again. I can't move now. It's just as well I've already decided to have a fuck-off lazy Sunday. All I've got to do at some point today, apart from eat and shit, is mix the cards for tomorrow.

I've got a friend named Jason who has a massive jeep. He calls it the Beast. He just rang me to ask for a favour. He wants me to follow him, driving his jeep, while he drives this small, single-seat German beamer car to a specialist showroom ten miles away.

Weird little thing, two wheels on the front and one on the back. It's called the Isetta. There goes my lazy Sunday as I head on down to his house in Essex. Fifteen grand he's sold this little car for. It's about forty years old, and it has to be delivered today.

His ten-year-old son Danny is with him, and he needs to drop him off somewhere after, so the boy gets in the jeep with me, and off we go. That little car he's driving is a nippy little thing. It's weaving through the traffic so easily, and it's a bit of a struggle to keep up with him, especially as I've never driven this car before.

I'm trying to talk to Danny, but I'm not getting much joy from him with his one-word answers to my questions.

I keep looking at him, waiting for a bit of conversation, but nothing. Maybe he's just one of those shy kids who don't like to talk much to anyone. He certainly didn't look like he was enjoying being with me. We're driving through this little town at about fifteen miles per hour, around these painted roundabouts on the road. His dad is about thirty feet in front of me. I asked him what he was doing today, and he didn't say a word. As I've turned a corner, I'm looking at him as I wait for an answer, and all of a sudden, he shouts,

'*DAD!*'

I immediately slam on the brakes to come to a sudden stop, but I'm nowhere near his dad.

What did you shout that for?

I'm looking out of the window, but I can't see anything there. Then, all of a sudden, a man slowly stood up from in front of the car, looking at me with a smile on his face, and then picked up his bike from almost underneath the front of the car and walked off to the pavement. I didn't see him fall off his bike when he turned the corner in front of me; I was too busy looking at little Danny. His instinct was just to shout out dad, and I'm relieved my reaction was so fast because I was two seconds away from disaster. I would have definitely run over the top of him had Danny not shouted out, and this car is at least two tons. Fuck that.

Jason picked up the fifteen grand in cash for the little car, then he drove the jeep to drop Danny off. I was quiet on the way home. For some reason, I decided not to tell Jason about what happened. He offered me one hundred pounds for driving the car, but I didn't take it.

MONDAY, 4:30AM

I'm walking up Tottenham Court Road to the first eight boxes outside the Dominion, and Timmy Tight Pants has not come in yet. By the look of the work of the weekend Cardboys, now all of the girls have gone back to explicit cards again. That didn't last long. I get a text from Terry telling me that the second cleaners will not be out this week. It's cold this morning, but at least it's not raining. I need to move fast to keep warm, so I strip the eight boxes quickly, and put my thirteen cards on the back, and thirteen on the side window. I hurry back to the car to get some more blue tack and open the boot to see it lying there next to my roller blades. These would keep me warm. Fuck it, I'll wear 'em. On go the blades, and in the next minute, I'm gliding up Tottenham Court Road to the next set of four boxes. It's a nice change being this tall in a phone box as I put the cards up. I can even reach the latecomers' cards that are on the ceiling easier too. It's a backward swoosh up Grafton Way, in a style like one of those ice skaters. I was turning corners like an ice hockey player, spinning around and jumping on and off curbs. Oxford Street, Euston, King's Cross, Soho, and back to the car in record time. It was six o'clock when I finished. I'd made myself six Hundred and fifty quid for the day, then decided to take full advantage of the time I saved and fucked off home. It's beautiful to be back in bed by six-thirty.

Again, I gave myself a fright after five hours of kip, waking up at eleven-thirty, thinking I hadn't put the cards up yet.

I refused to get out of bed that day before midday. A nice rest.

TUESDAY, 4AM

I set the central heating to come on at three-fifty. And I laid here till four. Just to give the house a chance to warm up a bit. I'm having thoughts of Mum. She would have loved to have woken up to a warm house. I wish she was still here, even if it was only to feel the house warm. I have her gold two-row knot ring on my little finger. It feels like there's still a connection to have something of hers on my person at all times. I'll treasure this ring forever.

This makes me think about the job I had in the clothes catalogue factory. It was a big place where they processed women's clothes before being shipped to outlets. There were rows and rows of clothes on coat hangers all tightly packed together; you could get lost in there. You'd get all hot as you had to rummage around in alleyways of fabric. The clothes there were a bit high-end, and acoustically, it sounded great.

When you spoke, your voice took on a whole new dimension by just stopping dead and not coming back at you as it does normally. That deadening sound is beautiful to hear, I'm so accustomed to hearing sound bouncing off two walls at sixty times per second—the deadening of sound. Like the sound of a large diesel car engine coming down a street when there is snow everywhere. It's nice to hear that deadening sound of the diesel engine. The way snow soaks up the ground reverberation to leave a more natural engine sound is worth pausing in the street to listen to.

The clothes warehouse paid a shit wage, but at least I had something coming in so I could chip in paying something to Mum each week. She was always happier when I was doing something. And she was equally happy when I brought home a nice outfit for her once or twice per week that fell off a coat hanger. That job didn't last too long, but at least Mum got about fifteen complete outfits. I'm getting a bit sentimental now; I'd better get up for work. I had a quick cup of coffee and a biscuit, or eight, and was out the door by four-twenty.

It's very cold out here this morning. I fucking hate it. The cold in my bones makes me lose a little weight. I gotta keep moving fast to try to get warm. Here we go, the first set of eight boxes. Even the handles on the boxes are extra cold today. I open the doors fast, and I fly through them, glancing up for the police as I dip my pockets two at a time for the next cards to go up.

A quick march up Tottenham Court Road to the next set of four boxes, and Timmy Tight Pants is there, taking all of yesterday's cards down in the last of the four.

'I'm not washing the boxes today Tony. No, I've gotta be somewhere this morning and I won't make it if I wash 'em all.'

I gave him one hundred pounds for last week, and he drives off down the road to the next set of four while I quickly smash my cards up in the first set. One to thirteen cards and out—whoosh! I go to open the door of the last box there, look down at my hand, and the ring is gone! My fingers have shrunk in this cold weather, and my mum's ring has slipped off somewhere.

I've gotta find this ring, so I run back to the first set of eight outside the Dominion and scour the ground all around and inside the boxes for the ring, but I can't see it.

As I'm searching the last box and surrounding area, I hear a single beep of a police siren before the blue lights start flashing. The van stops and out jump three policemen before one of them says to me,

'Stop right there a minute. You're looking suspicious. What are you up to?'

I've lost my gold ring. I'm just looking for it. It was my mum's, and it's just slipped off my finger somewhere.

'Well, what are you doing out at this time of the morning?'

I'm just putting some cards out.

'What, at this time? Why so early?'

Well, just so I can get the best positions. You don't wanna get down here late; otherwise, you'll end up having to put your cards up on the ceiling. The punter likes to be discreet and just look at the cards in front of him, more so than gaze up at the ceiling and worry about everyone knowing what he's looking at in there.

'I guess that makes sense. What else have you got in your pockets?'

Just cards.

He dips his hand in my pocket and pulls out a stack of mixed cards and looks at them.

'Busty Blonde. Dominatrix. Are these pictures really them?'

I dunno really. I don't think so.

'What, and they're using someone else's pictures?'

I dunno. I dunno which ones are real and which ones are not.

He puts the cards back in my pocket and says,

'Go on then, off you go. Hope you find your ring.'

Thanks, see ya later.

Mum's ring wasn't there, and the reality is that I've gotta just carry on with the round in the hope that it will turn up somewhere, but deep down, I know it's gone. I feel gutted about that. I march up the road, trying to walk in my exact steps while I look around for the ring. There's no ring, and I can't keep looking for it. I've got work to do.

Sorry Mum.

I know you won't be unhappy with me for losing your ring. I'm not happy about losing it though. Mum was a religious woman—a Catholic—and she never really pushed religion on us, apart from when it came to Christmas when she would take us kids to midnight mass with her. Either that or she didn't want to leave us alone in the house when she went. Either way, I didn't mind because at that time it was cool as a kid to be up at midnight, let alone go out at midnight. For a kid that wasn't into religion, how the fuck did I find myself being an altar boy! Standing there next to the big golden shiny candle holder, surrounded by all this other busy stuff, right in the middle of the church with all the people standing there gawping at me.

Wearing a cassock, that long black gown, and a cotta, which I thought resembled one of my sister's white blouses. This, I stuck on over the top of the cassock. The priest would do his shit, and I'd hand him a golden goblet of crackers, which represents the body of Christ. He'd lift up the goblet as a kind of blessing and say,

'Body of Christ.'

And then he'd eat one of those little white round crackers, and I'd have to go to him and hand him another golden goblet, but this one's got red wine in it. He'd raise that up high and say,

'This is the blood of God.'

And then he'd take a long fucking sip before wiping the golden cup's rim, where his lips touched, with an embroidered, glorified, towel sized cloth. Then he grabbed the crackers and walked to the front of the altar, where everyone was lining up to receive a cracker of their own. No one got a sip of the wine though. The crackers are cheap, so he can give them away, but a bottle of wine for three ninety-nine? Fuck that. I'd then have to take the rest of the crackers and the wine goblet out of sight to the back of the altar. No one else got to taste the wine, but when I got out the back, I'd down some proper glugs of it straight from the bottle. I'd walk back onto the altar feeling a bit pissed, and the priest would chat about one thing to the community while hiding a sinister side, the dirty cunt.

The church was situated bang on the end of the primary school playground, which, unknown to me at the time, was the priest's playground too. Come to think about it, the headmaster of the school might have been in on it too because he sent me and another boy called Bobby Lung to bring some bollocks thing or another to the priest's residence. I was only about nine or ten. When we got there, I remember being shown the sweets cupboard by the priest. He opened it up and said,

'Help yourself.'

Then he said to Bobby,

'Come with me, I want to show you something,'

and took him out of the room. I remember just standing there, looking at seven shelves full of sweets, and thinking, wow! I can have anything I want. It wasn't long before Bobby came running past the doorway with the priest trying to pull him back by his hips. Bobby was kind of laughing while he was desperately trying to escape the priest's grasp, shouting,

'Fuck Off. Fuck Off you cunt.'

The priest said to Bobby,

'Why, Don't you like it?'

I remember standing there with a Refreshers chewy sweet in my hand and thinking, don't like what? Bobby was not about to let him get away with any of it, whatever it was, thank fuck. I didn't understand then what was going on, but it didn't feel right, and I knew it was time to go, so Bobby and I made our escape, but not without shoveling handfuls of fucking sweets into our pockets. And to think that priest is probably still out there, preying on young boys.

By the time I get to the bottom of Tottenham Court Road, it's daylight and Terry has caught up with me.

'I tell ya, this is taking the piss. All the girls have gone back to picture cards; it's out of order. They'll end up stopping it.'

While he's putting up his cards and moaning away, I'm just listening to him.

'You're quiet Tony, what do you think?'

I don't think they'll stop it; they've been saying that for years ain't they? It's just part of London.

'Well, we should all refuse to put the picture cards out. That's what I'm saying.'

I'm freezing standing here, so we go into the McDonald's on the corner of Warren Street for a hot chocolate. There are a good few people in there who look homeless. One is half asleep on the floor, most have dirty clothes on, and their trousers are falling down low while they collect their coffees. It looks a bit like the walking dead in here—a zombie apocalypse. I turn to look at Terry, and he looks almost the fucking same as them, with his jeans not so clean and hanging down around his arse. We have a piss, grab our hot chocolate, and leave. The hot chocolate does the job in getting me warmed up, and it's not long before the round is finished, and I'm in my nice, warm car and on my way home. I'm out of weed at the moment, so by ten o'clock I'm calling my dealer to get some of that good stuff. He's very reliable and makes it over to my house within an hour after I call him. Customer service at its finest. Soots is his name; I don't know if that's his real name, but he's always got good shit on him. He turns up and immediately starts ranting about this good hashish he's got. I keep telling him I'm not interested in hashish and that I want weed, but he doesn't seem to pay attention.

'I've got some banging hash mate. You gotta try it.'

But I don't go for hash Soots; I like my weed don't I, You know that.

'Yeah yeah, I know you like your weed, but this hash is banging mate. You gotta try it.'

So I did. He rolled me a joint of this hash, and I only had three puffs of it before I could almost immediately feel the effect starting from my feet, all the way up to my brain. This hash was indeed a good lump of gear. So I decided to buy some.

'I've got five ounces left, so I'll do it for you for forty quid an ounce if you buy the lot of 'em.'

I'm thinking. Two hundred quid for five ounces doesn't sound too bad at all. In fact, that's a fucking excellent deal. I can sell some to get my money back and still have three ounces left for myself to smoke.

OK Soots, I'll have 'em. It's good shit, and I'd be a mug not to snap that up.

I hand him over the cash, grab the stash, and he leaves, taking the joint I rolled with him. That's like bringing a bottle to a bottle party and taking what's left home with you when the party is done. Tight git, got no class. I bite off a tiny piece from one of the ounces and roll myself another one.

A few puffs on that and I'm well fucking buzzing off this gear. He says it's Charis from the Himalayas. It's so dark and just crumbles so nicely without even burning it first—beautiful stuff. I spent the next five hours getting stoned out of my head.

5PM.

My phone rings, and it's Trilly.

'Hi babe. I'm just thinking of you, so I thought I'd give you a call to see how you are.'

Ah, that's nice of you Trilly. I'm fine thanks. How are you?

'Still pregnant. It's funny because I don't look pregnant, and I don't feel heavy or anything, but to know there's a baby growing inside of me makes me feel so happy. Can I come to see you?'

Of course you can Trilly. It'd be nice to see ya too. I'm busy now, but I'll be free by seven o'clock.

'OK, I'll see you at seven then. Bye.'

I can't believe how long the buzz from this hash lasts. It's better than all the weed I've smoked. My next-door neighbour, Stevie Duff, is a big hashish fan. I call him Stevie Puff because he's always smoking, and hash is all he smokes—no weed for him at all. It's the exact opposite to me, but the hash he gets is shit. I smoked his gear with him once before, and I think that's what put me right off it. Tasted horrible and burnt my throat when I inhaled and exhaled. I can still remember the taste when I think about it. Filth; he's always got a joint hanging out the corner of his mouth, and he's gonna love this stuff. He's been a solid friend of mine for years. Come to think of it, we did have one fallout many years ago. I got a bit flash with him over one thing or another. I can't remember the exact scenario, but I remember it breaking out into a proper fistfight, and then it all ended with him getting me into a headlock that I just could not get out of, no matter how hard I wriggled. I ended up using that time under his armpit just to rest. I was fucking knack-ered in that fight. It's the only fight I regret having because I loved him at the time, and I love him now. So I take the tiny piece of hash I chopped off and pop next door to see him. He's always very hospitable and has great parties. He's also got his doorbell wired up to a radio, and when you press it, it plays whatever the radio DJ is playing for six seconds. I love it. When I press his bell this time, I hear the song by a band called '**Space**', titled '**Female of the Species**', with the lyrics belting out *'shock, shock horror horror, shock shock horror'*. It felt like I was ringing on the Addams Family doorbell for that moment when I heard that.

Stevie opens the door, joint hanging out of his mouth with it stinking like some kind of burnt plastic. Fuck knows what he's smoking this time.

'Allo Tony, come in. D'ya want something to eat?'

Nah thanks Steve, I'm alright.

'How 'bout a drink? Can I get you a drink?'

Go on then, I'll have a coffee.

'How are ya?'

I'm alright. I've just got this bit of hashish for you to try. There you go, roll one out of this.

I hand him the small piece, and he rolls one up. He gives the piece back to me, which I put in the tiny little square pocket on my jeans. After taking four puffs of this stuff, his face got all serious as he looked at me and said,

'Fuck me Tony, what's this gear? My fucking legs have gone!'

It's good ain't it? Starts from the fucking feet and goes up.

'Yeah, it's incredible. I want some. How much you got?'

I've got three ounces of it to let off.

'I'll have them all. How much?'

Ninety quid an ounce.

'That's less than what I pay. I'll have all three.'

He gives me the money, and I popped back home, got him the stuff and went back home again.

I noticed when my clock turned from six fifty-nine to seven o'clock, and at that exact moment, Trilly rang my bell. I opened the door, and as always, she looked stunning. She gave me the nicest, warmest smile I've seen her give me, and we kissed passionately. She brought some ingredients and made a fantastic meal using radicchio, which she tells me is similar to red cabbage but with a more bitter taste. I dunno, I've never eaten it before. I had a bottle of nineteen seventy-six Chablis which I was storing, but I opened it tonight thinking we were going to share it together before she said,

'I'm pregnant, remember? I'm not going to touch a drop of anything while I'm in this state.'

I had a couple of glasses myself while we ate the delicious dinner, and she said,

'I'm not working tomorrow. Don't put any cards out for me.'

We had a great night together, and the sex, as always, was amazing.

'Why don't you take the day off tomorrow with me?'

No Trilly, I've got all the other girls I've gotta put cards out for.

It was tough waking up at four the next morning to go to work, but by four-thirty, I was dressed, had a quick cup of coffee, and was ready to leave.

'I'll be here when you come back. I love you.'

I love to hear you say that Trilly. I'll see ya later.

It took me fifteen minutes to drive into Tottenham Court Road, and although I was so tired, I was buzzing off love for Trilly and the thought that I'm gonna have a little family with her soon. I pulled up at my normal parking space and checked my phone to see a text message from one of the girls in Victoria saying:

'Don't put out my cards. I have a new number. Please come to pick up new cards before you start. I'll leave them in the little cupboard outside the front door.'

I had already mixed her cards with another girl's, so it was going to be a pain to sit there and unmix and mix them all again. So for now, I just emptied my pocket and threw the cards on the back seat of my car. It wouldn't take me long to shoot over to Victoria at this time of the morning, so I wasted no time in getting there.

It's quarter past five by the time I approach Trafalgar Square. I drive through Admiralty Arch and into St. James's Park and head towards Buckingham Palace. Just as I was passing St. James's Palace, I heard the whoop-whoop of a police siren behind me, and with the blue lights flashing, they pulled me over. I got out of my car and walked towards them. The policeman got out of his car and told me to step onto the pavement.

'Going a bit fast along there weren't you, What's the rush?'

He shines his torch into my car and sees the cards on the back seat.

'Putting out prostitute cards are we? I stopped you because there's been a report that you might be carrying a firearm.'

I knew exactly what he was on about; it was that incident at Euston Station that stuck with me, or stuck with the car at least. I explained the attack on me and how defending myself with the bin sounded like a gun and assured him that I didn't have a gun. Now, don't get me wrong, I do like a clean car, but this particular day the car was particularly messy.

'I'm going to search your car,' he said.

I'd put gloves on if I were you.

He shone his torch in the front footwell of the car, and after seeing the state of it, he said,

'On second thoughts, I won't bother.'

He then turned towards me and said,

'I'm going to search you. Lift your arms up.'

He stuck his hand in my jacket pocket, pulling out cards and putting them on the bonnet of my car, and then went straight for the little pocket on my jeans and pulled out the little piece of the finest hashish from the Himalayas. Rumbled. He smiled at me, smelt it, and said,

'Ooh, that smells good. What do you call this then? I'm arresting you for possession of a Class B drug. You do not have to say anything, but anything you say can and will be taken down in evidence and used against you. Do you understand?'

Well, nah not really. Not for a tenner's worth of puff. Can I lock my car?

It wasn't the best place to get pulled over, right in front of Buckingham Palace, on double red lines where you're not allowed to stop for one second without being liable to be towed away. He handcuffed me, then locked my car, then put me in the back of his car to take me away to the old bill station.

I'm sitting there thinking about the two ounces I've got left in the drawer at home and how they're gonna find it when they search the place. They've nicked my phone, and I've got no plan. At the police station, they book me in and all that shit and start talking about one phone call. So I call Trilly. She answers, and I say,

Hi Trilly, listen. I've just been arrested for a tiny bit of puff, so I just wanna tell ya that the police might be coming over to search the place, so you know what to do.

And that was it. I'm sure she saw me put the puff away last night. I was talking to her while I was doing it.

It was good to know Trilly had done something with the hash because they let me out six hours later without mentioning it. I really hope she didn't throw it away. It was eleven-thirty by the time I was walking back towards Buckingham Palace. In my head, I could see shitloads of parking tickets all over it, even a clamp on it. Or worse still, towed away. I got to the car, and there was not a single ticket on it. Checked the wheels—no clamp either. I opened the door, jumped in, and drove off. No battery on my phone, so I'll have to wait till I get home to find out what Trilly did with the puff. When I got home, Trilly greeted me with a big smile and kissed me.

What did you do with the puff?

'What puff?'

Did the police come round and search the place?

'Well, they came round, yeah, but they didn't search the place. I didn't let 'em in.'

They didn't try and force you to let 'em in?

'Well, they came round and said they've come to search the place, and I just said, 'Ooh, I'm just the cleaner here. I can't let you in.' They then said, 'Well, we can always go away and come back with a warrant,' and I just said, 'Well, you'll have* *to do that then. Sorry,' and that was it. When you said 'you know what to do,' I thought you meant don't let them in.'*

Ha, what a girl! You did brilliantly, but that's the thing, you see. They didn't even have a search warrant, but they still came around to search the place when they knew they shouldn't. Most people would have just let them in because they're "authority" without even seeing a search warrant. Not my Trilly though. You clever girl.

I had a party once. Someone had left the front door open a little bit, and everyone was inside having a great time and smoking. The place had clouds full of weed and hash in the air. I came out of the kitchen and saw seven policemen in my house walking around, gawping at everyone. Everyone was putting out their spliffs, chucking and hiding their stash anywhere they could. It was awful for my guests, and I wasn't having it. I told the DJ to stop the music, then I turned to the policemen and shouted,

OUT! C'mon, get out, you're not invited.

One of them said to me,

'But the door was open.'

It doesn't matter, it shouldn't be open.

I ushered them all out like a shepherd with my arms up in the air and waving. They did exactly what I said, and I closed the door behind them before signalling to the DJ and shouting,

PARTY ON!

The puff flowed again, and we were all in full swing quickly enough. Great party. At six that morning, a pal there, walked over to me and said,

'Tony, the missus sent me out last night at eight o'clock to get some sugar and milk, but then I heard your music and ended up here all night instead. She wanted the milk for the morning anyway. Thanks for the great party.'

I treated Trilly to lunch that day.

This was the first time I'd ever let the girls down by not putting their cards out. Then my phone started to ring, and it was one of the girls. Here we go. Well, I didn't have to explain myself at all, as she was so apologetic. She was saying she's sorry that I wasted all my time putting out her cards and that she was gonna pay me anyway. Then she rushed off the phone, saying she's busy, so I didn't get the chance to tell her that I didn't put the cards out. Then I had another similar call from one of the girls, apologising for me putting the cards out, but I told her that I didn't. She then told me that Westminster Council is clamping down again and that they collaborated with the telephone company to disconnect any landline numbers advertising prostitution. Overnight, the girls switched to mobile numbers, and the printers were hard at work. They're doing alright out of 'em. They don't give a fuck what they print on the cards. They're getting regular bucks for constantly printing 'em out. It's strange because there's the head of vice looking out for the girls, and yet they still punt around the notion that the law is about to change. But like I've said before, they've been mentioning that for years, but that's all it's ever been: talk. I think they just announce it once or twice every couple of years to keep the residents of Westminster happy. I fucking hope so anyway. I'm taking a nice wedge of dough, and I don't even wanna think about this job ending at the moment.

I do, however, have to drive around the West End again, collecting the new cards from all the girls. Trilly gives me a box of cards from the boot of her car before she leaves. That's one less I've gotta collect from. One thing doing this job has taught me is discipline. I've never been so focused on any job I've had. I'd struggle getting up at seven for the factory jobs, but this one is okay at fucking four in the morning because of the money I'm on. I got back home at nine-thirty, hungry and tired. I had a doggy bag leftover from today's lunch, thank fuck, so I heated that up and munched away. It tasted even better than earlier. Short rib croquettes and beef carpaccio with lobster mash. Only a little bit, but it went down a treat. I washed it down with a glass of wine and was in bed by ten-thirty. I must have fallen asleep about one-point-eight seconds after my head hit the pillow. I woke up at four and immediately went into a little panic because I realised I didn't mix the cards the night before. How could I forget that? Alright, don't panic. I need to be calm to work out a plan. The answer to that came easy enough. I just put a stack of one girl's cards in the front of my pockets and a stack of another at the back of the pocket. I wonder why I bother spending an hour plus each night mixing them anyway. That's it. No more fucking mixing for me.

Same old routine for me this morning. A quick scrub up of the teeth. Coffee, a biscuit, a few puffs on that Himalayan gem, and I'm out the door. When I get to Tottenham Court Road, I'm buzzing and in a really good mood. The cleaners have already been, so no need to strip any boxes. I still haven't got used to these Dominion boxes yet. Eight boxes, but they're just too close together. I don't like being in one place for this long. That's why I go so fast on these. Right, let's go. One, two, all the way up to thirteen and out! Next, thirteen and out. When I get in the last of the eight and start whacking the cards up, I look out the window, and there are two policemen standing on the corner junction of Oxford Street and Tottenham Court Road, staring at me. Clearly, they can see what I'm doing. I'm standing here, frozen in the box with a card in my hand, looking at them. I know what's coming next, but I didn't expect 'em to just turn away and walk off up Oxford Street. I'm just gonna carry on putting 'em up then. Fast pacing up Tottenham Court Road to the first set of four, the normal quick look around, seconds before I open the door, and I'm in. They may just be walking the block and catch me on this road, so I've gotta go faster to beat 'em. Definitely feels like the mouse and the cat this morning. Out of that box, quickly into the next, bosh, bosh, bosh. Cards are flying up.

I look out the window while I'm doing it, and a police car slowly drives past. The window is down, and the copper in the passenger seat is just staring at me as they drive straight past. I smash my head on the window, trying to see if they are stopping, but there's no brake light on the back of that motor. I continue to whack up the last of the four boxes and break into a little jog to get to the next set of four on the junction of Percy Street, looking out for the two old bill on foot and the patrol car that's on me too. I manage these ones without 'em coming back. Onto the next set of two across the road, in, and out! I just wanna get off this road. I'm quick-trotting down to the next two, opposite Goodge Street train station. There's always something going on there: you've got Paul the fruiterer setting up his stall, and the people who run the little café next door to the station that sell cheese croissants pressed in a grill. Then it's onto the next two, and the next, right up to the last set of four, and I go straight in. Cards are flying up at a good old speed. I get to the third box out of the four, and a police van drives past. They slow down a little to look at me and drive straight off again. What's going on today? That's three sets of old bill, and not one of 'em has stopped me. I wonder if it's just because they know me now? Maybe they just know I'm not someone that's up to no good. Fuck it, I'm just gonna carry on if they're gonna leave me alone like this, but I don't trust 'em. Feels like something's up.

I get to the last two boxes of Tottenham Court Road outside McDonald's restaurant and pop in there to use the toilet. There's a bloke in there putting a needle in his arm while another is sitting on the floor between two pisspots, looking like he's in another world. Fuck knows how they're getting away with doing that in here. I'd fuck off myself, but I need a shit. The toilet is surprisingly clean for a heroin den, but I still ain't sitting on that seat. The squat. I'll be squatting for the rest of my life. I'd better keep my legs strong because it ain't gonna be that easy holding that position when I'm older, especially now, when it's all taking some time to be delivered. But I push on through and force the situation to end sooner rather than later, and they're fucking groaning outside the door because the smack in their veins has started doing the business for 'em. I look up, and there's no bog roll. Bollocks! I've gotta talk to these fucking geezers.

Ere mate, you out there!

'What… me?'

Yeah, you. Can you get a toilet roll from the other toilet and pass it under please?

Ten seconds later, a dirty hand stretches underneath with a toilet roll in it. He drops it and proceeds to push it further towards me. Not only are his hands dirty, but they're bleeding as well, and now there's blood on the toilet roll, and the floor is wet in that bit, so all up the side of the roll is now wet too. I rip out the inner cardboard tube and start to take the paper from the half-inch of dry bit in the centre. Filth, but good enough to get me cleaned up before I'm out and on my way to Cleveland Street for those boxes. I go inside and find a bag of weed sitting on the shelf. Sweet! Packed full it is and… smells lovely. Don't like having this on me when I'm doing the round though, especially after what just happened with the hash. I hide it somewhere in the basement of one of the flats on Grafton Way and continue doing the backstreet boxes on the way to Oxford Circus.

FRIDAY

There have been police driving past me all week while I've been doing the rounds, and they've not bothered me at all. I've earned a good bit of dough, and I've got someone to do the afternoon top-up, which'll save me three hours each day. He's thirty-five, and he's got loads of kids from a few mothers. He does see 'em all though, I'll give him that. He cares. Just ain't got a pot to piss in. I trust him, and he's keen, so I set him up to do today on his own. I'm paying him eighty quid a day to keep the girls up for me. He's happy with that. All I'll have to do now on Friday afternoons, is go and pick up the money and cards for the next week. I'm out to a warehouse rave tonight in Shoreditch somewhere, so a sleep was definitely needed, which I did from midday till five.

Now, the raves in this part of London require you to have your "take care" head on. You see the boys that you know from your manor buzzing about, and you can just feel if a place has the potential to kick off. I went to the bar, pulled some notes from my back pocket, bought a drink, and put the money back in my back pocket. While I was standing there, looking around the tightly crowded space I was in, I felt a slight and slow rub up, and then down on my arse cheek. First, I'm thinking, is that a bird trying to get my attention? Then, in a flash, I saw a whole picture unfold in my head of a man sliding his fingers up and down my arse to get me accustomed to being touched. Then the fingers would go up and down into my pocket and up again with my wad of cash between the two fingers. I slapped my pocket shut and spun around to see a bloke quickly fix himself and stand still, trying to look all innocent with his drink in his hand, staring into the air. Does he really think I don't know what the fuck he was up to? Shall I confront him? He's probably got his boys in here with him too, and I don't know who they are, so I'd better be quiet about it. But it has put me on edge for the rest of the night. I didn't stay too long after that.

That's the thing about my area: you can easily get mixed up in all sorts of things. You know everyone there and spent time with some of 'em, so sometimes you have to fight to not get involved in anything. I remember one Sunday, when all the shops were shut, I was walking along a road where there's a community centre and heard the fire alarm ringing on it. As I walked closer, three or four of the lads that I knew came running out the door after robbing the place. One of 'em had a huge see-through plastic bag full of fifty pence pieces. He was struggling to carry it, wobbling but still trying to run. He ran straight into me and said,

'Ere Tony, take this. I'm going to run back in there quickly.'

I just held my hands up and said,

Nah. I don't wanna know.

I carried on walking, never saw a thing, and that was that. You could just see the path that these fellas were going on, and I didn't wanna be on it. It didn't stop me from helping 'em out just the once after that though. I got a job in a big supermarket in a place called Bacton. Another job I didn't respect. I was helping unload a lorry load of electrical goods. These same fellas that were always looking for an opportunity to steal something were walking past and noticed I was working there. One of them shouted,

'Tony. Chuck us over something?'

I looked at them, thought of the job, and thought, fuck it, and performed a quick, unnoticed underarm backward throw, twenty feet behind me to where they were walking. He picked it up and slung it under his jumper. It was a box of eight handheld food blenders. Fuck knows how much he sold them for, but that was the game around there. Hard to escape for some of them really, 'cos it was everywhere. There was a big freight parcel company, and when they came to deliver a parcel, they would get robbed. The driver would disappear up a block of flats or somewhere to deliver, and when he returned, his van would be empty. This happened so often that eventually they banned all their drivers from delivering anything there at all.

I'm thinking of Trilly a lot. She's gonna deliver my first child. She's still working, and her tummy is not showing much. She says she plans to carry on right up to at least three or four months pregnant, just whipping and beating the blokes, then quitting for good. She told me she's saved up four hundred and eighty thousand pounds, and I know that she's looking forward to having a family with me. And so far, she's been really decent towards me. Fancy that, me, becoming a dad. I ain't gonna be like my dad was with me; there'll be no beatings, that's for sure. I remember when I was nine, I can't remember what I did to deserve the punishment, but I know it was one of those delayed punishments—the ones where you have to wait till your mum or dad got home for the beatings. I hated waiting for that shit. I thought, if I go to bed, he'll come home, say he'll whoop me tomorrow, and then he'll forget all about it. That didn't work out; I went to sleep as planned but woke up some time later with the sniffles, like I had been crying. I didn't have a clue what was going on because I was asleep, but the blanket was off me, and I was cold. I leaned forward to grab the blanket back onto me and saw a big belt strap mark across the top of my leg. Now it all made sense. I couldn't believe that I stayed asleep and even cried, and yet I didn't feel or notice a thing when he whooped me. How was that even possible?

As my phone is ringing, I'm looking at the number thinking, who the fuck is that? I don't recognise it, and I'm not too keen to answer it for some reason, but I am curious as to who it is. I don't wanna miss out on anything, but I don't want anyone to have that "gotcha" moment with me. I know how I'll answer it…

Hello.

'Hello, am I speaking to Tony?'

Hello.

'Yes, hello, is this Tony?'

Hello, can you hear me?

'Yes, I can hear you. Is this Tony?'

Hello, I can't hear ya.

'Hello, can you hear me now?'

Hello, who is this?

'Hello, can you hear me?'

Hello, if you can hear me, can you ring back again 'coz I can't hear ya.

Then they put the phone down. Now, had they told me who they were when I asked, and it was someone I wanted to talk to, I simply would have said, oh, I can hear you now. But this person didn't. So they're getting blocked. The number ringing me now, I do recognise—it's Trilly. She wants to come over, so I arranged a date for Saturday night and got off the phone.

MONDAY, 6:30AM

Shit! I'm late. But I've gotta have a cup of coffee, which is the first thing I reach for, a quick bite, jacket on, and out the door. There's more traffic at this time, and it's seven-twenty by the time I get into Tottenham Court Road and park up. I rush to the first set of eight, and although a few Cardboys have been through, none of 'em have taken my space. I get to the next set of four, and again there are cards all up the backboard and side window, and an empty section in the middle just above the phone. I put all of my cards up in that space. Along the whole of Tottenham Court Road, my space was left open for me. This feels good. It makes me feel respected. After me, it's first come, first serve. I hit the backstreets, then the areas of Oxford Circus, Soho, Euston, and Kings Cross. Fucking nightmare when you come out this late, waiting around for people to finish using the boxes, not to mention the parking meters I'm now paying into. By the time I get back to my manor, it's ten-thirty. I'll have a good breakfast and sort out my place, but no morning sleep today. It's a punishment to myself for getting up late. Having Trilly in bed with me doesn't help, but when I walk in, the bed is made, the washing up is done, the whole place has been hoovered, and even my laundry basket full of clean clothes has been taken out and folded up neatly, including my socks and pants. Trilly has done everything and left me a post-it note saying, "Enjoy your day. I love you." My attraction for her now, after seeing all she's done here today, has gone up even more. Is she like this all the time, or is she putting on the mask and just acting this way to win me over? Like I always say, people can hide who they really are for a good one hundred days, and after that, well, let's just say the real person comes out. She's got my baby inside of her, and I wanna be around for that, but I am concerned about committing to her solely for that reason. I'm still finding out what kind of person she is. She might not be good for me, but at the moment, she's certainly doing things right by me.

NOVEMBER 4TH, 4:40AM

Terry has gone on holiday for two weeks to Gran Canaria, and he's left me his work to put out. Eight girls he works for. And they each give him five hundred cards to put out every day, which works out to two grand a week. So together with my cards, minus the five hundred quid a week I pay out to my top-up man, I'll still walk away with four thousand seven hundred and fifty pounds per week for the next two weeks. I've got twenty-one girls in total that I'm working for today. I had no choice but to start mixing 'em again for the next two weeks, just to make my pockets work. That's two girls mixed for the front of the pocket and two girls mixed for the back of the same pocket. Four girls in each pocket and seven pockets on my waistcoat used up, and it's fucking heavy. I'm counting my money, and so far, it's twenty-three grand, and I'm busting for a shit before I leave. I use the time sitting there to count what's left. Another four grand. I nearly wiped my arse with the last note I counted, so I put the cash stash in my waistcoat pocket and cleaned myself up. I've never saved so much money in my life. But I worry about its safety under the bed. Twenty-seven grand. What if someone comes in and just picks up the box? Fuck that. I'd better hurry up and secure my investments while I can. I know these cards are not gonna be around forever; I don't care how many years they've been going for, it won't last. That money won't last either if I don't do anything with it. And that idea I had seems all the more doable now. It's always been nice when I've gone to Brighton. There's always tourists there, a thriving, bustling town, and one of those flats I saw advertised for forty-odd grand there to rent out would be perfect. Bang in the middle of a holiday town. That's gonna be just right for me. I'll just save up a little more money and buy that fucking flat.

I'm on a steady pace down Tottenham Court Road, whacking up the cards as I go. Here comes another police car. Again. Just driving past me. With no bother from 'em at all. This will do; makes my job really easy. Right then, into Cleveland Street to get the two boxes there, now onto Maple Street and plaster the two boxes there. Then right turn into Fitzroy Street. This is good, I'm really moving. It's nice and quiet around here early in the morning. I'm in the phone box, grabbing some cards out of my pockets while I have a quick look around for police. I've really got a purpose and a dream that's gonna become a reality soon. All this good shit is happening to me, I've even had a—FUCK!…. Who's this pulling up in the Volvo? Are they plain clothes? Bollocks, they're plain clothes. Here they come, flashing their badges at me. I wonder if I can sweet-talk 'em out of busting me? Worth a go.

That's a nice car.

The taller copper grabbed my arm and pulled me towards the car.

'Show me what cards you've got on you.'

I grabbed a bunch of mixed cards from one pocket and gave them to him. He took one of each card and put the rest to the side.

'You got any more?'

Yeah, I've got more.

'I want one of each card.'

He continued to take one of each.

'You are a busy boy out here ain't ya. How much do you get paid for this?'

I do it for a service.

'What service is that then?'

Blow jobs.

He puts the cards in a plastic bag.

'You got any ID on you?'

Yeah, I've got my driving licence. Hold on, I can't find it. I know I've got it on me somewhere.

'I'm gonna have to search you.'

He begins taking all the cards out of my pocket, laying them on the car bonnet.

The feeling of my waistcoat getting lighter and lighter as he is taking them out is calmly satisfying. He's got one more stack of cards to take out, and I will be free from all that weight I have been carrying all morning. An empty waistcoat. He took the last one out, but disappointingly, it still doesn't feel empty. That massive pocket at the back of my waistcoat that I never use for cards is a little weighty, and my eyebrows feel weighty now. Oh shit, shit. I know why it's heavy, it's the money, it's the fucking four grand. And this fucking copper will soon be on his way to getting me to turn around or just sticking his hand in and pulling it out. Now he's telling me,

'Lift your arms up.'

I lifted up my arms, and he began to carefully search my left sleeve, then the right sleeve. Then he reached up and searched my collar and said those two words that had the potential to get me into a little bit of a situation.

'Turn around.'

I'm turning around slowly. I know this is it. He is gonna find it in about two seconds' time, but instead of going for the pocket deposit, he's bent down and now searching my sock. Now he's moving slowly up my left leg, he's having a good old search all around the trouser on the way up, now he's going for the other sock. He takes his time to search and move up my trouser leg. Fuck this lark, I'm just waiting for him to find it. Shall I run? Maybe not. I'm thinking of when D crept up behind me with the baseball bat, and that itch, and how it saved my life. Maybe something like that will happen now. Maybe he'll get an emergency call and run off before he looks in there, that kind of fortune can strike twice. The copper slowly puts his hand in the back pocket. I've been busted. He grabs and pulls out the wad of money before saying to me,

'That'll pay for a few blow jobs won't it?'

I'm—I dunno what I am. I can't think of anything to say, so I'll say fuck all.

'Where did you get this money from? Look, I've seen you out here before, I know who you are and what you do. I even know where you live, but unfortunately for you, you've got no ID on you, and with this amount of cash in your pocket, I'm taking you in!'

Well look at that. Handcuffs. That's a first for me.

All this, just for having no ID. I get taken to the police station where they process me into the system. They take my belt, my shoes, and then they take me to a cell and lock me in. There was plenty of time in there to think things over, and six hours later, I was released on bail and would have to wait to see if I would be prosecuted. I got back to my car in the afternoon and grabbed the parking ticket from the windscreen before driving home through heavy traffic. I'm thinking of the money under my bed, and this journey home is taking fucking ages. Home at last. Quick quick, stairs. Please be there, please be there.

AAHH!

The bed's messed up. Please be there.

IT'S GONE! Oh no.

My chest is hurting, this can't be happening. Did I put it somewhere else? The wardrobe? No, no, no. Duvet cover? On top of the wardrobe? I know I never put it there. I'll just check. No, it was under the bed. I feel sick. All that fucking money. Those fuckers came and took it. Oh no, there's fuck all I can do. There's fuck all I can DO!

WEDNESDAY, 4AM

These last two days, I've woken up with the first thought being my money. How am I gonna get it back? I ain't even got a believable explanation of where I got it from. My top-up guy has been doing a really good job out there, but yesterday, he didn't bring his ID in with him, and the police took him in too. They kept him in for a few hours. He was told he didn't have to go back when they let him go, but it put him off doing it. He was talking fast on the phone last night. I was way too knackered to take all that shit in, but I reckon I'll be doing the fucking top-up later on. I could do with staying at home today, but I have a quick cup of coffee, a banana and a biscuit, and I'm out the door. I pull up at Great Russell Street at four-twenty. My waistcoat is the heaviest it's ever been. I go into the first of the eight phone boxes at the Dominion, and just like I'm the fastest gunslinger in the West End, I go about the job with my fingers and thumbs and blue tack, whipping cards about with blind precision as I go from box to box as smoothly and as quickly as I possibly can. Two of each in a box, and eight boxes here, so just in these boxes alone, I've put up three hundred and thirty-six cards. I get to the next set of four, and I'm in. I've really gotta move fast now, a quick look around, and Tottenham Court Road is empty. Twenty-one cards on the backboard, twenty-one on the side glass. Bang bang! In and out, that's one hundred and sixty-eight cards in these four boxes. On to the next four near Percy and straight in. Second pack of blue tack, and I'm even keeping warm with the speed I'm doing. I'm on the third one of those four when I hear a vehicle coming slowly, so I stop what I'm doing, pick up the phone to my ear, and smile while I gaze into the skies, deliberately avoiding any acknowledgment of the police van driving past. I stayed with the phone pushed to the side of my face until I was sure they couldn't see me, and I was off again—bosh, bosh—and forty-two cards in every phone box on Tottenham Court Road were almost done. Time to reward myself with a hot chocolate from Macky D's as soon as I finish these, the last two that're right outside the restaurant.

My pockets are feeling much lighter as I've been cruising through the route of Oxford Street, Euston, Soho, and all the backstreets linking them. It's been one of those mornings, and I'm actually enjoying the day I'm having out here after all. Everything is going smoothly, and I finish the round by seven-twenty. I get back to my car and drive around the whole route again for a check-up before grabbing one of those toasted cheese croissants. By the time I get home, it's nine o'clock, and I've worked for just over a thousand pounds for the day.

I head to the post office to buy the postal order to pay off the last of the fines I accumulated this year. It's sixty quid I owe. I could just pay twenty quid over the next three months, but I decided to just pay it all off now and free myself from the headache.

The baby's on the way, and Trilly is very easygoing, easy to get along with, and she's so much fun. And she's doing everything to show me she's bang into me. It's good dating her. Fuck knows when I'm gonna introduce her to my family. I wonder what her family is like. Fuck me, I haven't even spoken to anyone about her. It's like she's just my dirty little secret, with my fucking baby inside her! About to retire from the game and wants to nurture a family, that can't be bad Tony. Will she even be good for me though? Even though I know she'll only be loyal to her feelings. I'm the only bloke that's ever fucked her for fuck's sake. I don't wanna do anything to fuck this up. And as long as she doesn't fuck up, and I don't put her off, we might stand a chance. Why would she fuck up such a thing? What if she runs off with my baby? Nope, that's not gonna happen. I will be in that baby's life. I went to sleep for a bit, waking up at midday. A cold afternoon. The Spice Girls have got a new song out called **'Two Become One'**. I keep hearing it on the radio, and it's growing on me. I reckon it'll be the Christmas number one.

I can't get hold of my top-up guy as expected, so I'll have to do it myself. I was getting used to not doing it too. At least it's more money for me.

TOP-UP, 2:30PM

It's a breeze today doing this top-up. I walked the length of Tottenham Court Road, and every single card is still up from this morning. I hit the backstreet boxes of Cleveland Street, Maple Street, Fitzroy, and Charlotte Street before weaving my way through to Oxford Street. It's so busy here. I get to Oxford Circus, and the cards in the four boxes there have been messed around with—there are piles of 'em blue tacked together, some are upside-down, and loads of cards are all over the floor. The boxes are in a right mess. There are people in the boxes as well, so I'll also have to wait for them to finish. Eventually, they do. Right then. Fuck it! I'll start this box afresh. I'm not interested in that 'Cardboy should never take down another Cardboy's work' bollocks today. These cards up here are terrible. I took 'em down, and my cards are going up nice and neat, but Oxford Circus in the afternoon, waiting for people to come out of the boxes is no fun. It's taken fucking ages to do these, but they all got the same treatment, and I move on to Euston, all the cards are still up here, good. Onto Kings Cross, Sweet! All cards up here too. So four boxes were all I had to do today. I walk back to Euston Station for the train home by four-fifteen.

THURSDAY EVENING, 7:30PM

That'll be Trilly at the front door. She looks very sexy, and her attraction level towards me is still crazy high. We're kissing passionately as soon as she walks through the door. Oh, my belt. Grabbing at my belt again. She wants it right here. She swiftly undoes my shirt buttons and gently claws at my chest, and with a short outburst of delightful laughter, she kisses my chest, then my neck, then back to my chest and continues to kiss me down along my stomach, gets onto her knees and pulls my trousers down. Grabbing and squeezing my cock tight, she sucks and licks it before standing up and turning around, she looks so good. I reached round and grabbed both of her tits, tickling and pulling on her erect nipples. Off we go again. Sex behind the front door. When we finally went to the kitchen to cook, it was eight-fifteen. We didn't finish eating until ten. Trilly said that she was thinking of stopping work sooner than she thought she would. She's just gonna grab a bit more money, and that's it. She said she felt a little twinge when she was whooping someone, and that got her a bit scared. Trilly and I are getting on really well. She brings a kind of coolness around me, she's nice to be around. But I've gotta be up at four in the morning, so it's off to bed for only four and a half hours of sleep.

FRIDAY, 4AM

No alarm clock as usual, and I'm up. Trilly is laying in bed fast asleep. She looks gorgeous, and I find myself standing there for five seconds just looking at her before grabbing that kettle for a cup of coffee and a few biscuits. I lean in to kiss her, but no. I don't wanna wake her up, so I quietly leave the bedroom and head out the front door by twenty past four.

It's payday today. And I've got the first week of Terry's work to collect, so that's twenty flats I've got to go to later. I'm not looking forward to that, even if it is to collect money.

The police are just driving straight past me on Tottenham Court Road today. It's as if they can't be bothered these days, but I don't wanna take the piss. I'll still pick the phone up when they pass—I can't have them take my cards, so a little respect encourages them to drive past.

At the last set of four boxes on Tottenham Court Road, there's a man in a dark suit inside the first one, taking all yesterday's cards down, and putting them in a big black plastic sack. He has a bow tie on. I'm gonna have to open the door on this fucker.

You OK mate? What are you doing?

This is sinful, and it shouldn't be allowed, and I feel I have done my good duty for the day by choosing to take down the cards from all the phone boxes on this road. And, I have completed my duty, first thing in the morning. The rest of the day is now mine. Tomorrow, it will be something else.'

You crack on mate. After these four boxes, you've got two further down across the road, then you cross over for the last two further down outside McDonald's, and you would have done the whole street. Well done.

He just smiled at me, and I went off to grab a cup of coffee and leave the man to clean all yesterday's cards. I'll put my cards up when he's done. Fuck knows where the cleaner is—maybe it's his day off. After my coffee, I finished the last eight boxes on Tottenham Court Road. I walk through the backstreets and straight into the phone box on a very quiet Cleveland Street. I'm whacking up the cards there when a police car comes around the corner, flashes the blue lights for three seconds, and drives slowly straight past. I'm standing there with a card in my hand, just waiting for them to stop and reverse up to nick me, but they don't.

They drive around the corner, and I'm thinking they'll be back around again in a minute, so I smash the cards up as quickly as I possibly can. One two three four five six—no time to look around—seven eight nine ten eleven twelve. Right then, where will those police be? Just driving down Conway Street I reckon, and then onto Grafton Way to get back onto Cleveland Street. Hurry up—thirteen all the way to twenty-one cards up and out! I'm not risking doing the side windows as well just yet, and instead of walking my usual route onto the next two boxes on Maple Street, I back up the other way, further down Cleveland Street and wait in a doorway for the old bill to come around, and there they are. They pull up slowly at the junction of Grafton Way and Cleveland Street, and I just watch them from the doorway as they slowly drive out onto Cleveland again and pull up at the phone box looking for me. Then they sped off. I quickly walked back up Cleveland, and straight into the other box to finish my cards, then round the corner to do Maple Street. I plastered the backboard of those two boxes before turning right onto Fitzroy Street to do the single phone box there. There's no sign of the police.

Walking through the rest of the backstreets, I make my way to Oxford Circus, leaving my car outside Mandy's flat on Grafton Way. The cleaners have been and gone, and there's not a single card in there. The roads are nice and quiet, with the odd taxi rumbling by, and I casually walk up and into the first box.

The cards are going up swiftly, but I'm just not in the mood to break the world speed record and still, my arms are doing their own thing and flying about in quick draw Edward scissorhands-style. After the four Oxford Circus boxes I continue walking down Oxford street to do the rest of the ten along there. Charing cross road is to be done today so I go there next as I've got three of Terry's cards that go there on a friday. I hit Soho after that before heading back to my car and driving up to Euston and Kings Cross and more boxes.

SUNDAY MORNING, 15TH DECEMBER

It's nice to have a lie-in now and again. I don't tend to do it that often, but Trilly is lying here next to me, and she's being as sweet as fuck. She's saying she wants to introduce me to her family before her belly starts to show. I do love her, and I've got shit to do, but if we're gonna make a go of having a family, of course I'll meet her folks. Mum, Dad, this is Tony, and by the way, I'm pregnant. That'll go down well. She's decided that she's gonna give up the game at Christmas. Good news I think. I'm pleased to hear that. I've not told my family that I'm gonna be a dad yet, and it seems that she's interested in us being a couple, which I would agree to if she asked. So far, she's been great. We had a good afternoon with great food and nice drinks before she left to go home at about seven tonight. I put the cards back to back in my pocket again instead of mixing 'em and hung the heavy coat up near the front door, ready for Monday morning.

MONDAY, 4AM.

It's pissing down with rain, and I'm not looking forward to going out in it one bit, but I run to my car and make my way to Tottenham Court Road. I got there at four-forty today, pulling into the side street and running through the rain to the first set of eight boxes. Timmy Tightpants is there. He's just finished these ones, and he wants his money. That's one hundred quid lighter for me. I'm loaded up with cards and proceed up the road, speed-carding my way into each box. I'm in front of the cleaner now, so I'm ripping yesterday's cards down and leaving them on the shelf for him. It's tempting to start collecting the blue tack off the cards myself with the amount of money I spend on the stuff—one pound fifty a packet now, and I'm doing four or five packets a day. Terry is coming back on Thursday, but he wants me to put his cards out that day, and he'll go back on Friday. Fine by me. Christmas is coming, and money is money. Even though I've gotta use my leather cloth in all the boxes in this weather so they stick, the good thing about the windows steaming up is that the police can't see you putting up the cards, so you can work away without fear. The whole round went without anyone bothering me. I got home soaked at eight-thirty.

It's nice to be able to afford good presents for loved ones this year. I've been buying one present for each person each week for the last six weeks, and I've spent two hundred quid on each person. I've got one more present to buy for Trilly. It is a bit too soon to be buying presents for her, especially as we are not exclusive, but it is Christmas, and she has my baby inside her, and she deserves it, so I think I'll buy her a nice watch. I have the top-up to do at three-thirty, so my plan is to go to Hatton Garden at one-thirty, the London hub of diamonds and jewels where every shop down there has a few carats on display in the window, I'll get the watch and do the top-up from there. In one of the jewellery shops, I'm standing there being served by an elderly couple, looking at the watch I'm going to buy her—it's a Tag Heuer. There's a well-dressed Arabian-looking man asking the old man to look at several diamond bracelets. These things must have been twenty grand each, and he looked like he could afford all of 'em. There was a buzz on the door, and a man standing there was waiting to come in. The jeweller pushes his button under the counter to release the locked door and let the man in. As soon as the man pushes the door open, the Arabian-looking man makes a grab for the five or six diamond bracelets laid out in front of him. I've gotta give it to the old jeweller though—he was quick, he grabbed the bracelets by the other end, but after a brief tug of war, The guy started punching the old man in the face to get him to let go, while the other guy wedged the door open with a stick, picked up the fire extinguisher, and ran in shouting and attacking the old man with it. He swung it at him, missed, and smashed the counter glass. He then grabbed some jewellery from there.

I backed off and moved outside to get away from it. The man ran out past me with a fistful of diamond bracelets, followed by the other guy with a little bag full of jewellery.

The old man ran to the door but just closed and locked it. I shouted to the old man to ask if he was alright, and he gave me the thumbs up and shouted to his wife to call the police. I didn't really want to be around when the police turned up, so I walked off and turned left into Greville Street, only realising then that I've still got the watch in my hand that I haven't paid for. I can hear a police siren in the distance, and I'm not hanging around, so I slip off to do the top-up.

THURSDAY,
19TH DECEMBER,
4AM

Today is the last day of putting out twenty-one cards in a phone box. The money has been great, but now I'm looking forward to a break from doing this, which is gonna be Tuesday, Christmas Eve. There's only Trilly working on the twenty-fourth, which is her very last day in the game, but I don't fancy working then, so Terry can return the favour and put her out for me. I drink my morning coffee and grab my heavy waistcoat. There's a brown envelope sticking out from the back of the shoe rack, and I recognize the red stamp on it as being another court letter. I ain't got the time to open it now, but I want all my fines cleared, so whatever this one is, I'll pay it straight away. I'll even go to court again to state my case to get a lower fine, depending on how high it is in the first place. I got to Tottenham Court Road this morning at four forty-five. It's so cold, and I forgot to press my blue tack to the heater blowers in the car to get it soft, which renders it harder to pull bits off and less sticky. As I make my way to the first set of eight, there's a group of seven smartly dressed blokes who are a bit drunk and look like they have just come from a nightclub, standing around outside the Dominion. I pay them no attention and continue into the first box, peppering it with forty-two cards, twenty-one on the backboard and twenty-one on the window, then into the next box to do the same. As I'm putting them up, I hear one of the blokes shout out to his mates,

'Chaps, look at this man putting up the cards,'

and he proceeds to open the phone box door to bother me.

'Hello mate. I've always wondered who put these up. Can you really ring them up and go round to see them?'

Yes mate, you can.

'Can I have some cards please?'

I gave him an assortment of about ten cards and continued to put the rest up.

'Are they open now? Can I go round to see them?'

They won't be open yet mate. Give it till about half-ten or eleven and you can go.

'No, I can't. I'm pissed, and I'm going home to sleep. I've been out all night.'

I finish the rest of the boxes there and move on to the next set of four, but the cold blue tack is giving me so much trouble. I return to my car, turn the engine and the heaters on, and push my tack onto the heat outlet to soften it up for ten minutes. I laid back in my seat waiting and the next thing I knew, I woke up at five forty-five with my tack almost melting on there. But I was warm enough to move faster, so I was off, walking like a speed walker and working the whole of Tottenham Court Road at an incredible pace. I hit the backstreets, Oxford Street, and all the usual places before getting to King's Cross at eight-fifteen, which is late for me. But the cleaner was there washing the boxes, and he's not on the payroll, so I'm glad I never got here earlier. I introduce myself to him and tell him I'm waiting for him to finish cleaning so I can put the cards up. Shortly after that, he collects his bucket, cloth and squeegee and walks off saying,

'All yours mate,'

These boxes are fucking soaking, so the leather cloth comes out to dry 'em first before I start carding them up. I complete all the boxes around King's Cross station before making my way back to the car, which is parked at Euston Station. I get there at ten past nine and collect another parking ticket. I left it on the windscreen as I drove home.

The fucking traffic made sure I got home at ten this morning, so it was a scrambled egg sandwich and straight to bed. At twelve-thirty, I woke up and thought of the brown magistrate's envelope. I'll pay this fucking thing off before Christmas. I opened it up, but it didn't look the same as the other ones, which were just fines. This one said in bold letters:

You must attend the court on Friday, the twentieth of December. Failure to appear on this date will result in a warrant being issued for your arrest.

Great, that's fucking tomorrow. I don't like the look of this, but last time I went to court, I got a twenty-pound fine.

FRIDAY, 4:30AM

I'm driving up to the West End, but I've had no coffee. I ran out. I've had a cup of tea, but it's not had the same effect. It's fucking freezing, and my blue tack is perched firmly on the heater outlet of the car. I might as well turn it over like a beef burger, spread it out a bit too so its heat can spread throughout its entirety. I intend to move fast today, so I quickly park up in Great Russell Street. Terry's back, so I'm back down to my thirteen girls—it's good to have a lighter load. I'm walking towards the Dominion. The cleaner is there, and so is Terry. He's very tanned and is taking down yesterday's cards in the other boxes while the cleaner is cleaning his first one.

Morning Terry, how was the holiday?

'Fucking brilliant, I didn't wanna come home. I could have stayed out there. It was fucking hot—well, seventy-four Fahrenheit. That's a lot hotter than here.'

Course it is, it's fucking Spain. It's two degrees here today. Can you do me a favour Terry? I've gotta go to court today, so will you do the top-up for me this afternoon?

'Sort 'em all out, and I'll do 'em.'

I gave Terry a few cards of each girl tied up together in an elastic band, and we walked up Tottenham Court Road together, stripping yesterday's cards from the boxes, leaving them on the shelf for the cleaner and whacking our cards up all over the back. We went on to do the backstreets together, Oxford Street, Euston, and King's Cross. I jumped in my car after that and drove home—another nice early one—and I got home at seven forty-five today. I ate a king's breakfast of a slice of bread and butter and went to bed.

FRIDAY 12PM

I had my best sleep at this time. That was great, and I've got the rest of the day to myself—apart from the court case that is. I had a nice bit of lunch, rolled a big joint, and chilled out for a bit with my guitar before putting on my suit and heading for the train station. I got to the court, which was busy with lawyers darting from one room to another, and a few people who clearly looked like they never wear a suit apart from at funerals and court cases, tugging at their collars and rearranging their trousers. I checked in and all that bollocks, got the metal detector treatment, and then went to sit down on a wooden bench against a wall to wait to be called up. Things are definitely changing slowly with all of this. We've gone from getting silly littering fines to paying hundreds for illegal advertising, and now I'm fucking forced to come here. How much are they gonna snatch off me today? I'm sitting next to this bloke from Manchester who asks me what I'm here for. Before I could even tell him to mind his own business, he began to tell me all about how he got in his car drunk and drove to his ex-girlfriend's house to win her back after she cheated on him. Another weak fucking pussy man with no emotional control or self-respect. No wonder she cheated on him. I was just about to tell him to shut up when a man approached me and introduced himself as my appointed solicitor. He told me he hadn't looked at the papers properly but had been allowed more time to go over them. He said he knew it was about my earnings, then took me into an empty side room and left me there, telling me we had a half-hour extension and if I wanted to make any phone calls, I should do it now. Then he left the room.

I rang Trilly, but no answer—probably whacking the fuck out of some bloke. Then I rang Terry, who's talking fast and saying he's got some news for me.

Hold on Terry, hold on. Slow down, now what's the news?

'That bloke that's been running around robbing all the flats has been back and robbed one of your flats in Gloucester Place. I went past there, and the police have put that do-not-cross tape up. There's a copper standing there guarding the place.'

Are you sure it's my flat?

'Of course I'm sure. My flat is across the square, and the girl there told me that the robber went in with a knife, stabbed the maid to death, and cut the girl's throat. I don't think the girl is dead though. She said she saw the ambulance take her away on a stretcher.'

I feel numb. That's my baby! That's Trilly. I can't breathe properly. Oh no, please lord, no, not Trilly, not my baby. I can't sit here; I've gotta go, but I don't even know where to go. Where is she? Who would know?

The solicitor walks back into the room and suggests I turn my phone off and hand it to him, as I will be searched before I enter the courtroom. I just want this shit over with so I can look for Trilly, so I do what he says and follow him to the courtroom. The judge was not smiling like the last one; he was looking at me as if I'd committed a crime. I'm looking at him, waiting for it all to start, and then they were off—chucking bits of paper in front of each other before they started to talk. I can't stop thinking of Trilly and the baby inside her, so I wasn't concentrating on what they were saying. I'm tearing up in knots inside my chest and trying to hold it together emotionally. All of what they are saying is a haze while I think about her. I couldn't give a shit about what they were up to. Just give me the fucking fine so I can fuck off!

The solicitor approaches me and says,

'Did you understand what the judge was saying?'

I couldn't even answer him straight away; I was in a trance. I was thinking of the baby and Trilly. So I asked,

What?

He said something about a guilty plea for a more lenient punishment.

Yeah, whatever. Guilty. I put the cards out, let's just get this over and done with.

I just couldn't think straight. Then after a while, I saw the plastic bag with a bunch of my cards in them being held up. Now I begin to recognize that copper sitting there—he was the one who took a card of each girl from me in the backstreets. Hold on a minute, guilty of what? I shake from my trance only to hear the judge say,

'You have pleaded guilty to the crime of living off immoral earnings. Prostitution is not a legal activity. These cards have been a nuisance to Westminster Council and the residents of Westminster, who have protested countless times for something to be done about it, to which the law finally has. The amount of cards that you were distributing is quite alarming. It is quite clear that you have some sort of control, like a monopoly, over vulnerable women. In today's society, there is no place for a criminal like you. I will be seen to be doing what I can to protect these women and to prevent predators like you from exploiting them for your own capital gain. We will have a short adjournment. This court will resume in thirty minutes, where mister Hemming can address the court before sentencing.'

That fucker's got it in for me. I ain't no predator, fucking wanker. I bet he goes to see the girls. The solicitor takes me off into the side room for a chat. He tells me he's pushing for a conditional discharge or, at worst, it would be community service and a big fine, but he doesn't know this judge's habits.

I don't want community fucking service. Can't I just have a fine and a conditional discharge?

'If only it were that straightforward. All we can do is present a good closing statement to win the judge over.'

But I know we ain't winning this cunt over. Besides, what fucking statement can I possibly write now to help myself? I can't just say that I put the cards out for a blow job. It's too late for that shit. I don't see the point in a fucking statement now. I shouldn't even be here. Let's just get this shit over and done with. I've gotta get out of this court.

The solicitor leaves the room again to speak to someone, and I'm there alone. My head is spinning. I can't get Trilly and my baby out of my mind. I haven't even met any of her family—there's no one to call to find out how she is. Please God, let her be alright. I know she's alright. I've gotta believe she's alright. I'll have to just go to the hospitals around the area; I'm bound to find her eventually. St Mary's Hospital. I'll go there first, as soon as I get out of here. Oh fuck, shit man, I can't think straight.

The solicitor comes back into the room and asks,

'Are you ready?'

I'm ready to get this shit over and done with and get out of here, that's for sure.

We leave the room together and walk the short corridor to court number three. There's more paperwork fluttering around between certain people in the courtroom, and I'm asked to take the stand. The judge then starts.

'Before I address the court's conclusion, is there anything you would like to say Mister Hemming?'

I feel like shit. I wanted to say something, but I'm not sure now. Someone has hurt my Trilly. I find myself full of sadness and holding back the tears as I say it anyway. But the words were not flowing out of my mouth like they should have as I spoke to the judge.

Well... I don't see myself as a criminal, and I think the girls provide a valuable service to people—some who may never experience any type of love. Everybody deserves intimacy, and if they cannot get it in the conventional way and find a willing girlfriend, then they'll never experience that girlfriend feeling. These girls can provide a temporary fix for that. I just ask that you take that into consideration.

The judge then says,

'Such nonsense. I have taken everything that has been said in this courtroom into consideration, but it does not change the fact that by placing these cards in telephone boxes, you are putting women in jeopardy. I am aware that this is not a one-off activity, and indeed you have been doing the same job for some considerable time. I will not be lenient on such activities that produce so many victims and family breakdowns. Above all of this, you have benefited financially from it. You did not and cannot prove the source of the four thousand pounds found on your person or the twelve thousand pounds found at your address. We know that these funds were accrued from prostitution and your involvement in distributing cards as a business. You are guilty of immoral earnings, and the sentence has to match the crime. I will therefore be passing down a sentence of four years imprisonment. That will be all. You may take him away.'

My mind is going crazy with all sorts of thoughts. What the fuck? Four years! For that? My fucking solicitor told me it would be a conditional discharge, or community service and a big fine. What about Trilly and my baby? I've gotta get out. How can I find out about Trilly? I don't know if I can handle this shit. I'm fucking feeling hot, and these fuckers are coming over to put handcuffs on me. What about my fucking house? What about everything? Those fucking old bill stole eleven grand of my cash!

They put the handcuffs on too tight and lead me away to a back fucking yard where there's a white security prison van waiting for me. I'm feeling claustrophobic even before they shoved me into the three feet by three feet box and took me away to prison.

How the fuck did I end up here?

THE END

Thank you so much for buying my book.

You've made it to the end.

I really hope you liked it? It took me two years to write, with the sole purpose of eliciting emotions in you, the reader. If you enjoyed it, you could do something really powerful for me. Simply leave a review. Together with the parting with your money to buy my book, it's the most powerful thing you can do to support me, and I thank you for taking the time to do so

Regards. Merv X

ACKNOWLEDGMENTS

Thank you to my team who have been so instrumental in making this dream come true.

Ray Shell: For mentorship, friendship and inspiration.

McVirn Etienne: For the coolest book cover photography ever. (mcvirnetienne.com)

Zeke: For your enthusiasm & being the Cover Model/ Mr CardBoy. (instagram.com/phyzeke.training)

Paul Waller: For cover design and support.

Becks: For wardrobe and being badass. (stayinyourlanevintage.com) (instagram.com/siylvintage)

Lewis Philips: My fellow writer for tips and reading through my work with a critical eye. (instagram.com/writersreads)

Desmond Herbert & Greg Baker: For friendship and kicking my ass when they felt I was slacking

Bradley Rae: For believing in me & offering your continued support. (instagram.com/bradleyraeofficial)

Emily, Evan & Noah: My three beautiful children, for being you & loving me.

Jared Alexander/JoãoInk: For being Editor and Proofreader. Also, for filming the Cardboy Trailer with a small crew of brilliant creatives. (instagram.com/jared.j.alexander, website: https://joaoink.neocities.org/)